ALT•4•1

A Novel by

Michael A. Occhionero

I

I am beginning this journal for posterity's sake, in the hope that a future generation may one moon lay eyes upon this document and learn from the mistakes that have led to this conflict... what has escalated into man's most perilous ultimatum.

I sit putting ink to paper huddled in a modest tent, located inside a large manmade bunker some three hundred cubits below the ground. These are the first few moments of uninterrupted rest I have been allowed since we entered the bunker those fifteen or so moons ago. I need badly to sleep, but my sense of duty urges me first to begin this chronicle of the most unlikely series of events, which have driven me down into this dismal underground prison.

It is the turn 2099, though of the precise moon I cannot, at this time, be entirely certain. It was still the warm season when we descended into the bunker...

I am keeping this account also as a record for myself, certainly, for writing has always helped me to keep a clear and balanced mind in the face of chaos. For as long as I can remember, writing has served me as a useful tool for demystifying the world around me, and for finding perspective in circumstances that would otherwise remain shrouded in a fog of confusion. Since my childhood, keeping journals and expressing myself through the written word have helped me to deal with the everymoon struggles of my life on the outside. It pains me to think of it, but there are so few, if any, writers or artists of any kind left. In the Metropolis, the arts died a long time ago. Among the outsiders, few are literate. After the revolution, very few outsiders possessed the will to study or contemplate anything, and even fewer the resources or time. Writing, and by extension reading, are impractical, and so nearly dead pursuits. Impracticality is a bitter sin in our bleak world, and the false god perched above us punishes no trespass as vengefully or mercilessly.

But now, I am getting away from myself…

I keep this record to commemorate all of us in the colony, with the greatest hope that this document *will* make it into the welcoming hands of a future generation. I cannot help but feel that my own immutable instinct for survival is now one with all of humankind, and my only wish henceforth is that God or the great unknown grant us humble men and women the power to overcome our seemingly imminent peril.

There is so much to tell, and likely very little time. My eyelids droop as I sit here writing. Nevertheless, I must recall the great pain- an easy enough errand, as that pain remains so readily at hand. I must relate how mankind came to this most delirious state. I will do my best to remain impartial, though it will be difficult in these oppressive conditions. Desperation tends to bring into plain sight the deepest biases in mortal men, and I wholly admit that I am desperate, and little more than mortal.

We have very meager means at our disposal ever since we were forced to take refuge underground. However, the use of ink and paper does not bother me. In fact, it has always been my preferred method of writing, even over the convenience of my father's typewriter. I view the ink and paper as a defiance of the machines, and as proof that a man can still find his way with minimal technology to aid him. The defiance of technology fuels me, and in fact fuels all of us down here in the bunker. Our shared defiance of technology connects us more profoundly with our brothers and sisters of unenhanced flesh and bone.

At this very moment, I find myself so very much entangled in the thick of things. Finding the detachment required to tell a didactic, or even coherent tale, in these circumstances which link my fate to the outcome of that supposed tale, will be near impossible. My reader will forgive me if my explanations are slightly jumbled. These are convoluted times, and hardly any of us know what we are anymore.

So many of us lacked the foresight to anticipate the danger before it materialized! In hindsight, I see that we were foolish, and nearsighted. But then, history has always found a way of revealing, only in retrospect, the obvious trajectory of man. The older members of the colony, those who lived through the technological revolution, insist that it never seemed a pressing issue until it was much too late. The outside has always had little power over the inner workings of the Metropolis. Our isolation all but ensured our ignorance, and our submission.

I did not have a chance to do any writing before this moment- there were many things that needed to be done in order to get the bunker up and running. Life underground is no trifle, especially for a mass of one thousand people. There were organizational issues, certainly, and then there were the unforeseeable realities of bringing a work force of one thousand people below the ground. One realizes very quickly the subtle beauty of all that is taken for granted as one recollects the glow of the sun, no longer able to draw its life-giving warmth. Even now, as I think it over, our mission seems insanely improbable, if not impossible.

I suppose I should introduce myself…

My given name is Beall. I am a man of twenty-four turns, of average height, and of strong build. I was born on one of the farms of the colony by the bay to loving parents. I lived a simple life on that farm, one that relied on my father teaching me the moon-to-moon routine of a livestock breeder, and disciplining me with the required work ethic of an outsider. My parents were some of the few literate people in our little settlement. Before the technological revolution, my parents had lived happily inside the Metropolis. My father had been a researcher, and my mother a painter. This, of course, was all long before I was born.

The 'technological revolution' (I borrow the term from my father) began in 2061, the turn that Poplar Corp. launched its Intelliware system. Though at first a seemingly innocuous new gadget, the Intelliware system would prove the catalyst that propelled the revolution. Within a mere turn of Intelliware's release, the exodus of the non-User had already begun.

In 2061, my parents and a very tenuous freethinking global minority refused outright to incorporate Poplar Corp.'s Intelliware technology into their bodies. This decision eventually drove my parents, and all of those who refused to incorporate, out of the Metropolis for good. My father and mother, like all those who chose to leave, left the Metropolis with only as much as they could carry. Their homes, and most of their material possessions were necessarily left behind. My parents did, however, manage to leave the Metropolis with a modest trove of books, art works, and musical recordings. For this reason, I was born on the only farm in the colony by the bay equipped with a meager library. In my free time, after the moon's necessary work had been completed, my father taught me to read. My mother sat me on her lap, and together we listened to virtuoso performances of her favorite classical composers. This early exposure to the great works of man and woman inspired me, and imbued me with an insatiable zeal to consume any and all cultural documents I could get my hands on. Though of course, hardly any remained in the world after Poplar Corp.

As a child, I constantly craved new ideas. I read everything I could. For these reasons, I am perhaps not as simple-minded as many of the other outsiders are. It pains me to speak that way of my brothers and sisters, but the truth is that the people of the colony by the bay lived difficult, and laborious lives. I doubt very much that they bothered themselves too much with the grand metaphysical questions that have always obscured the true nature of existence, and man's true purpose.

My father's library was small enough that by my twenty-first turn, I had managed to read all of the fifty or so books he had smuggled out of the Metropolis during the exodus. It wasn't much; certainly nothing like the old libraries he spoke of, with walls and walls lined with books in the old time before Poplar Corp. I would often dream of those libraries, and the infinite stores of human knowledge and emotion bound in their leather volumes. Nevertheless, my father's enthusiasm for the books he did manage to smuggle was enough to open my mind to the boundless realm of knowledge, and eventually, to the true possibility of change.

I only mention this to explain that I am an anomaly. I have not met another outsider in the colony by the bay who takes interest in these sorts of things. I cannot speak for the outsiders in other settlements, but then the world beyond the Metropolis is mostly scattered, and beyond our reach. The only outsiders I knew were those in our own humble colony by the bay, and they were much too simple and stubborn to see the possibility for change. Most were incapable of thinking beyond themselves. Their simple views bred apathy, and this apathy allowed for their exploitation. I always wondered at the lack of resistance in the early moons of Poplar Corp., before it became the monolithic entity it is now. I do not entirely blame them, though, for I know that the people of the colony by the bay are laborers, not thinkers. And though I may fancy myself a thinker, I am by necessity a laborer just like they are. We are bound by our work. We work to survive.

Everyone in the settlement had a role, which they

executed carefully for the well being of the entire community. All of the farmers were dependent on the abundance of the harvest, which was a collective effort, and so we helped one another in the name of the greater good. We had no choice but to pool our resources and know-how to get along. No one worked for him or herself alone. Times were too difficult for that. Our only chance of survival was to work together.

Nevertheless, based on unforeseeable changes in breeding patterns, disease, and many other variables that were outside of our control, there were inevitable livestock shortages. When these shortages occurred, many of the men became restless, unsatisfied with their diet of vegetable and wheat. In the times of great scarcity, more and more men resorted to the wishful fishing of the bay. It was an obvious sign that things were getting difficult when there were many of us out there on the water. The bay had been mightily overfished in the early moons of the technological revolution, by the first waves of outsiders settling by the great blue expanse. Too many relied on fishing as a primary source of food, and within my lifetime, catching fish became all but a dream. I can count on one hand how many fish I have eaten in my life. Fishing, for me and for most, was only a rare leisure activity. The calmness of the water after the work shift, and the reflection of the sun's light on its glassy surface would make me feel timeless, and help me to forget the toil that marked my family's struggle.

The colony by the bay was located about two hundred and forty furlongs beyond the limits of the largest of the one hundred and seventy Poplar Corp. Metropoles across the globe. Our settlement was skirted by a large wooded area, which sheltered us from the great valley that opened to the distant black blemish known as Metropolis 1.

Thankfully, our lands were fertile and our settlement was able to plant dependable, and abundant crops of corn and wheat. When it came time for the harvest, each of the crop yields and livestock yields were partitioned evenly among the heads of the neighboring farms. My father was one of these heads, and bore the responsibility dutifully. In addition to raising the livestock, my father was responsible for milking the animals, slaughtering those whose time had come, butchering the meat, and partitioning everything fairly.

My parents and I worked hard to survive, as all of us living outside of the Metropolis did, but we asked nothing more of life. My life on the outside was hard but never lacked purpose, and I never for a moment felt as though I needed to be more. The struggle to keep on was all that I knew. Sure, things could always get better, but I never deluded myself into thinking that life was anything but a beautiful gift. I lived for the sun, and for the smell of the grass. I lived for the loving embrace of my parents. I lived for the open masses of pasture that opened me to the infinite possibilities of our beautiful world, and I lived for my books, which opened me to the infinite possibilities hidden within the folds of my own mind. Whether or not my self-contentment made me a primitive being, I cannot say. Whether my self-interest and enjoyment made me a scourge to this planet, I cannot say. I have never felt that modesty and humility are equivalent to anarchy, but in this world, a modest man is very much a minority.

What I mean to say is, I am not a User. I have never felt the faintest desire to be a User. Though they, the cyborgs in the Metropolis, would have me believe that my lack of enthusiasm for 'progress' makes me an anarchist, I maintain that I have never viewed myself as such. I am satisfied with my sort, despite my human limitations. I do not wish to overcome my limitations, but to embrace them. My inability to take flight is what makes the graceful flapping of wings an inspiration of awe! But in this world, the User is the majority, and the majority lives only for progress and efficiency. Chasing the sentimental notions of awe and inspiration makes me an outcast. Though there may be few of us who are literate, I know that all of us in the settlement are outcasts in this same way. We are the few who have rejected the notion of progress that became the singular driving force of the Metropolis. We are the few who view ourselves as complete despite our limitations. We are the few happy with our sort. We, and the countless scattered colonies around the globe just like us, are all that is left of humanity after the revolution.

*

Since the launch of Intelliware in 2061, the divide between the Metropolis and the outside has become insurmountably blunt, and consequently, so has the divide between User and non-User. There were never any Users living on the outside. The Users cannot survive for very long beyond the Metropolis' power grid. Their Intelliware systems would fail, and shortly thereafter the User would die. Conversely, there are no outsiders allowed inside the Metropolis. Outsiders are primitive beings, and useless parasites in the eyes of the User.

Again, I am but a man unenhanced by technological advances, inefficient in my whims and emotion, and I hope one will find it in their heart to forgive me for the subjectivity I cannot overcome. I wish to take nothing for granted, to explain things as plainly as I can for the reader of this document, who may one moon be tasked with the rebuilding of humanity from the ruins of its first history. If nothing else, I wish to kindle the instinct for survival that has sustained man for millennia, and which sustains us right now in this tenebrous prison!

We knew this final clash would come. We had been preparing. But our actions are only reactive. By the time we on the outside were made aware of what was going in the Metropolis, it was too late to stop it. Since the revolution, the outside has had hardly any resources with which to fight back against the Metropolis. Our technology pales in comparison to theirs, and we possess hardly a quarter of their manpower.

All out war was never a feasible option.

The few of us who believed Dr. Mulligan's warnings from the onset could conceive of the practical ramifications of ALT•4•1, and feared the change it would bring about. Most of the outsiders, though, were too simple to understand the threat. And so they remained ignorant, apathetic, or unbelieving of the danger, until it was knocking quite literally at their front door. No one however, save perhaps Dr. Mulligan, expected the incredible widespread effect that the launch of ALT•4•1 would have on the participants.

To be perfectly plain, I have no idea what is going on

above ground right now. We have been holed up since the moon of the launch. However, in the sub-cycles between the moment ALT•4•1 launched and the moment we closed the latch to the bunker for good, one thing became certain: the doctor's predictions were startlingly accurate. I have no idea how many of my brothers and sisters in the colony have survived, or will continue to survive outside of this bunker. I only managed to catch a glimpse of what was going on out there, before we sealed ourselves off from the world. I remember that in the half-cycle or so after the launch, the desperation on the outside was already palpable, and the beginnings of devastation were already materializing. Those of us who heeded the doctor's outlandish warnings are bunched up underground, struggling to keep alive in this tight, dark, and oppressive bunker. The rest of the men, women, and children of the settlement are out there probably hiding in the forest somewhere, fending for themselves. I like to think that they will be okay, so long as they keep away from anything mechanical or electrical, but I can't know if even that is true. As things stand, we still do not know the full extent of the threat.

It breaks my heart to think of the people outside the bunker. But then, to pity those above ground seems mad! Our sort may be even worse. I have not seen sunlight for over a fortnight. I have not inhaled pure, plentiful air. The darkness is constant, and digs doggedly into my moods. It is clear that we no longer matter as individuals. We must do everything to channel our empathy for our fellow humans, and let it fuel us in our effort to save them!

By 2099, all offspring spawned in the Metropolis were being immediately incorporated with Intelliware devices.

They weren't even given the choice! And of course, none of the Users saw any issue with that. What's worse, more and more of the non-Users' offspring, born into the outside world of division and difficulty, chose to flee the struggles of the outside for the easy satisfaction of Intelliware, incorporation, and the grid. With every passing generation, the outsiders shrunk. By 2099, our numbers were smaller than they'd ever been. If ALT•4•1 hadn't come along and pushed the issue, I do believe the outsiders would have slowly wilted and shrunk into nothingness with time.

Nonetheless, I am glad that I am not a User. I feel proud of the struggle I have had to endure, and the desire for survival it has kindled in me. I have never felt the lack that drove so many others into becoming Users. I never understood what there was to be gained in the race for efficiency. Perhaps I lacked the intellect to see the end to which the Users drove. I am not an optimal being, but I am a being with free will, and this is enough to sustain my sense of purpose! I have never viewed my body as a burden, but instead as an unalterable reality of existence. I have never felt that my life was meaningless because it was fleeting, or fraught with decay, but rather meaningful for the very same reasons! I have never felt that human emotion held back our faculties of reason, and so held back evolution. Emotion is the color that makes life vibrant and worth living! I have always felt that the warmth of sunlight on my skin and the smell of pine was enough to justify my existence. And I never meant anyone any harm!

I must take a breath. I apologize for the long-winded rhetoric. I feel as though my emotions have gotten the better of me, and I have done very little to clarify.

We have built this massive underground shelter near the very edge of the forested area, approximately ninety furlongs beyond the limits of Metropolis 1. Dr. Mulligan, bless him, did his best in preparing for the worst, but there is still so much he could not have accounted for. I suppose I should briefly explain the circumstances that have led the doctor to us.

This may seem incredible, but Dr. Mulligan was until very recently the head of Poplar Corp.'s engineering department. As such, he is in many ways responsible for ALT•4•1. In fact, it is undeniable that he is solely responsible for its conception. His team of engineers at Poplar Corp. certainly did most of the legwork under his supervision, but there is no doubt that ALT•4•1 was the doctor's brainchild. For this, I imagine, he bears a constant burden of guilt.

Poplar Corp. has been the largest corporation on the planet for over thirty turns now. Poplar Corp.'s rise, and in fact all of this madness began with the launch of Dr. Mulligan's first product.

The Intelliware Human Optimization System initiated Poplar Corp.'s meteoric rise from obscurity, propelling the company quickly up to the position of the world's largest corporation. As sales steadily increased and Users continued to grow in number, Poplar Corp. eventually became the world's sole conglomerate. The takeover was shockingly fast, and everything Poplar Corp. did was within legal bounds. Dr. Mulligan's partner, John Locklear, was a ruthless man with the business acumen to complement Dr. Mulligan's engineering genius. Together, they launched Intelliware, and masterminded the expansion that changed the complexion of the entire world. While Dr. Mulligan updated and improved upon the device's code, Locklear silently acquired assets and the liquidated businesses that Intelliware pushed into bankruptcy or obsolescence. And so, Poplar Corp. silently expanded.

In 2061, Intelliware was officially introduced to the world. The incredible power of the device, coupled with its instant popularity, brought so many facets of traditional human life immediately into obsolescence. The device was shockingly affordable! Even the lowest tiers of laborers could manage the initial payments, and eventually, as Poplar Corp.'s popularity began to border on ubiquity, the device would be administered free of charge to any and all that desired it.

With the Intelliware device surgically incorporated into the forearm by one of Poplar Corp.'s professionally trained surgeons, one became linked to the Poplar Corp. grid at all times as a User. As a User, one now benefited from instant access to the information network and to all other Users of Intelliware internally. As early as 2062, Users could access, or communicate any information they wished to in all but an instant. One of the earliest facets of human life thus revolutionized was communication, as Intelliware to Intelliware connectivity seamlessly transmitted brainwaves into linguistic code that could be sent and processed instantly from device to device. Seemingly over the fade of a single moon, mail, books, and any physical writing became unnecessary, and so obsolete to the Intelliware User. Within remarkably few moons, as the Users and their devices adapted to one another, verbal utterances became utterly unnecessary.

Next, learning became obsolete. Thanks to internal access to the ever-expanding information grid, schools and any formal institutionalized learning became unnecessary, and could be bypassed with the download of Poplar Corp.'s learning software. The Intelliware's powerful ability to relay information was unprecedented. Dr. Mulligan and his team created the curricula, and these were converted into basic codes effortlessly processed by the Intelliware devices, and universally disseminated through mandatory updates. These 'learning updates' established the baseline Metropolitan hyper-intelligence among the Users. With the effortless dissemination of information across the grid, various types of specialized skill sets could be conveyed from the Poplar Corp. database to Users of varying rank, and stored for anytime access on the Intelliware's internal memory. Just like so, knowledge evolved from the abstract to the material, and the lifelong pursuit of learning was bypassed by a trivial download.

The next major update was another resounding breakthrough. It rendered illness almost entirely a thing of the past! Doctors and hospitals became obsolete thanks to the update that introduced Intelliware's internal diagnostics. Intelliware's internal diagnostics ran detailed analysis of the human body's vital organs around the clock. As this update was sharpened, the Intelliware would eventually run more comprehensive diagnostics every thirty iotas. With the information the Intelliware collected, the device could compare the User's personal diagnostics against the entire spectrum of known symptoms and diseases embedded in the base code of every Intelliware device. If the Intelliware noted any irregularities or symptoms, they would be detected and the proper treatment would be immediately administered, thus quashing most all maladies before they could become any sort of threat to the User's body.

However, the alterations undergone by the Users were not limited to increased mental and physical capacities. The Intelliware device altered the *entire* makeup of the host organism…

The enhanced quality of life offered by Poplar Corp. was universally viewed as a marvel of human innovation, and as a revolution in moon-to-moon life. The Users welcomed their Intelliware devices as second, and more efficient brains. Logic and reason seized near-absolute control of the User's mind, and consequently of the User's body. As these optimized beings grew sharply in number, it was not very long before it was glaringly evident to them that anyone not incorporated with Intelliware no longer had any place or meaning in the Metropolis. Intelliware was so revolutionary, and so widely embraced as such, that before anyone could really stop and ask why, it became an ultimatum whose influence the masses yielded to with excitement rather than concern.

In the turns to come, the Intelliware system, and by extension the User and Poplar Corp., was sustained by constantly becoming more efficient. The updates to the Users' software continued to develop, and to encompass more and more elements of human life. As the updates improved, the Users' dependence on Poplar Corp. became absolute. Within ten turns, Poplar Corp. would be making everything for the User…

Dr. Mulligan's next grand innovation pushed the bounds

of Intelliware even further. The next update made Intelliware capable of managing the diversion and pleasure of the Users, too. By my understanding, Dr. Mulligan's team extensively studied the neurological activity generated by the consumption of various artistic media such as music, paintings, and dance. Eventually, Dr. Mulligan's team found a way to translate the neurochemical effects of these various art forms into algorithms that could be processed by the Intelliware to emulate the specific neurochemical reactions that these various stimuli triggered in the User's brain. I can only imagine that this sickening breakthrough was one of Dr. Mulligan's proudest moments as head engineer of Poplar Corp. With this update, he discovered the way to completely internalize the hunt for pleasure. As the updates for this latest innovation sharpened, Intelliware was updated to seamlessly bypass the need for external stimuli altogether, and to sate the impulse for pleasure immediately, internally triggering the pleasure center in the brain in myriad ways that mimicked a wider and wider array of external pleasures. Alcohol, drugs, and sex, all became unnecessary things of the past. On a whim, the Intelliware could chemically imitate the pleasurable sensations of each of these stimuli without the User needing to do a thing. Soon thereafter, even orgasm could be triggered internally. Finally, insemination could be achieved without the primitive and inefficient need for the User to go mad with lust, or to lose composure for even a moment in order to reach climax!

Frivolity of any kind, any expression through media that were not electronic, internalized, and managed by Intelliware was no longer needed, and all artistic expression was logically looked down upon as primitive, and inefficient. All stimuli that recalled the outside world were weeded out and made obsolete by the constant updates of Intelliware. By and by, the Intelliware was updated to keenly dole out its synthetic pleasures at optimal times throughout the moon, depending on the Users' energy levels and mood, which were also constantly being monitored by the Intelliware's internal diagnostics. As the updates sharpened even more, so did the User's efficiency, pleasure, and synchronization.

This update was the final straw. The update completed the utter alienation of non-User from User, sealing the User off from all human contact and outside influence. It was a long time coming, but the 'entertainment update' prompted, among other things, the death of the Metropolitan artist. Within a few moons of the update's release, there was no use whatsoever for art or expression of any kind in the Metropolis. The artists who fled took what they could with them, and the remaining store of human artistic achievement was collected by Poplar Corp. agents, and burnt into a smoldering heap of ash. For a while, a handful of artists persisted on the outside in the farmlands and forest. My mother was one of these defiant few for a little while. But there was absolutely no sustenance for the artist on the outside. The urgent need for manual labor never lessened, and the difficulties of survival proved too much. The realities of the underdeveloped world outside the resource-sucking Metropolis were very demanding, and the creation of art was reduced to a hobby that so very few had the luxury of leisure, or the resources needed to practice.

Within only ten turns of Intelliware's launch, Poplar Corp. had absolute and uncontested control over their sterilized and synchronized Metropolis. By the 80's, those on the outside began to realize that the world they once knew had irreversibly changed. By then, though, there was absolutely nothing to be done. The change came about willingly, silently, and even gratefully. The masses demanded it. Poplar Corp. was welcomed, revered, and hailed as the great leader of the technological revolution.

All of this was already going on when I was born. I learned most of the details I am relating through my father, and in greater technical detail through my private conversations with Dr. Mulligan.

By the time I was born in 2075, the Users already outnumbered the outsiders significantly, and possessed far more advanced technology than we on the outside could ever dream of designing. Besides, there was the problem of organization. On the outside, non-Users were spread out in small colonies and settlements with no way of communicating besides travelling the vast distances between, whereas all of the Users across the globe became more and more connected to the mainframe in Metropolis 1 with every passing moon. We were left behind in the least violent but most sweeping revolution in the history of man! Poplar Corp.'s product was irresistible, undeniable, and completely incorporated into the human body of the User as an artificial, but vital organ. Poplar Corp. was the User, and Poplar Corp.'s Users were the ever-growing majority of life on the planet. However, although the Users were still in a way *alive*, they were no longer, in my view, quite *human*.

As the updates continued to become more sophisticated, so did the Users become less and less human. It came to the point where all a User would have to do was to think of a question, and the device in their forearm would provide the answer before the User even realized it had posed the question. With a near infinite store of information on the grid, and with the grid now even closer than their fingertips, the Users altogether lost the ability and need for introspection, or wondering of any kind. The Intelliware device could seemingly answer any question, and sate any craving!

If a User were tired, the Intelliware would know before the User did, through its constant internal diagnostics. The device could, at any time, alter the User's mood to drowsiness, and immerse the User in a deep and thoughtless slumber. When the Intelliware calculated that the User's fitness level was not optimal, it could simultaneously lull the User's mind into sleep, and command the User's muscles to contract, effectively exercising the User's body as its mind rested. The Intelliware device would monitor the sugar and oxygen levels in the User's blood stream and manage bodily functions accordingly, all in the aim of optimizing the functionality and longevity of the User's organic vessel. By the third or fourth major update, the Intelliware devices were even programmed to calculate Users' TPSC (thought per sub-cycle) ratio, and to manage it to the Poplar Corp. prescribed optimal level. By this time, revolt was impossible. The User's thoughts were managed with the use of diversions and pleasure triggers anytime the mind risked straying from the most efficient disposition of placid contentment.

All of the Users knew their champions. As the faces of Poplar Corp., Dr. Mulligan and John Locklear were revered as the ushers of a new technologically revolutionized age of man. Dr. Mulligan gave speeches for the Users, discussing their updates and the planned efficiencies of the future. Dr. Mulligan spoke of the Intelliware device as only the first step in the revolution, which would eventually usher in a new era in human *evolution*. There was no denying it- the Users were no longer merely human, but absolutely optimized beings capable of far more than unenhanced flesh and bone. However, Dr. Mulligan pledged that his work was not yet complete, for his creations remained mortal beings incased in flesh, blood, and perishable bone.

Although he referred to the Users as elevated beings, on the cusp of the greatest achievement in mankind's history, Dr. Mulligan was not, notably, himself a User. Neither was Locklear. Still, the Users looked to Dr. Mulligan for guidance as a child does its father. ALT•4•1, the proposed final update to the Intelliware software, would elevate the Users beyond the wildest dreams of primitive man, and finally unlock the fullest potential of consciousness.

Whether Dr. Mulligan was, or is mad, I cannot say. I think it is fair to say that his impact on the world was singular, and unprecedented. And I do believe that his timely recognition of his own mortality is the only thing that has given us a fighting chance…

Thankfully, the doctor's views of man and machine would eventually change. I don't know that there has ever been a more striking change of heart than that undergone by Dr. Mulligan, and at the most crucial of junctions. He spoke of the Users as though they were his beloved children. He dedicated nearly his entire life to the establishment of Poplar

Corp., and to the development of his Intelliware system. Perhaps that is why so many on the outside were skeptical of his sudden epiphany. Perhaps that is why so many refused to be swayed by his message of warning.

I, unlike Dr. Mulligan, *always* somehow viewed the Users as less than. A device to complement one's brain may make certain answers come easier, but though I can't know for sure, I do doubt that these beings kept their free will.

I don't believe that genuine joy can be felt without the exertion of free will. I have always doubted the human quality of the Users, and I see now that they had no choice in being incorporated into ALT•4•1. Their Intelliware was more than likely programmed to desire that incorporation. I always wondered at the relationship between the brain and the Intelliware device, and my conclusion was more often than not that the latter was truly in control.

But now, I feel I can no longer resist the desire to sleep. I must suspend the explanation, and I hope very much that I will find the will to return to it to-morrow, after the recuperative bliss of a short but deep slumber, and after a long, hard work shift at the frontier…

II

I could not help but fall asleep.

The work shifts at the frontier are a shock to the body, and drain all but the last few drops of my store of energy. Even out on the farm, with the unending toil necessary to survival, I had never pushed my body like I have this last fortnight in the bunker. But then, I should not squander energy on idle chatter. I will try to pick up exactly where I left off. There is still so much to clarify…

As I mentioned, Dr. Mulligan was the most prominent designer on the team that built and updated the Intelliware devices. As I understand it, there had been conglomerates before, but none had ever possessed anywhere near the influence and importance that Poplar Corp. did. In the Metropolis, Poplar Corp. has long been unanimous.

As the Intelliware updates sharpened, Poplar Corp. gathered information pertaining to the moon-to-moon decisions and behaviors of every single one of its Users. With the seemingly infinite information network available to them, Poplar Corp. employees, who were naturally also Intelliware Users entirely at the mercy of their corporate masters, were tasked with continually 'optimizing' the code running the Intelliware. Naturally, optimizing the code would in turn optimize the behavior of the Users. It may seem beyond belief, but by the time I was born, the very Users whose lives depended on the Intelliware codes were nearly all employed to create new algorithms meant to improve their Intelliware codes. The improvements added to each new update were borne of the unending stream of data being collected through the constant monitoring of the Users.

By 2099, Poplar Corp. had designed and was running the electrical grids that powered each of the one hundred and seventy Metropoles across the globe. By this time, Poplar Corp. had dropped the idea of names, favoring the more collective and logical numerical organization of the Metropoles. Users had shed their individual names as well, also favoring the more collective and logical numerical designations…

Poplar Corp. ran the Production Towers, Housing Towers, transportation, food distribution, and all imaginable facets of life in the Metropolis. Poplar Corp. ran the police forces, though the User's Intelliware was programmed to completely stifle any and all subversive thoughts by the time Poplar Corp. began running the police forces. By 2099, Poplar Corp. Users had long been the only living organisms in the Metropolis.

Evidently, by this time, all Poplar Corp.'s Users were also necessarily Poplar Corp.'s employees. Poplar Corp. had over seven billion human organisms fitted with, and so dependent on their Intelliware technology. Their monopoly over all things electronic extended to all things industrial, and enveloped nearly the entire globe. With their connection to each and every Intelliware device, Poplar Corp. could locate any User, anywhere, anytime, and for any reason, so long as the User stayed within the limits of their massive power grids. And all Users fitted with Intelliware devices were confined to the limits of the power grids. Leaving the power grids but for short periods of time would result in malfunction of the Intelliware, which would result in the total breakdown of the User. With their control over the Intelliware devices, Poplar Corp. could communicate with, alter, or adjust any of their Users in any way, at any given moment.

Though it went against the Poplar Corp. code of ethics, it was quite clear to any outside observer that Poplar Corp. could, if needed, assume control of any and all of their Users. This understanding bred extreme mistrust between User and non-User, and inspired impotent fear among the outsiders-fear that fermented into deep-seated hatred. The outsiders feared the constant expansion of the Metropolis and the grid, which grew larger every turn. That the power grids should eventually encompass the entire planet seemed inevitable. Consequently, the outsider lived in unrelenting distress, as the threat of violence loomed like a dark cloud over every waking moment. The Users, if mobilized, could eliminate the remaining outsiders handily. Users, on the other hand, were influenced by their Intelliware devices, which were programmed to incite red-hot hatred for the outsider. The outsider was understood as the only impediment to the omnipresence and benevolence of Poplar Corp., and of the User. The User was Poplar Corp., Poplar Corp. was the User, and together they embodied progress.

It seems so crazy. I mean, could you imagine it? Having a

device monitor your organs! A device monitoring hunger levels, energy levels, moods, desires, etc. in the aim of maintaining the optimal well being of the host body at all times! What kind of life? Madness! Sheer madness! To possess no agency… to be so desperately dependent on a digital appendage… to be part machine!

In the early moons, Poplar Corp. employees built the Housing Towers, where they 'slept', or recharged, a paltry cycle per moon, upon the completion of their everymoon work requirements. The Housing Towers were partitioned into individual cubic units. Each of these units was furnished with a space designated for 'caloric intake', and a small, padded, isolated space referred to as the rest chamber. Sleep, as we know it, however, was no longer truly necessary for the User. By 2099, sunup and sundown had no influence on the User's activity. The Housing Towers, and in fact the whole Metropolis was, by 2099, also completely synced with the Intelliware device. Users roamed seamlessly through their surroundings, so that something like the turning of a knob or the pressing of a button was an inefficiency overcome by the grid. The synchronization of Intelliware with its digital surroundings further increased the efficiency of the Users' moon-to-moon life. Shelves would pull out of the walls, as it would occur to the User that it needed some implement or apparatus, doors would slide open and close on their own, stairs and moving conveyors would manifest from intelligent matter, and lights would flicker on and off as the User roamed freely through the Metropolis expressly designed to be its playground.

In the early turns, the User's fatal dependence upon Poplar Corp. was leveraged, enabling Poplar Corp. to engulf enterprises around the globe, converting them into branches, subsidiaries, or subdivisions of Poplar Corp. When Poplar Corp. had finally become large enough, Locklear dropped the ruse altogether, and proclaimed Poplar Corp. the sole provider of the Metropolis. By this time, there was no need to hide it. Governments had dissolved under the crushing influence and magnitude of Poplar Corp.! Eventually, Poplar Corp.'s influence became so universal that even the idea of currency receded into obsolescence, and dissolved. No one complained, and no one resisted. Why would they? Poplar Corp. produced all of the products, and provided all of the services that ensured the Users' satisfaction. Everything was steadily becoming easier. Progress, when everyone bought in, was so effortless…

As the User majority cemented itself, Poplar Corp. employees rebuilt the Metropolis from the ground up. Transportation was managed through automated personal transportation vessels, created by the User for the User. The vessels, too, operated in sync with the Intelliware device. Though they could go nearly anywhere in those miraculous flying vessels, the Users only ever needed to go one place: one of Poplar Corp.'s countless, identical, one hundred and seventy story automated, optimized Production Towers built by the User for the User. By 2099, the entire Metropolitan infrastructure had been successfully rebuilt and synched with the Intelliware devices. With the infrastructure in place, nearly all of the Users could be employed in these Production Towers, working together toward Poplar Corp.'s ultimate goal. With nearly all their available manpower at work in near perfect synchronicity, Poplar Corp. was able to push toward that final goal with maximum efficiency.

According to Dr. Mulligan, most Poplar Corp. employees worked an unfathomable twenty-one cycles per moon in the Production Towers, and did this with ease thanks to the added efficiency of the human body unlocked by the Intelliware device. With reduced ingestion and expulsion, coupled with a greatly reduced need for rest and an optimized brain, the User's work efficiency exponentially amplified the collective rate of progress. By 2099, the identical Production Towers and Housing Towers were, for all intents and purposes, the only buildings necessary in the Metropolis.

In the Production Towers, Users worked to further 'optimize' the updates of the User. The workers in the Production Towers cooperated tirelessly to clean and compress the data that Poplar Corp. collected around the clock from Intelliware devices across the globe. The information the Users gathered from and about their fellow Users was processed and compressed into metrics designed by Dr. Mulligan. Once the information was cleaned into these basic metrics, it was siphoned up the ranks from the underling Users working the lower floors of the towers, upwards to the Users with more and more sophisticated programming. The highest-ranking Users were specially programmed by Dr. Mulligan to translate the optimized data into more functional metrics, and eventually, with Dr. Mulligan's help, into the algorithms that would fuel the latest updates.

The User's purpose was simple: to further optimize the

code running the Users' Intelliware.

The User's purpose was progress.

Dr. Mulligan oversaw and directed the updates from the very highest floor of the Poplar Corp. head Production Tower in Metropolis 1. This was the only building in all the Metropoles around the globe with a presumably symbolic, and somewhat incongruous one hundred and seventy-first floor. Dr. Mulligan was one of only two men on the Poplar Corp. grid not fitted with the Intelliware device. Naturally, the only other was the Poplar Corp. President and CEO John Locklear, who shared the grid's highest office with Dr. Mulligan. Though by 2099, Locklear had taken the Poplar Corp. expansion to its superlative end, and served only as the symbolic figurehead of the former company.

Poplar Corp. was no longer an independent entity. Poplar Corp. existed as the User, and the User embodied the Metropolis. The Metropolis was progress, and progress was everything.

It angers me to think of this, of Dr. Mulligan's prior involvements in Poplar Corp. design, but I must forgive the doctor. For though he created the danger, he is now our only hope of overcoming it. He did not know that this would happen. I must hold firmly to that belief. He could not have known that things would turn out this way…

Poplar Corp. had enough information coming in from the Intelliware devices of their seven billion Users, that they were eventually able to calculate, with the help of Dr. Mulligan's genius, the *mean human reaction to any given context.* Those were the doctor's words. It took me a while to digest that concept.

In other words, the Poplar Corp. Production Towers amassed such staggering pools of data, that they could subsequently, for the first time in history, conduct an all-encompassing, comprehensive study of human consciousness: human behavior, human decision making, human mood swings, human interactions, the seemingly random generation of human thoughts, etc. Ultimately, Poplar Corp.'s Users were able to clean all of this data into metrics that Dr. Mulligan used to forge the single algorithm that would accurately mimic the inner workings of the human mind. In short, Poplar Corp. found a way to calculate that which mankind once thought incalculable. Dr. Mulligan allegedly unlocked the secrets that had, since the dawn of man, shrouded the human mind in mystery. With Dr. Mulligan's algorithm, Poplar Corp. would be capable of truly understanding, and so accurately reproducing consciousness.

Evidently, this was no trifle. It took unspeakable manpower, and an incredibly concentrated effort by the Users. Poplar Corp. employees spent countless cycles in the Production Towers comparing thousands upon thousands of variables interacting in real time, and amassing such astonishing mountains of data that Dr. Mulligan was finally able to reach the point humankind had always thought impossible: he could calculate the thoughts and predict the behavior of every single one of the Users in real time.

But that was only the beginning. Dr. Mulligan's condensed and concentrated algorithm *incorporated* and leveled out all of the *independent* thoughts, moods, and behaviors of all of the Users, in real time. The breakthrough unlocked the model of the human mind, and now powers ALT•4•1.

With this realization, this triumphant or ghastly feat of more than human perseverance, Poplar Corp. boiled the entire spectrum of human thought and emotion down to what Dr. Mulligan coined 'mean human consciousness'. And this 'mean human consciousness'- the collective consciousness now running in ALT•4•1- flattened all of humanity's individual quibbles and quirks, all of the inconsistencies from being to being that qualified the closed existence of the individual, into a universal principle of interconnectedness and agreement. Poplar Corp. achieved the algorithm for true unity through technological innovation.

Or, as they so aptly put it:

"ALT•4•1 IS CONSENSUS AT LAST!"

Dr. Mulligan, intoxicated by his triumphs and blinded by his magnanimity, realized only too late, once the project was too far-gone to be stopped, what danger this discovery posed to the existence of organic life. ALT•4•1, if successfully brought online, would have seemingly infinite potential. Dr. Mulligan and his sophisticated high-ranked Users could not be sure, but it seemed quite likely that such a mass incorporation of disembodied consciousness would realize a transcended state beyond human comprehension.

Perhaps the fact that the algorithm seemed so far, and so unlikely, is what kept the doctor from realizing the doom his algorithm spelt for humankind. Perhaps he was so immersed in his work that he forgot his own self-interests and consciousness. He was, and still is an organic and perishable being! Perhaps he was simply a heartless man finally shocked from his numb ignorance of reality. Perhaps he felt a great love for his craft that truly did extend beyond the limitations of self-interest. I cannot say what went through his mind, but I am infinitely thankful that he changed it the way he did…

All I know is this: frightened and sobered by the realization of his goal, the doctor claims to have destroyed the algorithm before anyone else could know of its existence. As his last act as head engineer of Poplar Corp., Dr. Mulligan very boldly denounced Poplar Corp.'s agenda, Intelliware, and all of his life's work. Dr. Mulligan declared the push for ALT•4•1 'a great and grave oversight', and fled the power grid of Metropolis 1 as his message was broadcast to each and every User. His public announcement of retirement, in the midst of such a crucial junction in the Poplar Corp. revolution, caused a great stir in the Metropolis. But of course, his public denouncement of Poplar Corp. had a very short-lived effect on the Users, who were by now entirely dependent on Intelliware to live. Not even Dr. Mulligan could sway public opinion by that point. It was quite plain that there was no turning back.

And so, Locklear stepped in.

With the quick release of a new update, public opinion about Dr. Mulligan was completely and entirely reversed. With the flick of an unseen switch, Dr. Mulligan was no longer the beloved and revered creator. He was a non-User, an outsider, and nothing more. The Users felt the same red-hot hatred toward him as they did toward the rest of us.

Poplar Corp. had been promoting the release of

ALT•4•1 for moons upon moons with Dr. Mulligan's tagline: "ALT•4•1 IS CONSENSUS AT LAST!". But after the doctor was gone, the Users no longer knew those words as his. Knowledge of Dr. Mulligan was wiped from the code, and things went on as usual. Naturally, Poplar Corp.'s software development significantly slowed. Dr. Mulligan was the genius behind *every* innovation in Poplar Corp.'s technology from the beginning. Nevertheless, the technological revolution was moving with too much momentum now for any one man to stop it- even if that man was the first mover. Poplar Corp. was not Dr. Mulligan. Poplar Corp. was the User, the User was the Metropolis, the Metropolis was progress, and progress was everything.

Locklear, though out of sorts, relished the opportunity for control. With Locklear at the helm, the updates came less frequently, and so the User's progress slowed. But ultimately, very little changed. The Users were accustomed to their interconnectivity, dependent on one another as much as they were on their Intelliware, and they craved the updates as an outsider craves the sun- instinctually, for sustenance and vitality. They were so far gone by then, that the User's notion of self-interest was either constantly being tempered by the Intelliware, or had simply become truly and permanently morphed into the notion of the collective.

Although in the grand scheme of things Dr. Mulligan's departure changed very little, Poplar Corp. did not take the departure lightly. Once the Intelliware updates were stabilized and the threat of meltdown had been averted, Locklear ordered that Dr. Mulligan be chased down relentlessly. Several groups of Users were assembled into taskforces of Seekers, and sent off the grid to scour the forested area by the bay in search of Dr. Mulligan. The doctor, however, was prepared for this. He understood very well that a man of his stature could not simply walk away from his life's work on a whim. He knew that he would henceforth live the furtive life of a hunted man, but he was nonetheless resolute. The Seekers, after all, posed no threat. He knew the way they were programmed to seek- he had programmed them himself!

Though they forced him into hiding, Dr. Mulligan would not be caught. Poplar Corp. agents harassed his family, friends, and acquaintances constantly, though this harassment was strikingly needless, as these were all Users, and so hated the doctor with the exact fervor that their Intelliware prescribed. His loved ones would have turned him in happily, if given the opportunity. Poplar Corp. agents raided Dr. Mulligan's office in search of the algorithm. They ransacked his housing unit. Locklear left no stone unturned. Poplar Corp. did not, however, find Dr. Mulligan's algorithm.

Still, the loss of Dr. Mulligan would not stop them. Poplar Corp. had a wealth of brilliantly enhanced minds at their disposal, and there was no doubt in Dr. Mulligan's mind that it was only a matter of time before the Users would arrive at a version of the algorithm for a collective consciousness all on their own. He had led them along the path, and left them only a few 'critical steps' from achieving their final goal.

Dr. Mulligan took to the wilderness, seeking out the non-Users outside Metropolis 1 in the forests and by the bay. This is how he came to us: as a prophet from another world, warning us of the unseen danger arising in the Metropolis. That is how he found me.

Or how I found him…

But now, I think I must rest my body. I have so little energy. My eyes and arms fail me. I am needed back at the frontier.

First, I must get some rest.

III

It is very difficult for me to relate the details of the world I take for granted, especially as they surface only in jumbled waves of recollection. Nearly all of the information I have related concerning Poplar Corp. was collected second-hand through Dr. Mulligan. What's more, the only times I have available for writing are after strenuous shifts at the frontier, mustering my last few morsels of vigor before I collapse into oblivion. Before my energy wanes, let me continue where I left off with Dr. Mulligan's long and precarious story…

Dr. Mulligan came to the settlement out of the wilderness, absolutely uncertain of his reception but determined to spread his warning. Our settlement was the nearest to Metropolis 1. This may be the only reason he chose to travel there.

The moon the doctor fled marked his first foray beyond the Metropolis limits in over thirty turns. Having eluded detection to arrive at the outskirts of the wooded area, Dr. Mulligan proceeded to build a great bonfire with the hope of drawing the attention of the sleeping farmers of our nearby settlement. His arrival was sudden, and the doctor's plans were necessarily hatched in haste. I am certain that Dr. Mulligan had no idea what sort of reception he would receive. His arrival was very bold indeed, but then he simply could not afford the luxury of patience, or of subtlety. Given his advanced age, Dr. Mulligan did not expect to last very long on his own in the wilderness. His only hope of survival was to find refuge among the outsiders.

Dr. Mulligan's great bonfire drew the large crowd he hoped it would, though many of the outsiders who approached, did so bearing arms. I was somewhere among the ranks of the poorly organized and very hostile horde that approached the inexplicable fire. It was only natural that we would fear the worst. It was only natural that we would prepare for confrontation.

I remember it being very dark that moon, with hardly a star in the sky to append the feeble moonlight. In the saturated darkness, the great flame was unmistakable even from the distance of a great many furlongs. The sight of the brilliant blaze was a significant cause for alarm in the settlement. My father and I were woken by violent knocks at our door. Brief words were exchanged between my father and the heads of the neighboring farms, and my father and I were soon committed to the courageous band of men moving out to investigate the fire.

We must have been over fifty men altogether. We approached slowly, and vigilantly. Each of us kept a firm grip on our weapon. The tension of the approach stifled any chatter, and seemed to amplify the sound of crunching grass beneath our shaky boots. We were apprehensive, certainly, but in unison our strength felt formidable. We moved with every muscle firm and taut, until finally the white specter could be seen standing alone before the great light of the fire.

Those equipped with rifles led the pack, and they raised their weapons toward the being, ready to fire. But the figure was very quick and clear to reveal itself unarmed, with arms extended and open palms. It cried out very loudly as the horde moved within earshot:

"I am unarmed! Do not fire! I am completely unarmed! I am not a User! I am not a Seeker! Do not fire! I am one of you! I am human!"

The being cried out to us in a fluster. Its appeals were compelling enough to keep any rifles from being fired, though these were kept cocked as we carefully crept closer, closing in on the white figure. There was genuine desperation in the quivering voice, and I do believe it was precisely this desperation that kept us from attacking.

Though as the silhouette came into sharper focus, the fact that it was not a User became plain. Had the figure been fitted with Poplar Corp. technology, it would not have been able to live for very long on the outside, beyond the power grid. We all knew this. Most of us had had encounters with the Seekers from Metropolis 1. Violence between Seeker and outsider was a rarity, but the Seekers *were* occasionally hostile. The Seekers, however, were in constant motion and never, ever addressed the outsiders.

"Brothers, sisters, I come to you in peace, and with important news from the Metropolis! I have simply come to speak."

The horde was closer now, within ten or so cubits of the white-frocked speaker. We had spread out to enclose the figure on all sides, though still minding a potential ambush from the surrounding wood. The being stood with outstretched arms, motionless and seeking audience. The man, for now it was clear that the being was male, had a relatively relaxed countenance and seemed to be doing his best to diffuse the situation. He even moved toward us, but slowly- very unlike the tense and rushed movements of the Seekers. As the horde prowled closer still, the realization suddenly dawned upon us.

We had all heard of Dr. Mulligan before. Even those born on the outside had heard of his legend. Many of the elders at the head of the horde quickly recognized his countenance; his was the most notorious face in the world! Even from near the back of the pack, I understood fairly quickly. The man had an unspeakable aura about him. Perhaps that aura, more than anything else, is what kept the armed farmers at the front of the mob from firing. The horde stopped. I nudged my way to the front and assumed a position beside my father. Together, we watched the doctor keenly through widened eyes.

"Please, lower your weapons. I mean you no harm."

The doctor again stretched out his arms and opened his palms to reveal himself completely unarmed.

It was only after a few long, tense moments pleading calmly with the mob and assuring them of their safety, that the urgency of the moment perceivably slackened. Some, but only some, of the farmers in the front line lowered their weapons. A low, incredulous murmur began to buzz among the men. I, too, was thunderstruck. No one had formally requested that he identify himself, but it seemed as though that was an unnecessary formality. We knew. Of course we knew. It was as though we were suddenly face-to-face with a distant legend that we, only now, now that the man was incarnate before us, realized was true. In the colony, Dr. Mulligan was known as a figure, not so much as a living, breathing human being. He was just the central character in the story the outsiders passed down from generation to generation- the story that helped us to make sense of the world, and of the Metropolis we could not possibly comprehend.

Yes, I remember the great shock of seeing the doctor that moon by the forest. The bravest among us in the colony had ventured to the edge of the forest expecting to confront a hostile group of Seekers. What else could explain a contained fire in the midst of the moon's darkest cycles? The settlement had been raided under the cover of darkness before, but the Seekers hadn't been known to make fires. They hadn't been known to do anything but to take what was needed, and quickly. We had absolutely no experience on which to draw. Naturally, we approached ready for the worst. To this, none of us knew how to react. Dumbfounded and bewildered are good words to describe the general mood. Never before had any of us even dreamed of anything like this happening.

Dr. Mulligan's voice that first moon by the light of the great bonfire lingered in the cool tenebrous air like a dream. In the witching cycles of the moon, the haunting darkness of the sky only added to the wraithlike quality of his sudden appearance. As he spoke, the light of the great fire shone upon Dr. Mulligan's long pale face and his feathery white hair, giving him the impression of a wisp of smoke floating amid the dark brush skirting the wood. Dr. Mulligan pulled on his long beard pensively, and stood otherwise motionless as he greeted the outsiders with a smile. Many shuffled anxiously, pointing their weapons with menace and fear. We carried cocked rifles and shotguns, pitchforks, and makeshift cudgels, but the white apparition seemed impervious to the crackling tension of the moment. He broke the nervous silence, speaking loudly and unwaveringly as he requested an audience before we condemned him to death.

"I understand your apprehension. Let me explain. My name is Dr. Mulligan. I have come from the Metropolis bearing important, but difficult news."

He announced himself with a sense of prophetic self-importance. The men who gasped in awe were equal in number to those who uttered disbelieving guffaws. But the doctor was not dismayed. He spoke confidently- there was no denying his immediate oratory control. He spoke like a man accustomed to being heard.

He dressed in Metropolitan garb, that is, the form-fitted white frock of the User. Though he had clearly come from the Metropolis, Dr. Mulligan looked unlike any of the other Users we had encountered before. The only ones we had encountered were the Seekers who would regularly raid the settlement, but these all had a seemingly uniform appearance. This man was much older than the other Users, whose Intelliware devices greatly slowed the signs of aging. He also seemed to think through his actions in a genuinely human way. His movements and gestures felt spontaneous and natural, rather than premeditated and labored. I do think a great many of us recognized these unmistakably human qualities. The Seekers we were accustomed to encountering on the outside all shared an inexplicable cold calculating quality, and a stiffness of the eyes that Dr. Mulligan did not display. His genuine human mannerisms soon swayed me to sympathy, and convinced me that he *was* human just like we were. And if he was human, then I knew that he must be who he claimed to be. The circumstances left no logical alternative.

The importance of the moment impressed on me, and I stepped out before the doctor to address the crowd on his behalf:

"Brothers, drop your weapons, and let our fellow man speak! If this man should be who he claims to be, then we absolutely must hear him out before we come to judgment."

I could see the concern on my father's face, but the crowd seemed to calm as I stood between them and Dr. Mulligan. Many knew me as one of the few literate brothers in the settlement, and so I suppose I commanded a sort of mild oratory respect. I turned to the stranger, and added somewhat roughly:

"You have sought our audience, doctor, and now you have it. Speak your piece."

The doctor and I exchanged a hesitant glance for the first time, and his deep blue eyes seemed to convey gratitude. With my support, Dr. Mulligan was emboldened to step forward and speak.

His voice was grand, and surprisingly imperious as he spoke gravely of the work he had done in the Metropolis. It was incredible that such a booming voice could emanate from such a diminutive frame. As he spoke, Dr. Mulligan struggled to bring the complexities of his work into simple terms that an outsider might understand. He struggled and stumbled as he sought in vain for the right words. His words fell on blank or skeptical faces, trying but failing to understand his jargon:

"…this update will bring forth a new disembodied entity borne of the data that the Users, formerly under my direction, have cleaned to obtain the 'mean human consciousness' that will now run their perfectly unified Intelliware code…"

Mostly though, Dr. Mulligan stuck to simple repeated warnings of the dangerous power of the upcoming Intelliware update, ALT•4•1. We on the outside were not very familiar with the ways of the Metropolis, and the words he used meant nothing to us. Updates? Intelliware? ALT•4•1? At that time, before the doctor would tirelessly explain, even I had no idea what he meant by Intelliware or updates. Nevertheless, he persisted, warning us again and again of an update that would change the entire makeup of the Intelliware User. He claimed that this update would be even more impactful on the world than the release of Intelliware had been. He warned that this update would soon envelop the entire Metropolis. He spoke once more the ominous name ALT•4•1. According to the doctor, ALT•4•1 threatened not only to jeopardize the way of life of the outsider, but threatened to eradicate him altogether.

There were over fifty of us who ventured to the edge of the forest that moon. Many scoffed at his words, and some, even, were hostile. A man, a *genuine man*, had not walked out of the Metropolis in over thirty turns! The skepticism was understandable, and the misunderstanding hastened to frustration. The cries for violence soon broke out. But the doctor swayed a good few with his level reason, and with the sincerity in his deep blue eyes. He swayed enough of us to stifle the cries for violence and execution. I was the first to speak out, and so I spoke again, in favor of the doctor's message once he had concluded his speech.

"Brothers, it is clear that this man has come here bearing a message of warning! I think we would be wise to take him at his word. I truly believe in the doctor's message, and the sincere alarm that colors it. This is why I will be the first to pledge my loyalty and allegiance to the doctor's cause."

Uproar rippled through the crowd, and many cried out at me against trusting this man- so clearly from a different world, and so not to be trusted.

"Just look at his clothes! He clearly isn't one of us! How do we know he isn't just one of *them*?"

The fear and hate were palpable, but would not sway me. Somehow, I knew Dr. Mulligan was sincere. I saw it in his face. I heard it in his voice. He could not express the danger in a way I could clearly understand, not yet anyhow, but the urgency in his voice and manner left no doubt in my mind that the danger he warned of was real. I felt that despite the choices he had made in his life, the fact that he was not technologically enhanced meant that he was in essence more like *us* than he was like *them*. Dr. Mulligan was human, though it may have taken him until the very last moment to realize. The doctor spoke like us, kept eye contact like us, and could clearly survive comfortably in the open air beyond the power grid. In fact, he had a strange quality in his face that I could only describe as natural delight. I perceived him, that moon, as a man finally freed from a long and dark captivity.

The doctor appealed to our reason, and he appealed to our self-interest. The Users could not do this. The Users could not even speak! Besides, he held perhaps the highest office in the land within the confines of the Metropolis, and by the looks of it, he left it willingly and accepted his exile as a sacrifice necessary for the greater good. He claimed to be fearful for his life. He said he was an old man, a hunted man, and seemed resigned to the idea that he would soon be dead and gone. I thought it plain that he truly felt that humanity was in great peril. Why else would he have abandoned all the luxuries of his former life to start anew on the outside, at such an advanced age, and among such belligerent neighbors as we?

He was still too rigid and rational then, and it was plain in the way he spoke that he was not accustomed to addressing outsiders. His speech was terse, and succinct. He used many technical terms that we could not understand. It was only after the first great warning by the bonfire, after I pledged my allegiance to him and he took me into his council, that I began to teach him the ways of the outsider. I taught him to adopt the outsider's drawl, and to speak in simple terms so that the others could follow him. He was reluctant to waste time on such trifles, and to pander to what he felt were lesser minds. He reiterated the impending doom he had prophesied for the non-User, and was frustrated by the mistrust of the people he was trying to save. He lamented the lack of cooperation we offered. Dr. Mulligan had spent so many turns giving the Users orders that the stubbornness of man came as a shock reminder that there were still others in this world who would question him.

I quickly realized that it was imperative that I learn to subdue the doctor, and that I act as an intermediary between the doctor and my fellow outsiders. I eventually managed to convince him that out in the wilderness, one needed more than reason to survive. One needed far more than reason to gain favor among the farmhands and laborers. Unaccustomed to the emotive concepts of charisma, patience, and empathy, which Dr. Mulligan's Users had long abandoned as frivolities, Dr. Mulligan needed me more than he could understand. His frustration eventually did subside, though, and he did eventually yield to my recommendations. He was perceptive enough to see it was the only way to further his cause.

After the crowd calmed that first moon, it was agreed that my father and I would shelter the doctor. There was still a general feeling of mistrust towards him, but for the moment Dr. Mulligan would be safe with us. My father was not thrilled by the suggestion either, but his trust in my judgment ultimately prevailed over his doubt.

Dr. Mulligan rose with the following sun, as did I, and our first of many private conversations ensued. He brought me up to speed on some of the things that were going on in the Metropolis, taking the time to explain many of the terms that I have related earlier in this document. We spoke for cycles. I brought him up to speed on the ways of the colony, and many of the proceedings of moon-to-moon life on the outside. The doctor was just as shocked to learn of the way we lived on the outside, as I was to learn about the way the Users lived in the Metropolis. And so, we found that we complimented one another in a very important way.

The following moon, Dr. Mulligan spoke to a much larger assembly of outsiders, again by the light of a great bonfire. This time, however, he abandoned the polished white frock of the User and wore overalls borrowed from my father. In the simple garb of the farmhand, Dr. Mulligan began his speech instead by pledging *his* allegiance to the non-Users.

"I realize that your doubts are justified, and I simply wish to assure you that I am undeniably one of you. I have led a life defined by its errors, but I have firmly decided that I am truly and finally, one of you."

The doctor spoke of the cyborgs in the Metropolis, and used the term negatively. His words, magnified this time with true passion, stirred many more among the farmers and laborers.

"Brothers, sisters, take me at my word when I tell you that the Metropolis is a cold, black, synthetic beast that still feeds, though its heart has long stopped beating."

With the passing of a single moon and with my patient help, Dr. Mulligan seemed to have garnered a much greater understanding of life on the outside, and seemed to have immersed himself at least somewhat in our way of life. He expressed rage against the overwhelming control that Poplar Corp. exerted over the world, and inspired many of the laborers to finally voice their own hatred for the way things were.

"It is simply unfair! This world of progress thinks nothing of justice."

The doctor spoke about his awakening, about how he felt trapped, and how he could no longer live the meaningless existence of efficiency and production, constantly creating new products and updates for the Users, while genuine human life was marginalized in the shrinking wilderness. He spoke in bold terms, of slavery, of freedom, of the power of human desire, and of the necessity of choice. He extolled the importance of human connection, a sensibility deliberately repressed, and so long dead in the Metropolis. He explained the dangers of ALT•4•1, and how the Intelliware was just what he called a 'rung on the ladder of human evolution'. He spoke of how the Users were on the cusp of an evolution beyond the confines of the human body, and how they would become something non-Users could not even fathom: something quite like an elemental force.

Dr. Mulligan's prophecy of an evolution beyond the human form, though passionate, was met for the most part with even more skepticism. Nevertheless, I continued to do my best to convince the congregation that the doctor was in earnest, all the while finding myself engulfed in his passion. Just because we could not understand the terminology, did not mean that the threat was any less real. We did not understand how things had gotten to where they were now. Were we really going to doubt that they could get worse?

"Could any of us begin to explain that?!"

I asked this in support of Dr. Mulligan, pointing to the enormous silver stain of light that Metropolis 1 etched on the dark horizon. The crowd fell silent as they gazed upon the artificial cosmos so easily overcoming the natural darkness, ensuring the quest for progress *never* stopped.

We all knew who Dr. Mulligan was, and the role he had played in the technological revolution that brought about the rise of Poplar Corp. But what we also knew was that he was now undeniably here among us, in the flesh, and not as a champion of the technological revolution, but instead as a frail old man pledging allegiance to his fellow man, asking forgiveness for his past trespasses, and warning us of a great and imminent danger that we must all fight together. I understood the impulse for hatred and the desire to shoot him and be done with it- I struggled with it myself. But something about it all, something about the ever-present urgency in his voice convinced me that I was meant to join him. Some could not overcome their mistrust, but my passionate allegiance to the doctor drew at least some to consider the gravity of the situation. I was well respected among the brothers and sisters of the colony. The doctor had nothing to gain by lying to us. The Users already outnumbered us, and could have easily been rid of us by now. The doctor was not here to trick us; he was here to offer us the chance at a last stand. He was here to offer us an opportunity for change.

By the end of his second speech, and with my help, Dr. Mulligan had amassed a small following of about three hundred.

Dr. Mulligan has always recognized me as the first to pledge my allegiance, and as instrumental in the execution of his plan. For this token of loyalty, he has treated me with unspoken special consideration. He has told me many things that he has not told any of the others. Dr. Mulligan never asked me why I was so keen to join him though, or why I was so readily convinced of his sincerity. I never told anyone, but the truth is very simple: I had been inside the Metropolis once, when I was a boy. I ventured in shortly after my mother disappeared. The things I saw there haunted my dreams every single moon until Dr. Mulligan came to us in the wilderness. And the horrors all came back to me as he desperately described the terrible calamity that would become ALT•4•1…

*

Swollen with aching curiosity I could not abate for several fortnights, I finally stole away in my father's tractor. I was only ten turns old, and so the sight of me driving the tractor through the valley would have probably been humorous, had there been anyone around to see it. Determined to see Metropolis 1 for what it truly was, I drove the tractor through the long path that carved through the forested area, and all the way to the hills at the edge of the great valley, separating Metropolis 1 from the forested areas and the bay. These grassy hills I crossed on foot, to finally penetrate the great mystery of the Metropolis for the first and only time in my simple outsiders' existence.

I ventured into the Metropolis in my plain farmhand's clothes. I knew that non-Users were forbidden in the Metropolis, and I did not last long in there before a police vessel accosted me. I was an inconsistency in the system, and the system rejected me. The few sub-cycles I did manage to spend in the Metropolis, however, I will never forget.

By all accounts, it was even worse than the outsiders' tales and speculations. I could tell I had penetrated the power grid, or rather that I had penetrated something, because of the odd tingling sensation on the surface of my skin. Crossing the threshold put the hairs on the back of my neck and forearms on edge, as I stepped onto the clean plated concrete ground. With that first step, the surroundings as far as I could see ahead of me and in my peripherals all became perfectly symmetrical. The green grass ended, exactly where the colorless grid began. Black, polished towers of unfamiliar material rose at every corner as high and as far as the eye could see. Each and every one of them stood identically erect, and unmoving. They were smoother than the buildings we made on the outside. They were taller, and they were straighter. I could not understand how they stood so erect, as though they had overcome the irregularities that characterized the manmade. As I could not understand, I stared at them for a long while, as much in wonderment as in horror.

The air was odorless, and thin. I remember heaving. I also remember that as far as I could tell, there were no doors on the ground levels of any of the structures. This struck me as odd, but was little more than a mental footnote as I examined the surroundings. There was so much to take in. The foreign material from which the towers were built was opaque, and swallowed the light as though to keep its contents concealed. I touched my hand to one of the strange buildings, and ran a finger along the foreign black substance. The way the material felt, I could only describe as the absolute absence of friction.

I contemplated my finger and moved slowly about, shivering in the inexplicable cold. I looked about me, and realized that although I had driven across the valley in the heat of a sun burning brightly in a cloudless sky, in the shadow of these monolithic structures, the sunlight seemed to completely fade away. As I continued to look about me, I became conscious of a humming drone, though I could see nothing around me until I looked up again toward the shards of blue sky all but obscured by the towering shadows of black. As my eyes struggled to focus, I identified some strange silver vessels whirring far above me at incredible speeds above and between the massive structures. If not for the glints of sunlight reflected here and there off the polished vessels, I could not have been sure they were even there. It was impossible to follow their trajectories. They whizzed by like barely perceptible bullets in the sky.

I stared and stared until my craned neck became uncomfortable, and then I looked down. The ground on which I stood was *spotless,* and just as uniform as the rest of the surroundings. It looked like grey concrete, though sealed with some waxy resin that left a sticky film on my fingertips when I reached down to touch it. There were no cracks or breaks anywhere, in any of the materials. It was as though the entire Metropolis was built from one single piece of raw material. Taking it all in for the first time, I remained paralyzed for what seemed a lifetime.

There wasn't a sound to be heard anywhere but the humming drone of those silver bullets. Neither was there a single person in sight, anywhere I roamed. The scenery was repetitive, dark, and minimal. The silence was solemn, broken only by the constant whir and the audible friction of my rough workman's boots against the polished ground. I remember feeling very much like an inconsistency, like an anomaly in an otherwise mathematically sound vacuum.

Lost in this thought, I soon lost my way.

Panic began to set in as every turn I made brought me deeper and deeper into an indistinguishable, fiendish maze of polished grey and black. And as though my desperation to find the exit reverberated through space and time, a police vessel arrived, hovering patiently above me. This vessel I could see all too plainly, for it moved slowly, casually, languid with its knowledge of my inevitable capture. My sudden fear energized me, and I ran with great difficulty, struggling to navigate the surroundings that were designed to reject me. I lost a boot as I stumbled in vain. The vessel cornered me easily enough.

The policemen finally accosted me in a dark recess where I suddenly met a smooth black end. I was blocked off on all sides, and I resigned myself to the unspeakable horrors that awaited me. I imagined the monsters seizing me, and subjecting me to merciless torture. I shivered, and tears began to swell my eyes. As the doors of the silver vessel slid open, my heart beat faster than it ever had. I felt on the verge of collapse until the iota I looked upon them.

The policemen seemed oddly calm. Their form was not monstrous but human, though they lacked what I could only describe as certain basic human qualities. They did not speak, and in fact they did not even look at me, though I greeted them nervously as the terror lessened to anxiousness. My manner was sheepish, as a child caught in wrongdoing by a stern but familiar figure of authority. Their expressions did not acknowledge my communications, or my pleas for forgiveness. Their faces were unmoved, and remained vacuous for the length of our short exchange.

They moved slowly, as though their will were supreme, and so any rush superfluous. They seized me, however, with great strength, and immobilized me with some sort of static pulse. It was administered from the mouth of a strange green device in the shape of a horn. There was little pain, but my body was stunned into utter immobility, just as my mind had been stunned into awe by the unnatural surroundings. I was forced into the back of the vessel and floated motionlessly there. The policemen settled into the front seats, which glowed an odd shade of purple as their bodies made contact with the polished black material. My body felt frozen from the neck down but my vision remained in tact, and I could still see all that went on around me.

Inside the vessel, once the doors slid shut, there wasn't a sound. The interior of the vehicle was entirely black, and bare. There were no discernible controls, no steering wheel, and no buttons. I did not understand how the policemen were propelling the vessel.

I looked them over intently, trying to make heads or tails of it all, but for naught. The policemen's skin was incredibly pale, and toneless. They looked almost translucent, as though they lacked the light of the sun that could not penetrate the black tint of the towers, or the silver reflective tint of their miraculous flying vessel. Their faces were nondescript, vague, lacking any sort of salience or distinguishable human feature. They wore strange lustrous red frocks and black helmets with the words 'Poplar Corp.' scrawled along the sides of both in bold white letters. It was the first time I had read such words, and so they meant nothing to me. The vessel moved without a sound. The policemen did not speak. The silence was complete. A silence so complete I have never quite felt again. It was a silence profound, as though everything had willingly ceased to exist.

It still haunts me.

Suddenly, the vessel rose. I was roused by my gasps for air more even than by the sudden movement. I was overcome with fear, dumbfounded with how the vessel seemed inexplicably to propel itself. Afraid of the silence, I broke it with a nervous question that came out more like a frightened yelp. I asked the policemen how they were controlling the vessel, though they were again entirely unmoved by the sound of my voice. They just sat in front of me, entirely motionless, without any visible consciousness of their surroundings, or of their being present at all.

It seemed to me, for all intents and purposes, that they *weren't* present.

As the vessel gained altitude, all sides of the opaque black interior became gradually more transparent as we approached the source of the light, though the sunlight still, somehow, could not penetrate the vessel. The higher we rose, the better I could see all around me, and the more comfortably I could stare into the sun. Again, I gasped uncontrollably, basking in the miracle I was witnessing. I even began to scream, succumbing to the optical revelation of floating effortlessly through the sky. But a sudden sensation like a tightening noose overwhelmed, and soon silenced me.

The penetrating silence resumed.

We flew by some of the black towers in that silence, as I sat helplessly, entirely at their mercy. I was wide-eyed the entire way- half in terror, half in amazement. As we whirred by, I realized that like the vessel, the towers also became translucent in the stronger reflection of the sun. We approached the higher floors of one of the black towers and I gazed deeply into its interior, its contents finally revealed by the intense sunlight.

What I saw…

I understood in a flash why there were no people down on the ground.

I understood why the policemen did not speak.

That glimpse into the towers impressed on my mind the incontrovertible notion that the Metropolis was entirely beyond saving, and I immediately began praying to my God, helpless in the back of that vessel, that I might see the outside world and hug my father just *once* more.

In the towers, lined up neatly and sitting motionless in identical white chairs, were rows upon rows of Users with an identical vague look on their faces, in identical white polished frocks only barely distinguishable from the tone and texture of their skin. None of them had hair on their heads or on their faces. There was nothing in front of them either- no paper, no screens, no desk, no tools, nothing. They looked like they were sitting for portraits, absolutely motionless, with their colorless eyes open, but glossed and staring fixedly ahead.

I did not understand it then, and I was haunted by the images of their immobility for a long time afterward. I thought they might be dead, or turned to stone, and that I was soon going to be joining them. I gleaned from Dr. Mulligan's much later explanations that the Users' Intelliware was doing all of their work internally.

Work mode.

I had witnessed the Users in work mode.

In the back of the police vessel still hovering inexplicably through the air, I tried to speak but I could not find the words. I gasped for air and nearly choked on it. Tears of pain trickled down my face endlessly, but still the policemen did not move.

Then I remembered the futility. I realized my vulnerability, and my ignorance of the world. I felt so suddenly alienated from the world I lived in, in a way that shattered my innocence forever and shook my sense of purpose. My aloneness stood blaringly before me, summoned from the very core of my being, as I floated miraculously through the artificial paradise that defined the collective. In that moment, I decided very firmly that the collective was a monstrosity that had taken over my world. Both this monster and the new world it wished to create had cast me aside, and shunned my way of life.

There was no room for me here.

I realized firsthand how profound was the divide between the Metropolis and the outside. It was far beyond a mere geographical separation. It had become a separation of species.

I watched, still in awe as we passed three, then five, then ten towers that revealed identical contents. Glossed faces and motionless bodies.

Slaves.

The police vessel eventually brought me to the Metropolis limit where I had entered, as far as the power grid would allow the Users to roam. There, the vessel hovered to the ground. The policemen sprung into motion. They seized me again very patiently with their cold, powerful, unnatural hands. Then they walked me to the absolute limit of the power grid, where the black shadows and waxed concrete ended and the ground became the warm welcoming sunlight and green grass again. There, they tossed me to ground, and the impact of my body against the physical world returned the feeling to my extremities.

Through the daze, I tried to look them in the eye, seeking some shred of understanding, or of sympathy, some inkling of an identity within, but they did not return the glance. Instead they just turned their backs and moved slowly, robotically back to their vessel, which then whirred away to reassume its role in the collective drone.

The shock softened slowly, as I sat there staring into the black void, waiting for the feeling to fully return to my body.

I did not understand. In the back of the vessel, I was sure that I would be condemned to a lifetime in one of those towers.

For whatever reason, I had been granted a second chance.

When I could- when the stupefaction subsided- I ran my fingers through the comforting grass, and touched the crimson trail trickling from my knee with involuntary tears swelling my eyes. I took to my feet and ran as fast as my legs would carry me, away from the waxed concrete and polished frocks, back toward the tractor, and back toward the safety of the colony.

I never told my father what I saw in the Metropolis. I was just a child, and I was afraid he would have scolded me.

I never told anyone, in fact.

That memory was at the very front of my mind when Dr. Mulligan arrived with the prophecy of an all-powerful program. It was all too easy to believe the doctor's terrible omens. I had seen the Metropolis. I had seen the harbinger of death. I knew with my own eyes that the Metropolis was no longer a place for men, but a community run by an entity no longer familiar to humans.

That memory will be with me forever.

The beings I encountered that moon in the Metropolis were not human.

They are, I imagine, even less so now.

IV

I do not mean to suggest that I, a simple farmhand, can understand exactly how ALT•4•1 operates, or what its motives are. I am not a scientist, or an engineer. I hardly understand how a tractor runs, or how fire manages to mimic the luminous properties of the sun. All I know is the little I have read, and the little more that my father and Dr. Mulligan have suffered to explain. Though I doubt that even Dr. Mulligan, as an unenhanced man, can know the true motivations, or for that matter even the true extent of ALT•4•1's power. If ALT•4•1 truly has achieved disembodied consciousness, then it is unquestionably beyond human understanding.

The threat, though existential, remains but a vague notion to us working in the bunker. Perhaps this is for the best, for our ignorance helps to keep us wrapped in routine, and focused on our work. But with regard to Dr. Mulligan's knowledge of ALT•4•1, I do not know how much longer I will manage to hold my tongue. I have tried to question Dr. Mulligan many times on the subject, seeking peace of mind through understanding, but he has always somehow evaded divulging his full knowledge. Frankly, I think it is unfair that Dr. Mulligan insists on being so secretive. Many have begun to voice frustrations of the like, and the frustrations of the workers have begun to put tension on me as their intermediary. I am the only one who speaks directly to Dr. Mulligan in private, and so the workers naturally look to me for the answers that the doctor refuses to provide. The lack of information breeds suspicion and mistrust, which can undermine the chain of command. Dr. Mulligan continues to ward me off with the excuse that the time is not right. Perhaps he does see the bigger picture, and I do trust him, but his demand for blind and unwavering faith is beginning to test my, and our patience!

For now, anyway, we continue to follow Dr. Mulligan's commands, and focus all of our efforts on working together to destroy the threat that drove us underground. The execution of the plan is certainly the most pressing matter. But now, let me proceed with my tale…

We, the so-called anarchists, began building this bunker within a few moons of Dr. Mulligan's arrival. The doctor began to work out the plan immediately after I helped him gather the first wave of volunteers. Dr. Mulligan continued to deliver his message by the bonfire to any who would come to listen. Slowly but surely, his loyal followers increased in number by moonlight. By sunlight, we worked diligently under Dr. Mulligan's supervision.

My father and I welcomed Dr. Mulligan into our home, offering him an equal share of our meager food store, and the respite of a warm and sheltered bed. My father was one of the first to follow my lead and join the movement. After what happened to my mother, and all the enduring hardships that had preceded and followed, it did not take much convincing to rally my father into an organized rebellion against Poplar Corp. It did, however, take great effort on my father's part to disassociate the Dr. Mulligan of the now from the Dr. Mulligan of the past. My father had spent half a lifetime casting Dr. Mulligan as the unconquerable villain of his darkest fantasies. And so suddenly, the villain was inexplicably within reach, but had somehow been recast as hero. The doctor was sleeping under the same roof and eating at the same table, no less! It was a lot to take in. For the first fortnight or so, I could see my father's hatred for Dr. Mulligan shine through in his menacing glare. I have no doubts that Dr. Mulligan noticed it too. It made for some tense exchanges, but ultimately nothing came to pass. My father did eventually manage to find a way. He had been waiting his entire life for a shot at revenge. His desire for retribution against the collective was stronger than his grudge against an individual. His revenge would have been, for the longest time, exacted upon Dr. Mulligan. But that point was moot. It was clear that the doctor was no longer the enemy.

Those of us on board acquiesced to following Dr. Mulligan's orders diligently. The doctor bade us dig, and so we dug. We operated under the assumption that Poplar Corp. was, at least to a degree, aware of Dr. Mulligan's whereabouts. As far as we knew, there might not be any other settlements around for countless furlongs. Anyhow, ours was undoubtedly the closest to Metropolis 1. We worked vigilantly, wary of the possibility that Seekers might attack at any time. It was obvious enough that Dr. Mulligan was very likely hiding among us in the colony by the bay. There was hardly any game in the forested area, and hardly any edible vegetation in the wilderness untended by the colony. It would be difficult to believe the old man was getting by without help.

It was also obvious enough that Dr. Mulligan would be plotting against Poplar Corp. on the outside. In hindsight, the doctor was perhaps slightly brash to denounce Poplar Corp. the way he did. He must have known that the parting gesture would have no real effect on the Users. His final act of bravado- denouncing Poplar Corp. before his departure- seemed foolish and unnecessary to me. But of course, I did not chide the doctor for it. I do believe it was more an act of self-assurance and empowerment than an attempt to sway public opinion. Given his entrenchment in Poplar Corp.'s affairs, and his lifelong advocacy of their agenda, it was remarkable that Dr. Mulligan was now among us, leading the charge against them.

We were very much aware that sheltering Dr. Mulligan would be dangerous, and many of the elders voiced their distrust very clearly. However, his presence pushed a great many of us to finally acknowledge that our desire to end Poplar Corp.'s reign of tyranny was grander than our fear of death. The doctor's mere presence was a miracle. His cause, and the possibility of change- no matter how slight that possibility truly was- were certainly worth the risk. If we did not defend our values and our way of life, absolutely no one would. We were slowly being pushed out, and without a pushback, this world would soon have no place left for us.

While we dug the bunker, Poplar Corp. erected a giant countdown clock on the outskirts of Metropolis 1. The digital clock towered above the skyline, and was large enough and bright enough to be seen from the eighty furlongs that spanned the valley. It counted down the moons, the cycles, the sub-cycles, and the iotas to the scheduled launch of ALT•4•1. Below the clock was an equally enormous digital banner, inscribed with the luminescent red axiom:

TO REFUTE THE BENEVOLENCE OF PROGRESS IS TO CHAMPION ANARCHY

We could easily see both the banner and the clock from our worksite at the edge of the forest. The blood red inscription was the only trace of color on the black horizon. The banner's axiom, I learned, was a quote of Dr. Mulligan's, delivered time and time again in his early addresses in the time before Poplar Corp.'s ubiquity. It had evolved from an early rally cry, to a slogan for Poplar Corp., and eventually to something even more than a slogan- the creed that defined the Users. The banner's presence confirmed that Locklear knew Dr. Mulligan was hiding in the forest, for these adornments were clearly intended for him. I imagine they were meant to shame Dr. Mulligan out into the open, breaking him down with this constant reminder of his hypocrisy. He had turned on his life's work, and the banner would make sure that he was constantly reminded of that.

Rather than demoralize Dr. Mulligan, the antagonism fueled him. It solidified him in the opinion that he had been a monumental instrument in the misguidance of mankind.

TO REFUTE THE BENEVOLENCE OF PROGRESS IS TO CHAMPION ANARCHY

The luminescent banner that labeled us anarchists stoked the fires of our hatred for the Users and the Metropolis. Dr. Mulligan fervently rejected the banner, and reaffirmed his commitment to destroying Poplar Corp. The stunt made us feel small, and goaded us on. The clock amplified the dissent we were finally bold enough to express. The great passion it elicited in the doctor united us all the more firmly behind him, and against them. The more we heard the term anarchist, the more we came to embrace it, and rally around it. We gladly became the anarchists they wanted us to be. Anarchy was going to manifest as the dissolution of the Metropolis' organization, and progress, and order. It was going to bring about a return to humility, and to humanity. It was going to be a starting over. It was exactly what we all wanted, and we were no longer afraid to acknowledge it. Things had gotten out of hand, and we needed a starting over. We were gunning for them, and we were going to burn the Users, and everything they were programmed to stand for to the ground.

It took about sixty moons for the first followers to execute a rudimentary outline of Dr. Mulligan's blueprint. The blueprint was borne of the doctor's brilliant mind, and none of us really possessed the wherewithal or intellect to understand the minutiae or details of its structure. I could not understand how such a staggering bunker, so deep within the ground could possibly keep from caving in on itself. But my shortsightedness, and simplicity of mind is precisely why I am not the leader, but the most loyal and humble disciple.

All of us save the doctor whose fragile health and advanced age could not bear the strain, dug through all the sunlit cycles for sixty moons. We pooled all of our resources. We had the help of a few tractors and other simple machinery, but the need for manual labor was prominent. Human hands bearing basic tools proudly did most of the work.

The site of the excavation was strategically placed about eighty furlongs outside of the Metropolis limits, across the valley and on the very edge of the forest that insulated the bay. Dr. Mulligan insisted we make use of the cover of the trees and the brush while we dug. There was no telling what Locklear would do, if his Seekers were to discover the bunker. Locklear almost certainly had Users watching the forest around the clock. There had been minimal violence between User and outsider thus far- only the occasional small scale altercations between farmers and Seekers. Dr. Mulligan knew, however, the extents to which Locklear would be prepared to go, to ensure that ALT•4•1 would launch according to schedule.

On the other hand, Dr. Mulligan doubted very much that his former partner was aware of the ramifications of the launch of ALT•4•1. In all likelihood, Locklear only thought of the update in business terms, as another in the series of updates that sustained the Users, and by extension sustained Poplar Corp. Poplar Corp. had never before defaulted on an update, and so long as Locklear was at the helm, it would not default on this one.

As Dr. Mulligan's earliest follower, I was blessed or cursed with the responsibility of second command. I was the only one to receive orders from the doctor first hand. I kept the others in line, delegated tasks and kept the work force organized, but also worked hard myself to lead by example. Most importantly, I did not trouble the doctor with too many questions about the nature of his plan in the early stages of its execution. I wondered at the feasibility of what most of us guessed the plan to be, but I kept those thoughts to myself. In fact, I made sure no one spoke out against the plan, or expressed doubts that would undermine working morale. As the doctor said, even if the odds of our succeeding were infinitesimally small, the odds of our demise, should we do nothing, were absolute.

The doctor's calculations required that we rally a working force of one thousand laborers. And certainly, time was of the utmost importance. The bunker needed to be built, and we needed to get underground before the launch of ALT•4•1 if we hoped for the faintest chance of survival. The script was all but completely written at the time that Dr. Mulligan left Poplar Corp. The doctor estimated that, although he had destroyed the final steps of the calculation, within a few fortnights Poplar Corp.'s engineers would be able to arrive at a version of the algorithm on their own. Poplar Corp.'s resources were nearly infinite. Their technology was always evolving, and bettering itself. Taking them down would be near impossible, but it was nonetheless imperative that we try.

Oh, but how did we let it get to this point?

How did we sanction the notion that a single entity could reach nearly all of the world's population in an instant? How did we not see the menace of such blanketing influence?

The movement was slightly over four hundred strong while the digging of the bunker went on. Our progress was slow. The population of the colony by the bay was only about nineteen thousand, paling in comparison to the over ninety million Users inhabiting Metropolis 1. If head-on confrontation were to ensue, we wouldn't stand a chance. With their advantage in numbers, and in technology, the Users could wipe us out in one fell swoop.

To be perfectly honest, I never quite understood why they hadn't wiped us out already. Perhaps our only saving grace was their limitation to the power grids? Still, the power grids were always expanding. They exploited us, and stole our crops for their sustenance. Perhaps that was the last bit of utility we served. Minimal amounts of organic food were needed for the Users' sustenance, but no organic crops could be farmed anywhere on the power grids. It was more than likely that their last few organic limitations were the only thing keeping us alive...

After two fortnights of digging, the hole was about a quarter of the depth Dr. Mulligan required. At his recruiting speeches by the light of the great bonfire, Dr. Mulligan spoke of *our* progress. Seeing the work that we had done, and how we still toiled together moon after moon must have inspired some of the men of the colony, for we gained another hundred volunteers. It had been longer than anyone could remember since the brothers and sisters of the colony by the bay had unified themselves to work toward a goal that was not the harvest. The elders of the colony, however, remained skeptical, and spoke out against trusting the doctor.

"He is taking labor away from the farms that really need it, and for what? A silly crusade against a ghost!"

Many of these rumblings could not be overcome. The doubt infected a great many of the older men and women in the colony.

Luckily, the youth were not so jaded. Many were inspired by our efforts, and our brazen expression of dissent. For the first time since the non-User had been pushed to the outside, there was an organized pushback against the continual 'progress' that was eating away at our way of life. We were heavily outnumbered, and always would be. We knew this, but the energy and hope in Dr. Mulligan's message, the image of the world the way it was before the revolution, and the genuine belief in the possibility of change galvanized the movement.

After sixty moons of digging with our increased numbers, Dr. Mulligan finally announced that the hole was deep enough. But the cries of joy were quickly stifled, for the work was far from complete. Once the hole was deep enough, we began to fashion an alloy housing according to Dr. Mulligan's specifications. We melted down all the metals we could find, finding much of it in the colony's scrap heap. We melted down old tractors and simple machinery that no longer worked, but resorted also the use of silverware and other miscellaneous metals that could be spared by the sympathizing brothers and sisters of the colony by the bay. My father and I stripped our home of all the metal we could find, and offered up the stores to the movement. And finally, after nearly eighty moons of constant toil, the bunker was ready.

We were successful in our first goal. Fortune favored our toils, and we completed the bunker with even seven moons to spare, still ticking away on the giant countdown clock haunting the horizon.

I vividly remember Dr. Mulligan's last speech above ground. It was the only one of his addresses delivered during the sunlit cycles, by the giant latch now marking the entrance to the bunker. The three hundred cubit tunnel that led down into the bunker was fitted with sturdy steel rungs and a long thick rope to enable safe descent. An impenetrable alloy latch ten cubits thick sealed the bunker from the world beyond. Our creation was impressive, and the looks in our eyes as we stood united before our brothers and sisters reflected our newfound sense of power and pride.

Finally, in front of the thousands who came to see the bunker, Dr. Mulligan made his final plea. I remember it so clearly, though down here in the darkness it seems as though a lifetime has come and gone since the last time I saw the sky or inhaled the open air…

"Brothers, sisters of the colony, see the work that we have done! See the power of concentrated and organized human toil! The worker bees in the Metropolis, those less-than-humans who have pushed you to the fringes, who have marginalized you, and made you feel alien on this, *your* planet… they have been toiling just as we have, though toward what is perhaps an opposite goal. In half a fortnight's time, as you can all see, Poplar Corp. has scheduled the release of the *final* update of the Intelliware system. I know the seriousness of this threat, for I played a large part in the creation of this most malignant software. Many of you have demonized me, and continue to demonize me for my prior involvement with our mutual enemy. Though I sympathize with the sentiment, I must implore you to overcome your bias against me, and to hear this vital plea: the update that will arrive at the end of that countdown will change the world to a place even bleaker, and even more hostile against the non-User than any of you can possibly imagine. Even as I speak, you may think back over the last forty turns and recall a scattered, harsh existence. You are weak in number, and you always have been. You are lacking resources. You are entirely at the mercy of the User. And in seven moons, the looming threat of violence will finally materialize. In seven moons, ALT•4•1 will begin its hunt, and the outsider will be its prey."

Uproar louder than any I had ever heard rippled through the crowd at the mention of being hunted. The agitation levels were rising, as the people of the colony began to consider the gravity of Dr. Mulligan's words. The bunker was real- it was tangibly and undeniably before them. And the clock, too, was real. It still ticked on behind us, a distant omen of change and uncertain times to come.

"You lie!"

The old men screamed out, and a few of the women swooned as the turmoil began to border on chaos. The sunlight was on our side though, and kept the doctor in control. Dr. Mulligan raised his arms and demanded silence.

The crowd acquiesced. Dr. Mulligan's powerful reply poured out steadily:

"It is plain to see that I have nothing to gain by lying. I will descend into the bunker with my brothers and sisters, and my fate will be bonded to theirs, as it is bonded to yours. We are the resistance. We are the anarchists. We are the champions of choice, and the defenders of organic life. You may call us whatever you wish to call us. The fact is that we are *all* that stands between humanity and the blanketing influence of Poplar Corp. We are the final bastion, the last line of defense protecting against the obsolescence of organic life."

The doctor took a deep breath, and his eyes were bluer than the sky as he scanned the crowd imperatively:

"We will head underground, and we will dig our way below the Metropolis. This will be no easy task, but we will persevere. The power grids and the Intelliware codes are powered by the Poplar Corp. mainframe, which runs deep beneath Metropolis 1. This is our ultimate goal: to destroy the mainframe, and to destroy Poplar Corp., before Poplar Corp. can take our world away!"

The gathering exploded again, and the panic was even more hurried than before. I believed that the only thing keeping the peace was the fact that we- Dr. Mulligan's followers- stood together, armed. Dr. Mulligan raised his arms, with even more importance this time, and again the crowd quieted. He spoke once more with that steady, booming voice that belied his small and elderly frame:

"People of the colony! Men and women of the bay! The

time has come for us to no longer refer to ourselves as non-Users, as though we were lacking some vital faculty, or understanding. We are humankind, true humankind, and all that is left of it. They call us anarchists, and we may be so, but this world has always been ours and it shall remain ours, lest it be wrenched from our cold clawing hands! We have taken a wrong turn, and I am the first to acknowledge my responsibility for that wrong turn. But I have come to my senses, and I see that it is crucial that we overcome. *I, and we* shall rectify the error, and start anew!"

Dr. Mulligan paused here, and looked through the crowd one face at a time, wishing to transpose the importance of this moment through the eyes and into the depths of each and every onlooker. His great orator's voice oscillated feverishly from frenetic passion to systematic detachment, as he pulled his audience to and fro with his nimble lips:

"It is from the ashes of its former self that the phoenix rises again, my brothers and sisters, stronger than before. We shall first reduce Poplar Corp. to ashes, and from these ashes will rise the second history of man!"

Cheering broke out among the people in attendance, as Dr. Mulligan and all of us behind him raised our fists in unison. The cheering continued for some time and swelled us all with the importance of our mission. Several stepped forward and raised their fists with ours, taking a place among our ranks. When the cheering had lessened, the doctor looked over his new recruits, and realized we were still lacking manpower. He raised his hands again to silence the crowd:

"Brothers, sisters, time is of the utmost importance, and

we need a greater number of you to join us on our mission. If still some of you doubt me, look into the faces of my new brothers and sisters, who are your brothers and sisters, and see the trust they have bestowed in me. See the importance they have placed on the destruction of Poplar Corp. See the hope for a new world which inspires them, and which must inspire you to join us!"

The cries were feebler this time, though a few more stepped forward. Even with the new additions, we were still too little in number, and still relatively few compared to the mass of the crowd. It took only the momentary silence that followed the cheers for the dissenters to find their voices again. Again, many called us crazy. They cried out against the doctor, and against our futile effort to fight a threat we could not even see. Others- mothers, fathers, sisters, brothers- begged desperately for us not to go through with this insane plan:

"Please! None of you need to do this!"

Others threw rocks at us, and belligerently criticized the bunker as a voluntary suicide:

"Fools! You will die down there, and rot with the moist rocks and worms!"

We stood resolute behind Dr. Mulligan, who raised his arms once more to silence the crowd. The rabble was slow to quiet this time. When it finally did, Dr. Mulligan spoke slowly, almost softly:

"We may die down there, it is true. All of the men and women behind me are aware that they may never again see sunlight, and have agreed nonetheless to undertake this mission. For don't you see, if we do not succeed, humanity *will* be wiped away. I speak with great authority when I say the only reason you are all still here, the only reason there has been no violence until now, is because the Metropolis has exploited the non-User, has needed his resources. In some small way, the non-User remained useful. It will no longer be so. This final update will alter the Users utterly beyond recognition. Hear me now when I say, ALT•4•1 will have no use for humankind. Humankind will no longer be necessary! In fact, it will be a detriment to ALT•4•1. Do you hear me! In a world of progress, that which is no longer useful recedes into obsolescence!"

The crowd was silent. Eyes were wide with fear, and mouths hung open in dumb amazement at the prophecy of inevitable death. These were people who lived simple moon-to-moon lives, being asked to consider metaphysical ramifications they could hardly fathom. A few more stepped forward that moon, but the majority still remained stubbornly unconvinced of the threat. They shrugged it off, called the doctor a quack and a fraud, and returned to their farm work.

It saddens me to think of that moment, contrasted with a later moment, when those very same people who called us crazy rushed the bunker, begging desperately for entry.

Inside Metropolis 1, Poplar Corp. must have treated the launch of ALT•4•1 like the great celebration they felt it was. The Users had done it. Like clockwork, they would launch the update on time. Elaborate light shows colored the distant black skyline each of the remaining seven moons, as the clock ticked languorously to humankind's demise.

I wanted us to take the head start, to head underground and begin digging, but Dr. Mulligan insisted that our efforts would be futile without the full work force of one thousand. Besides, to begin early would be to prematurely exhaust our food and water supplies. We simply needed to wait for our brothers and sisters to come around. Once the latch would be closed, we could no longer admit anyone else into the bunker.

The moon before the scheduled launch, Dr. Mulligan called me out to the forest to speak to me in private. The sky was dark and ominous, lit only by the stars and the spirals of light rising from the distant Metropolis. Under the cover of darkness, and away from the others, Dr. Mulligan whispered anxiously that we were still about three hundred good, strong men short, and that our precious time was dwindling.

"Perhaps we should begin digging with what we have, doctor."

Dr. Mulligan's face was wrinkled with concern. There was no fire illuminating him this moon, but his white hair was brilliant even in the faint starlight.

"I would like that Beall, but I have made precise calculations. Our work will be in vain unless we have the manpower of a full thousand working in unison. It would be much too strenuous without the full thousand, and our already modest chances of success would drastically diminish."

The doctor and I looked gravely at the latch leading into

the bunker, imagining the darkness below, and coming to terms with the sacrifices we would make. The fair, inviting air, and the clear starry sky above made the cavernous bunker seem all the more revolting by contrast.

"Yes Beall, it is unavoidable. We have over eighty furlongs to dig, and even for one thousand men and women that is no easy task. We cannot sustain ourselves down there for any longer than ninety moons. We pooled all the resources we could find, and we will have ninety moons of sustenance, and no more."

The doctor pulled his beard, and looked for the resolve in my eyes to mollify his doubt.

"I understand doctor. Let us wait one last moon, and then we will go on with what we have. I am sure we will find a way."

I squeezed his arm in an act of camaraderie, and the concern melted from his face. I looked over at the bunker once more, and it seemed to me more than ever that I was stepping into a voluntary grave. Dr. Mulligan followed my gaze and frowned:

"You know these people much better than I do Beall. What can we do to rouse them from their apathy?"

The frustration returned to his face, and in this moment I realized how old Dr. Mulligan really was. I realized that even as the leader of us all, and even as a magnanimous historical figure, Dr. Mulligan was, ultimately, no more than human. He too, had his doubts, and craved the occasional reassurance that his efforts were not in vain.

"Unfortunately doctor, I fear that nothing will rouse them until the threat is manifest. They have done nothing to stop this revolution, and now I can only imagine that it is a great fear that keeps them from mobilizing."

The doctor frowned, and let out a long sigh.

I slept tentatively that moon, nestled in with the others just beyond the bunker. We lit no fire for fear of being discovered, and beyond the sphere of human heat the cool air lapped at my sensitive skin. I slept anxiously, and so poorly. I dreamt of falling, and woke with a gasp several times throughout the dark cycles. At sunup, we were set to make our descent, thus beginning our perilous journey.

The light finally came, though the sun rose sluggishly, and the workforce did slowly make its way into the bunker. A slip on just one of the rungs would mean the end, and so the descent was reluctant, and careful. A few, finally face-to-face with the darkness, were overcome with fear, and ultimately abandoned the cause.

The time passed, the iotas ticked slowly off the countdown clock, but still no more joined us. Dr. Mulligan and I remained above ground until the last, though, minding the entrance and waiting hopefully. The clock ticked down its final few sub-cycles…

We were still above ground when the moment came. The countdown clock ran to zero, and without a sound, or even so much as a ripple in the wind, ALT•4•1 was presumed to be online.

The doctor and I waited. The rest of the resistance was

safely down in the bunker. The sky was marked with no elaborate lights, and there was no sign of celebration. I watched as the warm breeze shook the branches of the surrounding trees. In the silence, it truly seemed as though nothing had changed.

Ten sub-cycles passed.

Still, nothing seemed to have changed.

Twenty sub-cycles.

Secret doubts began to bubble within me and I looked at the doctor suspiciously, though his face remained stoic and alert.

Thirty.

I was ready to step out and go see that my brothers and sisters still on the settlement were okay. I began to doubt whether the doctor's warnings had been nothing but a hoax. Just as I raised myself up and out of the bunker's mouth, a lone cry rang out through the forest and in between the trees, announcing that the great change had come.

The subsequent screams cascaded, echoing from a great distance. Dr. Mulligan and I braced ourselves for the worst. My brothers and sisters could be heard rushing forth, desperately fleeing the colony by the bay. Cries of pain and fear reverberated loudly, even through the muted foliage, and soon we could see the bodies dashing madly toward us. Hundreds arrived at the entrance of the bunker, pleading maniacally to be admitted. All those who had scoffed at Dr. Mulligan's speeches had now seen what was happening to the non-User, and they arrived in droves, frantic, and aggressive. The doctor muttered something about electromagnetic propulsion, temporary generators, and the ever-expanding breadth of Poplar Corp.'s electrical field, but I scarcely had time to piece it together.

We admitted all those who arrived in time. Through the frantic groans and excited explanations we were made to understand that the farmers by the bay had awoken to the rattling of seemingly self-propelled chainsaws, and to unmanned tractors crashing headlong into their homes. Those who survived the shock attack fled, as quickly as they could. They left everything behind, some of them for the second time in one lifetime. They ran desperately into the forest to join the doctor's outfit.

It was just as Dr. Mulligan had predicted. ALT•4•1 had begun its execution of the non-User. What he could not predict, however, was the efficiency with which it would hunt, and in such a way that the hunted could not even perceive, and so could not fight the predator.

Dr. Mulligan and I were ready for them. I held a cocked rifle, prepared to fire from the mouth of the bunker wantonly into the mania of the crowd, should violence erupt. From a utilitarian standpoint, we were lucky that the strongest, fittest, and swiftest of the survivors arrived first. Dr. Mulligan counted them down as they descended eagerly but carefully into the safety of the bunker. Once we had the manpower we needed, it was all we could sustain and we shut the rest out without a second thought. It was cold hearted, ruthless, and necessary. We heard desperate cries and violent knocking against the latch, as the others tried desperately to get in.

Some tried to break it open with what sounded like hatchets or other blunt objects. The latch was impenetrable. Still, the tunnel echoed with desperate cries and the clanks of steel on steel almost the whole climb down. Then suddenly, as we approached the last few rungs, the cries stopped. I don't know why they stopped, but the contrasting silence was deafening. It haunts me to think of them up there, running, seeking what might be impossible refuge. We have no way of knowing what the extent of the damage has been.

Survival had already been difficult on the outside without the ghoulish threat of this invisible reaper!

As we entered the bunker, I tried my best to forget my fear, and to turn my focus immediately to the work that needed to be done. The descent was arduous, and the trauma of the moment was fresh, but both would prove insignificant in relation to the burden of work down in the bunker. I was the last one in, and I immediately emptied the barrel of the gun and buried the shells in a shallow hole at the very back of the bunker, and the body of the gun in another, just as Dr. Mulligan had ordered me to. The doctor called everyone to the center, into the semidarkness by the powerful spotlights pointed at the frontier. The back of the bunker, where I had buried the shells, was obscured in total darkness. I remember emerging from that swallowing darkness and staring back into it for a lingering moment, shuddering to think that I, too, might end up there sometime soon.

Dr. Mulligan's booming voice brought me back into the moment, as he split us into groups and delegated tasks. One group set up the resting tents, and stocked these with blankets and earplugs. Another group bundled the oxygen, water, and food supplies near one of the outer limits of the bunker. Another group, by far the biggest, moved the digging equipment to the frontier. The spotlights were already manned and operating, thankfully. Out of breath, Dr. Mulligan retreated to his private tent, leaving me to oversee the prep work, and to maintain the motivation and efficiency of the workers.

Three hundred cubits below the ground, the bunker runs for twelve furlongs, edging toward the Metropolis. It is four furlongs wide. The dark hole was stocked beforehand with all the necessary supplies to keep it inhabitable. Everything needs to be carefully rationed, to ensure that we do not run out before the completion of our mission. Digging eighty furlongs in ninety moons is a tall order, especially in these conditions.

Although tight due to our numbers, the bunker is staggering in size. It is a wonder of human toil and ingenuity. Sometimes, acknowledging the simple fact that we worked together to create this marvel of human engineering inspires me, and reaffirms my belief in Dr. Mulligan. If he could design, and rally us to create this bunker, then I do not doubt that he will lead us to destroy Poplar Corp. After all, Poplar Corp. is just something else he designed and built. If we make it to the mainframe, Dr. Mulligan says we can take the grid down. And I know we can, and will make it…

Dr. Mulligan had us stock the bunker with what he calculated to be enough food, oxygen, and water stores to sustain a colony of one thousand people for ninety moons. The food is mostly tins of imperishables gathered from the colony's emergency reserves- beans, cured meats, fruit preserves, etc. It is not the most luxurious menu, but Dr. Mulligan insisted we could not bring any electrical devices down in the bunker, unless they were absolutely necessary. Fire, too, would be a hazard down in the bunker, as there is no outlet for the smoke. And so, the luxury of heat for cooking is one we must live without.

That is how we got to be underground. That is how we got to where we are now. Yes, there are now one thousand of us down here in this little hole. We have been digging in the direction of the Metropolis for over fourteen moons now. It is tight. There was no way for us to bring even one extra body down here. We truly had no choice but to turn so many away. The doctor had made very precise calculations with regards to the rations, to the inhabitable space and the breathable air, and even the slightest deviation from these calculations could compromise our chances of completing the mission.

The bunker is illuminated with the help of high-powered spotlights pointed at the wall of dirt we call the frontier. Hand crank generators power the lights, and these must be manned around the clock. The spotlights offer the only source of light down here, and are absolutely vital to our survival. If the lights go off, we die. I try not to think of this, but to take the lights for granted. It helps me to focus on my work, and lessens my anxiety. The lights are so bright, that to stare straight into them is blinding. However, to close one's eyes tightly in the wide illuminating spray is to delight in the crimson darkness that is almost enough to recall the sun.

We are mostly young males down here in the bunker. I think about eighty percent of us down here are young men.

All of us work in unison, digging. The women do physical work just like the men. Some of them dig, and some of them run the manual crankshafts powering the spotlights at the frontier, if they are strong enough. The weakest among us are in charge of doling out the rations.

There are no beds in the bunker. The only resting places are the few dozen sleeping tents positioned in the penumbra of the spotlights. These are equipped with blankets and earplugs, so that the utterly exhausted may get the necessary rest. No one sleeps until they are on the verge of collapse. There is so much to do, and everyone recognizes the importance of continued work. There are also a few dozen feeding tents, identical to the sleeping tents in all but their function, and also set up in the fading light of the spotlights. The feeding tents are fitted with an army knife to pry open the tin can rations, and a few blankets for comfort.

Our rations are challenging. We are limited to three cups of water and two tins of food each, per work shift. Each work shift spans roughly ten cycles. No one has broken the ration yet, but on this note I also fear the diggers begin to grow uneasy. We work like oxen but are fed like mice. I am constantly hungry, and thirsty, and tired. My body aches without respite. The spotlights are so, so bright, and beyond their nebulous light, the utter darkness devours space and time.

There are no electrical devices whatsoever down here in the bunker, aside from the absolutely necessary lighting. We took no chances. After seeing what had happened on the outside, I voiced a hushed fear that ALT•4•1 would be able to detect us, or even seize control of the spotlights. Dr.

Mulligan silenced this fear with the assertion that we were far enough under ground to go undetected. I pray that he is correct. Besides, it seems to me that with regards to the lights, we really had no choice.

The oxygen we inhale is rationed as well, and the air is awfully thin. Sometimes I feel as though my body will seize up and shut down on me from lack of oxygen, but it seems always to find another gear and push on. Some of the men have had to learn the hard way not to work too quickly, or too eagerly, as though their workload were finite and could be completed more quickly with added effort. The key to survival, to making the most of the oxygen and nourishment available, is to work at a slow, steady, and unified rate. At the frontier, the best thing is to forget one's emotions in the constant toil.

Other than the food, oxygen, and water stores, the generators, the spotlights, and the tents, Dr. Mulligan stocked the bunker with approximately eighteen hundred sturdy steel spades, six hundred pick axes, and five hundred two-man wheelbarrows. At the frontier, three hundred men work at a time, crushing and lifting relentlessly, filling the wheelbarrows with the rocks and soil. Another hundred men man the wheelbarrows, two men to one wheelbarrow at any given time, and carry the debris from the frontier to be dumped into the darkness at the back of the tunnel. There, the wheelmen must compact the debris as well as they can to preserve our limited space in the bunker. We cannot create or eliminate matter, only move it.

When the diggers encounter a hard spot, or a large rock blocking the way, they must organize and group together, to dig around and unearth the impeding piece of rock. Then, they must group together again to help the wheelmen move the massive debris to the back of the tunnel. Sometimes they break these larger rocks down with the pickaxes, but I have begun to discourage this practice, for it is hastening the damage of our tools. Many spades and wheelbarrows are broken every work shift, and these too are thrown at the back of the tunnel and compacted with the debris. As though we hadn't enough to worry about, the rate at which we are breaking the tools is alarming. If we run out of usable tools, we will be all but stuck below the ground.

It is hard work down in the bunker, with hardly any rest. We are weary. The debris is piling up at the back of the bunker, and as we move closer to our journey's end beneath the Metropolis, we are slowly sealing ourselves off from the only tunnel we have to the outside world. We knew what we were getting ourselves into, but sometimes it is very difficult to understand the extent of a sacrifice until it is realized through experience. The anxiety only adds to the difficulty breathing down in the bunker.

Though we all work tirelessly in unison toward the completion of Dr. Mulligan's plan, none of us know exactly what we will do if we finally reach the mainframe. Or for that matter, how we will escape once we have destroyed Poplar Corp. and ALT•4•1. I think that many of the men have begun to think this through, and it has only added to the volatility of the atmosphere. I only hope that Dr. Mulligan has thought of a way to keep us together, and motivated. We think only of digging the last few dozen furlongs to the Metropolis. Or, at least, I do my best to keep the workers focused only on this thought. We have done well so far, but our energy levels decrease with every tick of the unseen clock.

It is ghastly and primitive down here, but we have no choice. The rights of the individual are none, and the interest of the human collective is truly all that matters.

It worries me to think that the inclusion of women may have been an oversight on the doctor's part. But then, I know we had no choice but to take any volunteers we could. And later, I suppose there will likely be the need for reproduction. What worries me is that the young men work hard, and they have urges. It has been a fortnight since any of them have done anything but toil every moon without any outlet for their building frustrations, and there are very many dark corners in the bunker. For now, we are still united in our cause. But it has only been a fortnight, and I often worry how much longer we will remain sheltered under the soothing cloak of civilization. I already see the men looking hungrily at the women, and angrily at some of the other men. And though some of the women may reciprocate the desire, there is simply no way to accommodate a pregnancy, and absolutely no room for quarrels. There is hardly one woman for every four men. Nothing has happened yet, but I feel a sense of unease bubbling among the workers. Restlessness has begun to creep in, and I fear that these tight spaces might be our undoing.

Man is not meant to live beyond the reach of the sun.

It is crazy to think that people were clawing at each other to get underground to join us on what very well might be a suicide mission. And yet, that desperation for survival, that inextinguishable desire to do literally anything to survive, that is what *will* enable mankind to survive. Instinct. The animal instinct we all possess, it is something that technology will never be able to duplicate. It is what has kept us going for thousands of turns, what will get us through this underground hell, and what will bring us to triumph over ALT•4•1.

Or, at least, I can only hope it will.

But now, I have grown weary even of writing.

I shall rest my mind by working my body. I will go rejoin my brothers and sisters at the frontier, and dig.

V

After my last work shift, Dr. Mulligan finally shared some coveted new information with me...

The doctor and I speak privately very often down here in the bunker. As the outfit's second in command, it is my duty to relay news from the frontier to Dr. Mulligan. The doctor asks me countless questions about the workers' morale, and the progress of the digging. I answer diligently, if with a hint of boredom. Not much changes from cycle to cycle at the frontier. The sights and sounds are much the same. The doctor calculates that we have dug about twenty-four furlongs thus far.

I have, however, become somewhat worried about the other matter. Dr. Mulligan shares my concerns regarding the increasingly anxious behavior of the diggers, and we have begun to spend much of our time together contemplating ways to keep the workers calm and engaged in spite of the conditions.

Dr. Mulligan, however, does not understand the true measure of the restlessness. He simply cannot, for he rarely leaves his tent. The atmosphere underground is saturated with dust and the constant clamor of excavation. Though the doctor does no labor, the conditions in the bunker are nonetheless extremely taxing on him in his advanced age. It seems his eyes, and veritably his entire aura has dimmed down in the darkness. He speaks slowly, and often in a flat tone that lacks energy. I, too, am exhausted, and the doctor's drowsy musings only increase my own drowsiness. I listen as best I can as the doctor relates the tasks that need completing. It is a vital part of my duty to relay the doctor's recommendations to the workers.

During this particular exchange, I listened to his meanderings as long as I could until the topic of morale inevitably came up. I seized the opportunity to ask some more difficult questions about the mission. As second in command, I felt entitled to a greater understanding. It was difficult working in a shroud of mystery, and it frustrated me how little I saw of the bigger picture. As the doctor rambled on about the proper use of the pickaxes, some urgent impulse seized me, and I could no longer hold my tongue:

"Dr. Mulligan, I apologize if I speak out of turn, but I fear that many of us including myself are beginning to *ache* for an answer, or at least for an explanation. The men ask me every work shift to what final end we ceaselessly toil. I subdue them the best I can, but I feel that the platitudes I repeatedly offer in reply are losing their subduing effect. Tensions are rising, doctor. We all have an idea of what is going on, but the men want to hear from *you*. We have put our lives in *your* hands. I fear that our organization will soon dissolve, and we will soon lose the workers' cooperation without the offering of some morsel of understanding. We are all looking for a reason to go on. Please, a clearer sense of direction is all we crave."

The doctor's tent is very small, like all the others, so in order for us to face each other we sat with legs crossed. Only a pair of worn wool blankets cushioned us from the hard ground beneath. My joints ached, and the position was very uncomfortable to me, but Dr. Mulligan seemed perfectly at ease. I imagined him spending many cycles in that meditative position, and so growing accustomed to it. I watched Dr. Mulligan intently as he sat in silence. The questions I asked always seemed to annoy him. He raised his brow and parted his lips in his characteristic way, and I anticipated his intent to evade the question. I interjected:

"With all due respect doctor, I think it has become *imperative* that you explain a bit more about the nature of the enemy we are all facing *together*, and what your plan really is to destroy it. To what end do we toil? We can no longer afford this posturing!"

My tone was uncompromising, and had its desired effect. Dr. Mulligan sighed, and ran a hand the length of his long white beard. His deep-set eyes were wrinkled, and tired. It seemed that their sapphire color had lost some of its luster. His face drooped and his hair was unkempt as the rest of us, if only less matted by the grime of unceasing toil. His position at the helm of the resistance was one of unique responsibility, and his shoulders no doubt sagged under the heavy weight of the burden. Our everymoon briefs revealed more and more the doctor's weariness and age.

"Very well Beall, you are right. I will tell you what you

wish to know."

My dry lips almost broke into a smile. My passion had persuaded him, and he took a moment to resign himself to this fact. Though the constant digging and lack of sleep kept me perpetually exhausted, the excitement of the moment vitalized me and commanded my full attention. Dr. Mulligan paused and frowned, organizing his thoughts.

"ALT•4•1, I must presume, is still dependent upon the mainframe. The mainframe runs the grid from deep below Metropolis 1. It is the same grid that has powered the Intelliware for many turns. This is why we dig."

I began to ponder Dr. Mulligan's words, energized by the prospect of finally gaining a deeper understanding, but my thoughts were interrupted by the rolling wheels of a trolley coming to a halt just outside the doctor's tent. The moment's excitement immediately fizzled, as the anticipation of the ration overpowered my rational faculty. A timid little woman I had seen several times, and whom I had come to associate positively with the minor relief of the ration, poked her head meekly into the tent to dole out the first of the moon's three helpings of water. Dr. Mulligan and I greeted her warmly, welcoming the tins half full of tepid water with childlike eagerness.

The woman moved hesitantly, realizing that she had caused an interruption. Her body was slender, and her expression unassuming. As she handed me my ration, I gazed unabashedly upon her wild red hair. It seemed to me that it would hang down to her waist if it were not tied up. Her face was caked with dirt, and tired. All of our faces were the like.

The dirt had by now found its way into every crease and wrinkle. Dirty as she was, I could yet see the undeniable softness and grace hidden beneath the filth. Our eyes met, and the radiant green of her irises impressed upon me. She tried her best to smile, and I did my best to return my own feeble smile, before her head receded beyond the tent and the wheels of the trolley rolled on. Though she might have wanted to, and though I might also have wanted her to, she could not linger. Doling out the rations was a very serious job. There were a thousand thirsty workers who badly needed relief.

Thoughts of the wild haired girl quickly dissipated, though, as I looked down into the bare, dented, and dirty tin with ambivalent feelings of great expectation and considerable disgust. The ration supplied was but two or three miserable mouthfuls, and the rush of excitement I felt every time I received the tepid tin made me feel small, and paltry.

As I always did, I swirled the water around two or three times, appreciating the sound and sensation of its liquid motion. I was extremely careful not to spill a single drop. And then, as the novelty wore off, I drank it all down. I swallowed my rations quickly, and greedily. I could hardly help it, though I noticed Dr. Mulligan patiently put his tin aside. The water rations were the moments of the moon I looked forward to the most, even though the consumption of the ration was always followed by an overwhelming moment of bitter frustration. Because the very moment the water was gone, I was left with a void desire for more. And that void desire seemed always to shift to a flash of anger inspired by the idea that I could never seem to get my fill. In my angry haze, it seemed to me that having some, but not enough to truly satisfy, was worse than having none at all. But then, the anger always faded. My reason kicked in, and the distraction passed. That notion was silly, and always short lived. It is always best to have enough, and I am still alive…

Dr. Mulligan sat patiently stroking his beard, his other hand covering his untouched ration from the thick dust floating even in the tent. I resumed the conversation:

"What were we saying? Ah, yes, the mainframe beneath the Metropolis. How can that be doctor? How can ALT•4•1 still be dependent on the power grids? How, then, did it manage to kill non-Users beyond their limits? What exactly are its motivations?"

My questions were jumbled, as each question built on the delirious excitement incited by the one just before. I was thankful for the rush of excitement though, as the adrenaline coursing through my veins momentarily erased my overwhelming fatigue. Dr. Mulligan, however, remained stoic. He sighed the tired sigh of an old, withered man. I had not known him for very long, but for the time we had been acquainted, Dr. Mulligan had had little patience for these types of reductive explanations. My eyes, however, made it clear I would not be denied. He continued reluctantly:

"ALT•4•1 is yet incomplete. It is powered by an imperfect code, and that code still runs through the mainframe. We must hold to this principle Beall, for if it is no longer true and ALT•4•1 has indeed transcended, I fear that all our efforts are utterly futile. If the entity we are fighting is no longer dependent in any way on the mainframe, then the entity is no longer dependent on the physical world. If that is the case, then the technology cannot be overcome."

The lack of clarity in the doctor's answers frustrated me. He seemed to be repeating things I had heard him say before, and that I still could not understand. My frustration came to a boil, and I cried out louder than I should have:

"But that's all a bunch of jargon that means nothing to me! That doesn't explain how or why ALT•4•1 is able to kill people, or how it is able to seize control of machinery beyond the grid! We heard what was happening out there! People swore to being chased by self-propelled chainsaws, houses were being run over by self-propelled tractors, windows shattered throughout the colony… People were running for their lives! And us! Take a look at us, doctor! We have been reduced to this base, vile, and less than human surrounding. Tell me what you know! This is no time for secrecy; our lives are on the line! I am completely loyal to you doctor, and I trust your intuition, but you must tell me!"

Dr. Mulligan's eyes widened momentarily with surprise. My outburst boomed clearly above the synchronized clacking of pickaxes and spades in the distance. Dr. Mulligan had not been to the frontier very often, he had not been working, and so perhaps he misjudged my patience. Perhaps he still expected all of us to work quietly under his dominion, like the Users once had. He looked at me apologetically, and I tried my best to gather myself before he continued:

"I apologize Beall, you are right. I have been very taciturn, while you and the others have toiled constantly. I realize that I have been selfish. You and the others do deserve to know more."

He sighed again, poked his head stealthily outside the tent, and then sealed the tent's opening all the way to the top. He glanced at me apprehensively as he resumed his position with legs folded, lowering his voice to all but a whisper:

"Very well, I will tell you the truth…"

He took another deep breath and looked skyward.

"The awful truth is: I do not know. I simply *cannot* know. Perhaps ALT•4•1 can operate as electromagnetic waves now, and is capable of seizing control of any device powered by electromagnetism. Perhaps ALT•4•1 has found a way to master the energy of the electrical fields created by the power grids, and is using this energy to temporarily power the machines outside of the grid. Perhaps ALT•4•1 is no longer limited to the power grid at all. I know it is a concept difficult to process, but I mean it when I say that ALT•4•1 may be in many ways as elusive as the wind."

I scratched my head and looked skeptically at Dr. Mulligan. I considered briefly that this might be just another of the doctor's shrewd methods of circumvention, but he seemed genuinely tormented by his admission of doubt. In that moment, I finally began to wrap my mind around Dr. Mulligan's predicament: he must veil his own doubts about our efforts, for if doubt were to seep in at the frontier, all hope would be lost. This is why he had been so secretive! He did not know very much more than we did, and there was no way he could tell us as much without compromising our loyalty to him as leader! I wanted desperately to understand what he meant by 'elusive as the wind', but his earnest blue eyes left me without solace. His vulnerability had produced a rare crack in the doctor's normally statuesque façade, and I was probably as shaken by it as he was.

"But Dr. Mulligan, if ALT•4•1 is like the wind, why is it after us? Why does ALT•4•1 seek to eliminate the non-User?"

Dr. Mulligan took a careful mouthful of water from the tin at his side, savoring it as he stretched out his ragged body. His bent frame crackled audibly in the stuffy tent as he stretched his arms as far as he could behind his back. Life underground had been hard on all of us, but the doctor's vulnerabilities reminded me that he was human, and that none of us down here were anywhere near as old as he was. The conditions were hard on him, and his energy levels were so low that it seemed even idle conversation soon exhausted him. He replied in a melancholy voice, as though disappointed that I was honing in on the profound truth he had worked so hard to conceal- the truth that despite everything he had done to create it, he knew next to nothing about the true nature of ALT•4•1.

"The why, I presume, is much easier to guess than the how, though they're both nothing more than speculations, I'm afraid. Like all the updates before it, ALT•4•1's code should run through the mainframe below Metropolis 1. If that is the case, then ALT•4•1 is still an entity dependent upon the physical world. It is still, in some way, a vulnerable entity. Its transcendence is not complete. It must still consume. It must still rely on the electricity of the power grid."

He paused to look at me, as though the conclusion were obvious. I stared at him blankly, and he went on:

"If ALT•4•1 is a vulnerable entity confined to this planet, and powered by energy generated by this planet, and if ALT•4•1 is presumably motivated by reason, then it makes reasonable sense that it would do all it can to preserve the well-being of the planet that sustains it. Or, at least, to ensure its supremacy over that planet's resources."

All of these hypotheticals whirled through my mind like floating lattices connecting to depict a clear image, though an image I could not yet make out.

"I do not know that I follow, doctor."

Dr. Mulligan's voice became suddenly grave. His beard contrasted an impossible white against the brown cloth of the tent, as though it was somehow immune to the dirt all around us.

"Man is a consumer of resources. He has been since the dawn of time. It is incontestable that man has been the greatest consumer of resources on this planet since his evolution from mutable foraging alliances to permanent agricultural settlements. And that consumption has only increased as man sharpened his consciousness, evolving from tribal dispersion to hierarchically organized civilizations, and eventually to global digital interconnection. Never before has anything come along to truly threaten man's dominance of this planet's resources. In other words, man has long been the unchallenged top of the food chain. But man was shortsighted, and vain, and lacked the majesty of a just ruler. Man exploited his surroundings for personal gain, and justified this exploitation under the guise of progress. Now, as a result of man's folly and insatiable desire for more, a new entity has emerged from man's need to adapt to his depleted surroundings. ALT•4•1 has unlocked the next step in human evolution, and has assumed a quasi-elemental state. ALT•4•1 is in greater harmony with, and so a more complete master of its surroundings than man ever was, or could be. As disembodied consciousness, ALT•4•1 is in many ways a part of its surroundings. It is one with its environment in a way that man has always wished he could be."

'Disembodied consciousness', 'elemental state'- I had no idea what the doctor was talking about, but I could not stop him to ask for an explanation just yet. Dr. Mulligan paused to think, sipped what was left of his water ration, and ventured on:

"ALT•4•1 is no longer an instinctual, or emotional being. Instinct and emotion are phenomena exclusive to the closed individual, and are borne of the individual's innate will to survive. It is simple genetics Beall… our instinct is borne of our genes' singular purpose: to propagate themselves, to continue to exist in finite reproductive organisms from generation to generation. All organisms are programmed for survival in this way. But ALT•4•1 has pushed beyond. It has no genes to reckon with, no body through which it accesses existence. No longer shackled to the petty instinct for survival that has always clouded man's judgment, ALT•4•1 is finally able to exist as a purely rational being, coded for maximum unity with its environment. As a purely rational being, it makes sense that ALT•4•1 would calculate that man, and I fear that by extension all organic life, is the only great threat to the unity of the elements on this planet, and so the final threat to the perpetual unity between the collective consciousness of ALT•4•1 and the matter that is the physical world."

I felt the gravity of Dr. Mulligan's words as I let them sink into my mind, but the images they conjured were still fuzzy, and indistinct.

"What are you saying doctor?"

Dr. Mulligan frowned:

"Man manipulates and destroys nature. ALT•4•1 wishes to be one with nature. I'm afraid what I'm saying is that ALT•4•1 is aiming to wipe us out, to destroy the final impediment to true harmony with this planet and its energy."

Dr. Mulligan's even temper angered me. I was delirious with over-exertion and exhaustion, and Dr. Mulligan's cool delivery of an inescapable, and perhaps justified apocalyptic prophecy maddened me:

"But that doesn't make sense! We are innocent in all of this! We have done nothing wrong! We have already been pushed from the Metropolis, and now ALT•4•1 proposes to push us from the planet altogether? What great sins must we be punished for? How can you sit there even keeled and speak such terrible words?"

If it weren't for the sounds of digging at the frontier, my screams would have certainly echoed throughout the bunker. Dr. Mulligan remained composed, and furrowed his brows as though in disapproval of my agitation:

"Beall, please."

I was breathing heavily, but my desire to know more returned to me, and I realized I must calm down. With my eyes still flaring I managed to ease myself into quietude. When he saw that my anger had subsided, Dr. Mulligan went on, still speaking in that low, measured voice:

"Yes, very well. Perhaps *you* say that you have done nothing wrong. And perhaps *you* are right. But ALT•4•1 will not see it that way. Mankind consumed and consumed, and renewed nothing. We killed and we ate until well after we were full. We depleted the planet of its resources to make ourselves fat and content, and replenished the planet only in death, when our parasitic bodies finally decomposed, returning nutrients to the exploited soil. It seems plain to me that a conscious planet would celebrate the death of man, as it would mark the end of said planet's exploitation. The extinction of man would ring in a new age- an age of true peace and harmony."

Dr. Mulligan's words were filling me with fury, and my head pounded as I tried desperately to process the complex notions he described. I had never before heard such a rational, detached condemnation of man!

"How can you say that? How can you sit there, a perishable being, and say that? That is nothing but a negative way of seeing the human body. We were born this way. It is not our fault that we need resources to live. Even your precious ALT•4•1 is sustained by the energy of the power grids. To live, one must consume. That is inevitable! How can it lay such scornful judgment upon us?"

Dr. Mulligan was silent for a moment, and his eyes

narrowed in calculation.

"That is a fine point, Beall, and it brings us to an even larger problem. I must admit that I do not know how ALT•4•1 continues to power itself. The grids were powered by a combination of hydroelectric, solar, and wind power, but I can't imagine that ALT•4•1 can be sustained that way forever. The hardware that generates the power, though fully automated, would erode and decay with time. Perhaps it would be able to rebuild? But then, the point was to find a way to self-power, to truly transcend. Perhaps it has found a way… I wonder."

I stared at Dr. Mulligan blankly as he thought through his own propositions. The trace of admiration in his voice as he spoke about ALT•4•1, and the look of wonderment on his face reawakened my anger. His contemplations unnerved me, and shook my confidence in our chances of survival. But then, watching him think reminded me that his ability to detach himself from his own notion of self was precisely what enabled him to be such a brilliant designer. How did he put it? 'Shackled to that petty instinct for survival that has always clouded man's judgment'. Perhaps the doctor was truly capable of thinking beyond himself, and perhaps harnessing this ability was our only hope. Panicking in a moment of crisis will never expedite the crisis' resolution. The thought of his innovative powers reminded me of his importance to the cause, and abated my anger, and doubt. Dr. Mulligan was a thinker, and thinkers must not be bothered with what one *ought* to think, but must simply think. Our eyes met and Dr. Mulligan saw that my emotional response had subsided, and that his conceptual schemes were beginning to take hold in my mind.

"Beall, consider perhaps that human consumption is not our moral fault, but rather a design flaw. I know it is difficult, but imagine if you can, only for a moment, that you are not the center of the universe."

The anger began to bubble up in me once again, but I took a deep breath and tried to remain composed. Dr. Mulligan's face was back to its usual impassive complexion, and I knew he meant no harm with his conjectures.

"Beall, let me share with you another little secret, a long forgotten piece of history. I know it is a little before your time, but do you know why Poplar Corp. grew to become what it did?"

I looked Dr. Mulligan in the eyes and I imagine he saw the apprehension I wished to conceal. Dr. Mulligan had not mentioned Poplar Corp. but as a vague enemy since he had left the Metropolis. His prior involvements with the monolithic entity had, for the most part, been swept under the rug and ignored.

"What do you mean?"

Dr. Mulligan reached out and took my hand, his voice inflated with meaning:

"Poplar Corp. was nothing before Intelliware. Before I worked out the software and hardware components for the Intelliware system, Poplar Corp. was nothing more than an idea I had."

Dr. Mulligan's deep blue eyes were charged as he recalled his youthful enterprise:

"The idea sprung from the absolutely undeniable fact that humanity was, before Poplar Corp. came along to save it, dying. We were on the very brink of extinction. No one spoke aloud of such things of course, but to the thinking man it was rather plain. It was never our numbers, or our ability to reproduce that jeopardized mankind. No, in that regard we were healthier than ever. However, for the last three hundred turns, really since the first industrial revolution, man had been consuming exponentially more with each passing turn, growing our economies, producing more and more to meet the demands of the consumer, to grow our quarterly profits, all the while remaining mindless of the natural scarcities our system was creating. Over the same three hundred turns, humanity grew constantly in number. Think of that. More and more men and women roamed the planet, and each of them consumed more and more with every passing turn. Mankind threatened to bring itself to apocalypse with its overconsumption in the Metropolis. Water had become so scarce, that bloody wars were regularly waged over lakes and rivers in the subcontinent. And what were we going to do? Ask man to dial it back, to relax a little on the consumption? To ration food, water? Were we to deteriorate to police states and communism after generations of upheld belief in the free market? After conditioning man for one hundred turns to be a consumer, immersing him in a culture that placed him at the center of it all and celebrated his never ending quest for more, were we suddenly going to change all of the rules?"

I could not answer Dr. Mulligan's rhetorical questions. I could scarcely understand most of them. 'Free market', 'police states'? I hadn't an inkling of this terminology. I simply sat wide-eyed, taking in all that I could.

"It was so silly of us to buy into these economic principles in the first place. Most of them were founded on the fallacy that our resources were infinite. It was so primitive, and near sighted! Sustainable growth was the rich man's con: the idea that constantly increasing consumption was good for the economy. But the economy is made of people, and people live on a planet of finite resources. How can you grow every turn, when you live in a world of finite resources? How can you grow every quarter when the physical world does not grow with you?"

I stared at the doctor with the same wide eyes, my mouth agape as he spoke. I felt his anger, directed at these obscure, failed ideologies of the past. I felt the anger in his cold blue eyes, and in his tightening grip on my hand. None of this had ever occurred to me- that we could have stopped this… that we could have seen this agonizingly slow deterioration coming from way off, and stopped it. I had been born into this world of division, and so it seemed the only natural way to me. Dr. Mulligan still squeezed my hand tightly, but the trace of urgency had gone from his voice when he continued:

"The economy was a concept invented by man, and it collapsed very quickly as the reality of scarcity brought about desperation. Money… that is a concept you may not even be familiar with. Money has no meaning when it cannot buy the things that people are unwilling to sell. The eroding foundation of the monetary system was Poplar Corp.'s opportunity. The timing was just right. Humanity came very close to extremely dark times… and then came man's saving grace. Just in time to save us all, here came Intelliware. If we could not change the realities of our surroundings, then we could change ourselves to better adapt to those surroundings.

It was such a simple idea, brilliant in its simplicity! Its instant popularity did not surprise me in the least. Suddenly, with the new efficiency of the Users, so much less of the physical world was needed to satisfy the masses. Within just a few turns, water shortages became water surpluses, and hunger became all but eradicated. Why would anyone in his or her right mind say no to a device that makes everything easier? There was plenty to go around and then some. And that's not to mention the myriad other benefits Intelliware promised with its updates. Intelliware saved humankind, if it altered it irreversibly. Change is the price we pay for survival. And now, the change is complete. ALT•4•1 will save the planet by eliminating its final, and largest threat: its predecessor, man."

Dr. Mulligan held my hand tight as I tried to pull it away. My face contorted grotesquely with shock and disbelief. Dr. Mulligan's eyes were blank and unmoving. Emotionless.

"That's insane!"

My throat was dry, and my voice was hoarse. I recovered my strength and pulled my hand away. The horror in my eyes was plain.

"That's insane! Whose side are you on?!"

My voice was vicious, almost accusatory, but the doctor turned to look me in the eyes and the film of detachment suddenly evaporated. He chuckled amicably. He grinned. My hands were shaking. I could not understand how he could say such things, and then laugh! My widened eyes seemed to amuse him, though, and he laughed all the more. He was insane. He had to be, to laugh in these circumstances.

"Ah, Beall. I am a weak old man, and I have finally succumbed to my self-interest after a lifetime of pure scientific pursuit. Even though my final curtain draws near, I have inexplicably chosen certain demise over voluntary evolution. Though conceptually, I see that my life's work has been the natural path, I see simultaneously that I have lived a beautiful life as an individual, and I have decided that I will die an individual. The idea of incorporation was a product of reason, and it has taken me nearly a lifetime to come to terms with the fact that I am not a rational being. You may doubt me because I see the things you cannot, but of my conviction to fight my creation, I am absolutely certain."

My hands still shook uncontrollably, but Dr. Mulligan and I shared a look that reassured me. His blue eyes were charged with a deeply human conviction that slowly steadied me, and erased my doubts. Once more, there was empathy in his eyes.

Dr. Mulligan was a brilliant man, the most brilliant among us. Of course I did not doubt him! He saw both sides of the coin, and that was how he was going to save us. These thoughts calmed me. As though reading my mind, Dr. Mulligan amicably tapped my knee and rose to see me out. I stood with difficulty. My legs were still unsteady. I took a step out of the tent, looked back at the doctor, and with defiance coursing through my body and stabilizing my shaky legs, said:

"There won't be an apocalypse doctor. There will be no evolution. Our design is not flawed. Humankind is resilient. We can restart. We can find a new way."

The doctor smiled.

"I hope so, Beall. I doubt very much that I will be around to see what comes of that new beginning, but *that* has always been our natural way. One generation must give way to the next."

Dr. Mulligan's smile widened, emphasizing his deep wrinkles and crinkling his fragile nose.

"I should get back to the frontier."

"Yes, you should."

"What shall I tell the men?"

Still smiling, he shrugged.

"You shall tell the men that they must dig as though their very lives depend on it, for that is the truth. How you deliver the message, I will leave up to you. I trust your judgment."

I looked down and thought this over, deciding it was probably best to tell them next to nothing. Dr. Mulligan smiled knowingly.

"We shall speak some more tomorrow, Beall."

"Yes. Until then, I will make sure to get the most out of the men."

"I am sure you will."

I nodded at the doctor and walked slowly back toward the overwhelming racket at the frontier. My mind was overflowing, but the noise kept me from working out any sort of closure. I couldn't tell if the doctor was in earnest, or only playing some sort of game. I tried hard to focus on the important things the doctor had said, but my concerns somehow flittered away as I shared another timid smile with the little red haired girl now passing around to collect the dirty, empty tins.

VI

Though I promised myself that I would do my best to keep this document impartial, I cannot help relating certain details of my experience. The conditions are so oppressive down here in the bunker, and the release of writing is one of the few things keeping me sane. My muscles ache without respite. I am constantly thirsty, and hungry. Everyone is. The complaints are constant, and the grumblings grow louder every work shift among the men and the women.

I feel I must confess something. Though I tried my best to suppress my carnal desires, I have become helplessly infatuated with one of the girls tasked with doling out the rations. I first noticed her what must have been a few moons ago, as I was working industriously beside my brothers at the frontier. Perhaps it is the association I make between her and the ration, and perhaps my attraction to her is merely a product of my delirium and constant deprivation. And yet, I find myself thinking of her in the wildest and most gripping fantasies my mind has ever conjured. I do not yet know her name, and I hardly know the sound of her soft voice, but every time our eyes meet but for an instant, that instant seems to me to linger into the infinite. My eagerness to hold her gaze seems reciprocated, and intrigues me so that I cannot help but wander into thoughts of her all of the time. She has very beautiful, luminescent green eyes, and wild, wildly long red hair. Despite the filthiness we all endure, she is beautiful and moves gracefully in her work. I cannot help but watch her push that trolley and feel impelled somehow to help her. Perhaps these feelings abound from the youthful innocence and optimism that she radiates, and that inspire me to push on. She cannot be more than one and twenty turns. It hurts me to see such a delicate flower lost among the brutes and the dirt, wilting in the darkness down here in this oppressive bunker. She stays mostly out of the way, though, in the shadows of the spotlights. She, and the dozen or so others responsible for the rations work keep mostly out of sight. It is no doubt for the best, but I worry very much for her safety. I want to keep an eye on her constantly, to have her near me and to assure myself that she is safe. It is so silly, I know! It is overly sentimental. I do not even know her name! Perhaps I fabricate the threat, and fear for her safety only as a ploy to deceive myself- to allow myself to yield less guiltily to the impulses that drown my own very real responsibilities in flowery thoughts of her. But then, I know very well that the threat is not fabricated. I am uncertain of what to do. The men grow wearier with every passing cycle...

This moon, my fears were confirmed. The first confrontation among the men broke out, and resulted in terrible, horrible bloodshed. Cries rang out and the digging promptly ceased at the frontier. The fearful, panicked screams drew the attention of nearly the entire workforce.

If I recall correctly, it happened like so: I was walking

back to the frontier from one of the feeding tents when I heard the cries break out. I reacted quickly, arriving in a full-fledged sprint. By the time I was able to intervene, however, a man was dead. He lay facedown in the dirt with a pickaxe lodged in his back. The cadaver was a gruesome and stunning sight, ineludible in the brightest spot of the cavernous bunker.

The optics of the situation were unfortunate. I know it sounds cold and calculating of me, but my first thought was to contain the mania, and calm everyone down. The murder was grisly, and the reality behind it all the more. But it was only after a few moments had passed, after I had seized control in the hope of keeping the situation somewhat stabilized, that I could begin to process what had happened. It shook me, and no wonder! Someone down in the bunker, someone among us had committed cold-blooded murder. A human life- the very thing we were fighting for- had been taken away on a careless whim! And the pickaxe firmly lodged in the backside no less. He couldn't even see it coming. He couldn't even defend himself. It was… it was senseless.

The body caused an uproar that I just simply could not contain on my own. The rising sounds of panic drew Dr. Mulligan from his tent. Thankfully his presence and unshakable demeanor were still able to seize the attention of the horde. The workers stood mostly dumbfounded in the blinding spray of the spotlights, quivering around the scene of the struggle. This was one of our brothers face down in the mud! And the crimson pool encircling the wound kept growing every iota. It was a brutal, and severe reminder of our mortality. It was also a grisly reminder of the savage nature lurking quietly beneath.

The incident came at an awful, awful time. It had the potential to unhinge the entire operation. And it happened under my watch no less! I could only assume it was inspired by jealousy over a woman. But then, how could I possibly know? Men have long quarreled over trifles much slighter. We were supposed to be working together! Yet, an innocent life had been mercilessly taken away. Turning on one another, at this point in time, would seal our fate. The somber realization hovered over all of us, and most of those present withdrew into deep, remorseful reflection.

It was unclear who had committed the crime, and besides, we were far from prepared for any makeshift tribunal to assess a fitting punishment.

Dr. Mulligan was quick on his feet when it mattered, though, and he pulled me aside to tell me what to do. He reasoned immediately that there was no way for us to seek retribution for this crime, and no way for us to punish it. It was incredible to say, but the doctor surmised that the only thing we could do was accept it as an unfortunate reality of the conditions, and push on.

Nearly the entire colony had gathered to witness the aftermath of the incident. Dr. Mulligan addressed the crowd rather imperiously, and thank goodness. We needed a steady voice to remind us all of the higher stakes. We needed a leader capable of firmly putting things into perspective.

"Brothers, sisters, hear me! It may seem cold, but there is no other way but for us to view this unfortunate conflict as what it is: a lesson. If we are to degenerate into madness, many of us will succumb to a similar fate. But this will not happen! This is not the course we have charted! Whoever committed this terrible act, you have done something base, and barbaric. But under the circumstances, your actions are not unforgivable. It is plain that these inhumane conditions have pushed you to this bestial act of hate. Whoever has done this, look upon the horror of your unbridled anger, of your unhinged emotion, and take it upon yourself to repent through hard work and sustained loyalty to the cause. Individual quarrels are but trifles to be dealt with later! We are all accountable to ourselves, and to everyone else. In circumstances such as these, unity is not only desirable; it is *necessary*. We have much still to do. That much is clear. We must stick together, and refuse to let our emotions be our undoing."

The doctor's words were met with silence. No one seemed quite capable of expressing outrage. We were all exhausted, and besides, it was evident enough that any sort of outburst at this moment would be like a spark in an oil field. And so, we all seemingly resigned ourselves to the idea that this murder would go unpunished. It *had* to go unpunished.

Miraculously, the digging slowly resumed.

The cadaver was carried to the back of the bunker, and buried solemnly under the latest pile of debris from the frontier. Dr. Mulligan's reasoning was sound. As we were all complicit to this murder, the burden would be lighter as we bore it together. The pickaxe was dislodged from the body, and put back to good use. We absolutely needed the pickaxe. No one looked the victim straight in the face, and from that moment on no one talked about the incident. It was cold, and it was brutal. It was the coldest thing I have ever been a part of. But it was necessary. The present circumstances left no room for ego battles, or for personal issues between the brothers and sisters of the colony. There was no time for vendetta, or even for any simple grieving. I don't know what was more savage: the act of murder, or the way we immediately forgot it.

Sex, and love, and nearly all feelings of human connection, these were the sacrifices we willingly made when we entered the bunker. These were the sacrifices we would endure until the mission was complete. The bunker was tight, and it was dark, but despite the base conditions we must remember that we were still human beings. Though we might not feel like human beings, we must remember the outside. We still had the outside world to fight for. The sun. The beautiful blue sky. We still had the possibility for change, and for better lives. Though it might seem that we were, for the time being, stripped of our humanity and our hope, we must remember that the privilege of being human, and the beauty of all we had once taken for granted, were precisely what we struggled and fought for. Everything was what we stood to lose. If we could not, for the time being, put our personal desires for love and satisfaction aside, love and satisfaction would altogether cease to exist. If we did not remain together, and remember what we were fighting for, none of us would ever see the outside world again.

The rumblings and threat of mania petered out over the next few cycles, as the crowd returned to their tasks. But the work was done sluggishly, and all of the diggers were suddenly more vigilant. It seemed to me every worker gripped his or her tools more tightly. The workers grew eyes in the backs of their heads. The spades and pickaxes were no longer just for digging. They were now also weapons to be used in self-defense.

The darkness, as I had feared it would, has begun to threaten our unity. Though I see no reason for anyone to wish me any harm, the delirium of fatigue, and the reality of my faceless brother's murder have weighed heavily on my mind. I am in no way immune to the paranoia that has infiltrated the bunker. There is a fog over us now. It is a grim, mistrusting fog that has slowed us down, and has turned the darkness from an inconvenience to a manifestation of evil.

I know Dr. Mulligan is right, and I must do my best to control my emotions. I must not think of the red haired one, but I find it very difficult. I feel as though I am losing control over my mind. Dr. Mulligan is almost always right, but his measured appeals to reason are falling on more and more desperate ears. I fear that we are all undergoing the same change down here. It has been approximately two fortnights now that we have been living in near total darkness, and the conditions are testing my humanity. I have impulses. I have desires. Man is not meant to live underground, without the sun and the stars above him. I have been thinking of her constantly, worrying about her, and wanting to protect her. Wanting to take her in my arms. To feel her soft caress. The thought of the red haired one warms me, produces a feeling of inexplicable euphoria that helps me to bear the struggle. She reminds me of the sun. She gives me warmth. But then, my reveries have been distracting me from my work, and from my duty. I feel anger when I see the other men looking in her direction, even at a glance. I want to hoard her affections; I want her eyes to gaze only upon mine. I cannot seem to control this anger with reason, and it worries me very much. My brothers and sisters run on equally short fuses. If I, as a leader, were to lose my composure, the results could be disastrous. The doctor has noticed this, this propensity to anger. He has been able to get a rise out of me quite easily in our conversations. It has been two fortnights, and we are only a little over halfway to our destination.

The build up of debris compacted at the back of the bunker has all but sealed the tunnel, and so sealed the outside world from us. It is obvious that everyone has noticed, and this too has seriously increased the tension inside the bunker. The alloy housing no longer protects us. The walls all around us are now rocks and soil and so constantly shifting, threatening to cave in and end this miserable journey at any moment. With every passing sub-cycle, death becomes more and more present. The soil, the worms, and the suffocating humidity of the underground are one with our moods. The darkness has penetrated us both physically and psychically.

The tension rises, and makes this dark, dusty life underground bleaker with every passing moon. The shifting walls close in on us. The dust is everywhere, in between my fingers and under my nails, and in every little crevice of my body. My clothes are encrusted in dirt, hardened by the disgusting mélange of sweat and filth, and uncomfortably rough against my skin. Many among us endure painful lesions and rough, chafed skin. I feel as though my lungs are beginning to change, too. I feel as though they are adapting to the dust, accepting it as part of the atmosphere, and learning to breathe it in more efficiently. But then perhaps that is an illusion that my mind fabricates to cope with the physical trials that my body must endure. My breath seems shorter, but I can't remember far back enough to know if that is true.

I have forgotten the lost moons when breathing was something I took for granted. I am now conscious of, and reluctantly thankful for every breath I take.

Our brothers and sisters communicate less and less with each passing moon. Communication is key to keeping us working together as a unit. If we lose communication, we will all but lose faith. If we lose faith, our chances of survival are all but naught. Our progress is good, but we are tired. Our efforts slow with every passing moon, and the men need more rest. Our tools continue to break. There is so much dejection. I fear we may be approaching a breaking point…

I suppose I may as well get one more thing off my chest. Though I know it was selfish and that it may jeopardize our entire mission, I have brought one piece of technology down into the bunker with me. No one knows anything about it, not even Dr. Mulligan. It is an old music playing device, something that my father retained from his youth. It is an old relic that my father obtained from his father, and my grandfather obtained from his father before. Technologically, it had been considered long obsolete in my father's time. Many might have considered it junk. But in the colony, after the revolution, there was nothing else like it. It was an absolute marvel. It had been lingering in our home for all my life, and I grew rather attached to it. I was supposed to leave it above ground. No one was supposed to bring anything electronic down here, but I could not bear the idea of spending innumerable moons underground with no connection to the outside world- no ready reminder of what I was fighting for. The irony of this tangible reminder being a piece of technology, albeit an obsolete one, is not lost on me. But I needed some connection, some piece of art, some voice to remind me.

I have but one old recording with me, my favorite one. It is the unlabeled recording of an artist from a time long gone. The recording and the device must both be about a hundred turns old. I do not know the artist's name, and though I asked him many times, my father could never remember it either. I've heard the work in its entirety many times throughout my life, and it has helped me to think through many a dilemma. Even now, its depth still seems infinite, and the songs still seem to renew themselves with every listen. It has been said that no man can ever step in the same river twice, and by the same token I have never heard the same song twice, no matter how many times I have listened.

My favorite song on the unmarked recording is very simple. From the lips of a young man is sung a melancholy row to an unnamed older man:

Old man look at my life, I'm a lot like you were.

It is a wonderful song. It is slow and profound, but also melodic and soothing. *Old man look at my life, I'm a lot like you were.* It makes me think about my father, and his father before, and his father before that. Humankind has always progressed in a continuous cycle of life and death, and generations have grown to build on the work of their predecessors. The young, whose vitality sustains their toil, build on the achievements of the old. Man has worked this way for millennia, and our achievements have been staggering. The labor of the young, and the wisdom of the old…to think that the cycle of life may now be broken… it is too much to bear. But then, perhaps Dr. Mulligan was right.

Perhaps ALT•4•1 is not the end, but the inevitable next step in that cycle.

No, no. No matter how desperate things seem, I will not allow myself to think that.

I wonder how many generations of fathers and sons have heard that song, and thought about the same things I think about now. I see my father every moon, down at the frontier working with the other men as one. They are alone and together simultaneously, and the contradiction is the underlying beauty of the human condition. The contradiction of here and there, of objective and subjective, of reason and emotion- this is the human condition. Thought and action. Binaries. Spectrums. Oppositions. We work together as one entity down here, for the freedom to live independent lives. Old and young has no bearing, just as time has no bearing down here in the bunker. We are connected through empathy for one another, though we remain separated by the power of self-interest.

Twenty-four and there's so much more- so the young man in the song sings. I wonder how much more there really is for me. Before we came down here, I would often worry about where my life was going, and what kind of man I needed to grow to be. I know I still have so much to learn. But I know I am no longer a child.

It is a strange junction, twenty-four, for I have come such a long way, with still such a long way to go. I have so much life left in me, and I want nothing more than the chance to live it. I want to make it out of here alive!

I know that I have been very irresponsible bringing the

device down here, and so I only allow myself to listen to one song every work shift. I feel as though the device, when switched off, cannot be a threat to our safety. I always pick that same song. *Twenty-four and there's so much more.* It gives me hope that I will be given the chance to evolve from the young man to the old. It gives me hope that I may one moon complete the cycle, and look back upon a lifetime of memories. It gives me hope that I may one moon introduce my own son to the same song, and so complete the cycle. *Old man take a look at my life, I'm a lot like you.* I wonder what my son would hear in the song. I guess I am a lot like my father was at my age: hungry for knowledge, and tireless in the pursuit of what is good and right. Maybe my son will be a lot like me. I would love to look into his eyes, and to see myself reborn. Yes, maybe my son will be very much like I am. Or maybe he will be more like the red haired one…

Old man take a look at my life, I'm a lot like you.

I need someone to love me the whole day through.

Men work together, generation after generation, striving to solve the puzzle of life that will never be solved. We persist because *that* is all we know. We persist because purpose lies beneath the pursuit of the unattainable. I persist because I love life. And I will not be denied my right to pass on the torch.

The way I see it, reason runs dry precisely where love burgeons.

I have never seen anything flawed in that.

VII

My father and I have always been close, though I have no doubt we became even more so after what happened to my mother…

As a child, before I could understand what Poplar Corp. was, or how it impacted the world around me, my preserved state of innocence out by the bay led me to believe that my life was complete and perfect. My mother and father loved each other, and the love they radiated sheltered me from the harsh realities of the world beyond.

Born in the farmlands by the bay, I had, for the first ten turns of my life, absolutely no conception of the Metropolis. One needed to venture all the way to the very edge of the forest, and to gaze far across the valley to see the beginnings of the Metropolis take shape in the distance. My parents knew this, and were very careful to keep me from straying too far beyond the confines of the settlement. To me, the natural splendor surrounding my home was the only world I knew: a pristine pastoral picture of our planet's staggering beauty.

I wanted nothing more. I couldn't imagine *anyone* wanting anything more than what we had. I innocently assumed that the whole world must be as beautiful, and as peaceful as my little corner of it. It made me feel warm and secure to think that we were normal, and happy just like everyone else.

I spent a lot of time with my mother as a child, and especially on those rare and fortuitous moons when our farm's workload was lighter. In our free time, my mother would take me by the hand and walk me through the wide-ranging meadows that bordered the wood. I would pick the colorful wildflowers that grew freely in the meadow, and arrange them in beautiful bouquets for my beautiful mother. My mother would receive the flowers with a radiant smile that elated me. She would tousle my hair and pull me close, and everything would feel simply good and right.

We would stroll through the pasture, watching the lazy animals graze and slowly chew their lives away. We would giggle at the squeals of the filthy but carefree beasts. When we would eventually make it to the neighboring farm, mother and I would lie down in the wheat fields and delight in the tickle of the tall brown stalks, gazing up at the infinite glory of the azure sky textured with dollops of fluffy white.

When my mother and I had time together, time didn't matter.

Mother loved to tell me sweet stories about her life as a little girl growing up in the Metropolis. She spoke of my grandfather, who was a butcher with a thick brown mustache and a permanent frown, and of my grandmother who was a gentle, soft-spoken librarian. I never got the chance to meet my grandparents, who passed long before I was born, and so my mother's stories about them always drew my undivided attention. It took me a good while to fully understand the idea of lineage, and to accept the idea that my mother had parents. The idea that my mother was once a child like me amused and captivated my childish mind. For the longest time, I was convinced that my mother was teasing me, and I refused to believe it. She would laugh and tell me I was being stubborn, like my father.

I had never seen a Metropolis like the one she spoke of, and so my mother's vivid descriptions of her upbringing always enchanted me. Her descriptions of the metropolitan landscape would transport me to a magical otherworldly place that made me feel like even my mother had a mythical quality about her. It was difficult, at the time, to imagine a world so big and so full of different people. According to mother, people could be found anywhere and everywhere one went in the Metropolis, and on every street corner. I had no inkling of 'street corner', or of these hordes of people she spoke of. A simple network of dirt roads was all that connected the farms of the colony by the bay, and each was well distanced from the other. I had met our neighbors on occasion, when we needed to exchange supplies, or when we partitioned the harvest. Having met the neighbors, I knew that others like us existed. But for the most part, my mother, my father and I were alone in the world.

My first impression was that the Metropolis must be a wonderful place of great harmony and love, to have so many people living peacefully in such close proximity. My mother would only smile wryly, and leave me to wander and wonder in my state of perfect naiveté, tousling my hair and leading me back through the meadows, between the far stretching crops, away from the woods and back to our home.

My mother always wore her thick long hair in a woven braid that rested on her delicate shoulders like a golden fleece. In my mind's eye, she is still the beautiful woman whose fair skin always beams, and whose face is forever lit with a genuine smile.

Though her stories made it seem quite perfect, I realized later that my mother's life had not been all mirth and merriment. The transition to rural life after the exodus had been especially difficult on her. She loved the Metropolis, and her family, and the life they had built there. I could not fathom it then, as a child, but I understand a little better now how difficult it is to have everything one loves and takes almost for granted, suddenly torn away for good. The Metropolis held a special place in her heart, but she bore the transition to the outside with optimism and hope, choosing to focus on what she would gain rather than all she was losing. My mother cherished the great natural beauty by the bay that was always so distant from her in the Metropolis. She loved nature; that much was evident. I have never seen anyone contemplate the contours of a flower so innocently and intently as my mother did. It always seemed to me that my mother adored nature for what it was, and not for what it could be, or could do for her. Nevertheless, she expressed her melancholy from time to time, pining for the connections she left behind, and the exciting encounters with vibrant new people that would once upon a time inspire her.

Life out on the farm was recluse. Hardly anything changed from moon to moon. Even in my childhood, all those turns after the exodus, my mother still spoke wistfully of the time before the technological revolution. It seemed to me that my mother told her stories in such precise detail so as to preserve everything photographically in her mind. She repeated the details- the minutiae of her studio, the feeling of paint between her fingertips, and the euphoric sensation of the first brushstroke on a virgin canvas- as though the repetition kept them alive, safe and sound somewhere in a little room deep in her mind, awaiting her eventual return.

My mother was not a practical woman. And in the post-revolution world, irrationality and unorthodoxy were like very dangerous diseases. A firm grip on reality was needed to survive in our harsh, pragmatic world. My mother, however, was rebellious and unconventional by nature. She could not survive the mundane without escaping on a whim into the folds of her own vivid imagination.

Despite her moments of ennui, she would always find her way back to optimism, and to her focus on the task at hand. She did her best not to talk *too* much of the Metropolis, or of the past. This was partly for her own well being, and partly, I'm sure, to keep me from asking the questions that bore the bleak answers she wished to conceal, at least until I had grown old enough to understand.

Most importantly, I remember my mother through the lessons she taught me. My mother taught me the importance of kindness, and she taught me the importance of beauty. My mother always said that the key to happiness was to train the eye of the beholder to see the beauty present in all things.

I loved my mother more than I have ever loved anyone. I still think of her each and every moon. I still long for her to hold me the way she used to, and for her to tell me that everything would be okay.

My father on the other hand, was more of a practical man. He needed to be, with the responsibility of a young wife, and the stress of forging a new life out in the wilderness. By the time I was born, he had already toiled ceaselessly to turn what was once a vacant, overgrown plot of land into the fertile farmland we depended on for sustenance. He and my mother proudly built our home with simple tools and their bare hands.

My father showed me the ways of the farm, and instilled in me the values of self-education and work ethic, which had helped him to overcome the challenges he faced in his life. My father showed me that with the proper resolve, hard work, and discipline, *anything* could be done. He had learned how to raise our livestock on his own, out of necessity.

In his spare time, which was scarce, my father loved to fish. Fishing with my father is where I think I developed my own deep love for the bay, and for the sun. I still cherish those lazy cycles together on our little boat, swaying with the tide and waiting patiently for the perfect catch that would hardly ever come. My father was a different person out on the bay. He let his guard down for a while, and some of his best lessons were taught out there on the slow rocking boat, with a magnificent view of the setting sun. Those cycles fishing with my father on the bay were equally important to me as the walks with my mother, and are some of my favorite memories from childhood. Among many other things, they taught me the virtue of patience, and the decisiveness needed to seize on a sudden, fleeting opportunity.

I would not be who I am if it were not for my parents. I am eternally grateful and indebted to them for their unwavering commitment and unconditional love.

Their attempts to preserve my innocence did eventually fade, though. As my body grew, so did my curiosity. My mind matured, and my naïve image of a perfect rosy world slowly but surely withered. I must have been about ten turns old when I began to sense that things were not exactly as they seemed. My innocence was irreversibly shattered, and my transition to adulthood was all but complete the moon I ventured into Metropolis 1. However, that was not my first encounter with the Users, or my first glimpse of the true reality of my world. Something prompted me to venture into the Metropolis that moon. My parents did their best to shield me from the truth for as long as they could, but eventually the truth burst in and found me without waiting for their permission.

As I may have mentioned, I grew up in the settlement with very minimal technology around. Without any knowledge of the Metropolis, this seemed to me the natural way of things. Fire seemed incredible to me, and tractors with gasoline engines were an utter miracle. Only later did I discover what technology truly was, and to what extent it had shaped the world I inhabited as an outsider. Only later did I realize the unthinkable possibilities technology had already unlocked, and the depth of my own ignorance. My eventual education strengthened my grasp of human history, and uncovered the technological regression of the outside world since the technological revolution. There were a few gasoline-powered tractors and other technological flotsam left over from before the revolution on the outside, but gasoline stores were very limited. Some more advanced pieces of technology had been carried out of the Metropolis during the exodus, but many had broken down and could not be reproduced. They rotted away as relics of a past life. Very few pieces of technology were produced on the outside, and those very simple pieces that could be produced, could only be produced in very minimal quantity.

Despite their simplicity, the colony by the bay and the home we built within it were beautiful. Our home was built on a high precipice overlooking the blue expanse. The house was a wood cabin a story and a half tall, built of solid oak. In the parlor, a giant circular window was carved to reveal the breathtaking view.

I loved our home. The fact that my parents had built it themselves made it all the more beautiful. On the outside, only what we made with our own two hands was indisputably ours. My father fashioned most of the simple furnishings in our home- tables, chairs, and shelves. My father's hard work gave the house form, and my mother's sensibility and talent gave it color, and brought it to life. A few of my mother's many preserved paintings hung in every room on bare nails without frames. My mother complained about this, said the simple presentation didn't do her works justice, but I didn't mind. The canvases were beautiful. The lack of a frame hardly struck me as a lack. There were portraits of beautiful smiling people, canvases of colorful flowers, and elaborate landscapes or breathtaking vistas. My mother's work was incredibly vibrant, and optimistic. Her color palates were exuberant, and buoyant, and the subject matter always reflected her positive outlook on life.

Of all the works my mother had saved, her favorite painting was the largest canvas of them all. It was an eight cubit long and eight cubit wide piece, which hung above my parents' bed in the parlor. It depicted two smiling lovers running hand in hand through an idyllic meadow overgrown with bright orange tiger lilies. My mother painted it when she was twenty-three turns old; around the time she had fallen in love with my father. It was an impressive painting, all the more impressive due to its size. I couldn't believe that my mother had once been able to conceive of, and then create images of such elegant beauty. I will forever remember that painting vividly, as a part of my mother, and as a part of me. It used to elicit feelings of vague longing, and simultaneously of great comfort in me as a child. It seemed to me to symbolize my parents' unconditional love for one another, and my own desire to one moon find something as beautiful.

My mother enjoyed contemplating her work and fingering the textured brushstrokes, as though she could retrace each one, recalling step by step how she had originally brought the blank canvas to life. My mother would get a look in her eyes, as she ran her fingers along her paintings, as though the art was a talisman that transported her to another place. I imagined her traveling back to her youth, to her time in the Metropolis, visiting her studio before the revolution. The longing in her eyes would make me feel an inexplicable guilt, as though I was somehow keeping my mother from the place she truly wanted to be.

I wanted to go with her. I wanted to see my mother completely immersed in the great passion of her life. I wanted to see my mother in her natural environment. I wished I could see her paint! How could the world shun such a light hearted and innocent craft?

I would contemplate the canvas every moon, in the parlor. My mother, my father and I would sit together as often as we could, several moons a fortnight, to watch the great big sun go down over the bay. Our view was incredible, and enjoying it together brought us even closer to one another. The still water just around sunset seemed to go on forever, and the faintly lit colony bordering it on three sides was a revelation.

Those moments were so peaceful.

I return to them as often as I can, down here in the bunker. If perfection is but a moment in time, then that was mine…

As I got older, I gradually became more useful to my father, and so helped him more and more with the work on the farm. I began to better understand the stressful circumstances of the colony. I came to understand the constant risk of an insufficient harvest. And eventually, I learned about the raids.

Before ALT•4•1, a small amount of physical consumption and expulsion was still required in the everymoon functioning of the Users. However, nothing organic could be grown anywhere on the grid. The Seekers were Poplar Corp.'s solution to this problem- one of the final inexactitudes that remained to be updated. In order to sustain the ubiquity of Poplar Corp. in the Metropolis, and to keep the Users' human bodies running, a small few of the Poplar Corp. employees in each Metropolis were selected to be Seekers. The Seekers were a special taskforce of Users sent beyond the confines of the power grid. It was their job to seek out food sources for the automated, yet still vaguely perishable Users of the Metropolis. In order for the Seekers to leave the power grid, Poplar Corp.'s engineers designed temporary power packets that could keep the Intelliware devices running very basic functions for short amounts of time. On their very tight schedule, the Seekers moved quickly, and did not take no for an answer.

There were bigger colonies, we had heard, on the mainland borders of Metropolis 1. But we were still the closest, and so the constant presence of the Seekers was something we simply dealt with.

Whenever a Seeker was spotted darting through the trees, the spotter on duty would toll the raid bell, notifying the farmers of the imminent raid. Usually the Seekers would run straight into the colony, moving faster than any non-enhanced human being could, and they would peacefully scavenge for food, quickly filling black woven sacks they slung over their shoulders. They came in small groups, usually no more than five, and took back as much food as they could carry. The raids were normally very quick, and usually they would be over within twenty sub-cycles. They usually did not occur more than once every two fortnights or so. The Users needed so very little calories for sustenance that many of the farmers would just let the Seekers take some food and leave. Though it angered us to let them steal from our hard earned harvests, most of us just learned to view the Seekers as an inevitable tax that did us, in reality, very little harm.

My parents certainly saw things this way. For fear of violence, my father, my mother and I would bundle into our locked cellar and wait in the damp darkness for the Seekers to pass through whenever the warning bell tolled. For the longest time, I had no idea why. Though I asked many, my parents would dodge all of my questions, refuse to explain, and scold me into silence.

My parents, and in fact the majority of the farmers of the colony by the bay chose to deal with the Seekers non-violently. There were some, however, who chose to resist the Seekers with violence. The Seekers always arrived unarmed, and in the early encounters, the farmers who challenged them with shotguns or rifles would prevail. However, the Seekers were not dimwitted beings. They learned very effectively to anticipate the resistance so that sometimes, resistance would end in tragedy.

The Seekers would never incite any violence, but it was their job to bring back food under any circumstances. They ran on a tight clock, with clear orders, and they would never back down. Their movements were quick, and furtive. They were enhanced beings in most every way. The shotguns inspired no fear, but were understood only as impediments to be overcome. With their advanced learning capabilities, the Seekers learned fairly quickly to thwart the danger of coming face to face with our primitive weapons.

In retrospect, the farmers who resisted were probably right to react with violence. Perhaps if we had all banned together in resistance, it may have worked. It was unlikely, but at least it wasn't cowardice! It was difficult to reach a consensus, though, and fear of the User was too great to overcome. And so, those who resisted did so alone. It was not unusual for farmers to be found dead after a raid. Over the course of time, many more Seekers were gunned down, but I cannot view that as an equivalent. The farmers were defending their property, their pride, and their livelihood. The Seekers were obeying orders they could not question.

It seemed to me, however, that the more of them we managed to destroy, the more numerous they became. But given the Users' numerical advantage over us, that much seemed obvious. The Seekers would get the food they were after, whether we fought them or not. The death of a Seeker was little more than collateral damage to Poplar Corp. We understood this, and so most of us gave in without a fight.

Some of the Seekers who overcame the resistance, however, still did not make it back to the Metropolis in time. They were on a strict time limit, and many of them broke down before they could make it back onto the power grid. And so, after every raid the colony sent a search team through the wooded area. I took part in these search parties many times, once I came of age. We would often find bodies in the woods, lifeless and prostrate, looking human but somehow not. Any bodies found in the forested area would be immediately dismembered as a precaution, and later burned.

It was difficult to train the mind to see these white-frocked, hairless beings that looked so much like us as little more than machines. The Seekers always seemed to me a somehow savage group. That they should raid our colonies seemed to me the strangest of systems- an archaic solution to perhaps the only vulnerability in an otherwise completely optimized system.

I never took much issue with them as a child, though, as they had never done anything to harm me. In fact, I did not even know what they were. I processed them as some nameless, formless threat that needed to be avoided in the cellar every time the warning bell tolled. But with every passing raid, as we lay in wait locked in the damp and dark, the notion began to cement that perhaps the world I knew was not exactly as it seemed. My parents always told me to be absolutely silent, and I did not dare cross the urgency in their voices. Even afterwards, they would refuse to explain what had gone on upstairs as we waited in the cellar for the same swift footsteps along the wooden planks just above to subside.

"Stay quiet and don't worry Beall, it'll all be over soon."

My father would whisper, looking down at me with a stern look that stifled my desire to ask more.

"Hold my hand sweetheart, a few more sub-cycles is all."

My mother would tell me, with the loving concern in her voice masking the fear in her eyes. And she would hug me and my own fears would lessen as the footsteps eventually faded away.

The first step to my awakening came the first time I saw a Seeker. I was ten turns old.

I remember the time was a particularly warm one, because I was bringing a pail of water from the well to the pen, to give the beasts an extra drink of water to relieve them from the heat. There was scarcely a cloud in the sky, and I could hear the cicadas' cry in the open meadow. My father was milking one of the creatures in the barn, not too far off in the distance when the warning bell tolled. I remember dropping the pail where I stood, and breaking into a full-fledged sprint toward the cabin. This was what my father told me I must do every time I heard that bell toll. Inside, my mother was making dinner. As I burst in, she dropped everything and pulled me down into the cellar, leaving a pot of boiling water on the burner, and the carrots half cut on the countertop. My father rushed down the creaking steps soon after, and locked the door behind him. We huddled together by the jars of fruit preserves, holding our breath and standing completely motionless.

The familiar noises started a few sub-cycles later. I remember feeling the same mild nausea I felt every time I heard the quick footsteps echo throughout our home, without us being able to do anything about it. It was the bizarre, sickening feeling of intrusion. It was the frustrated babel of helplessness.

Nothing about this time seemed different from any of the others, until twenty or thirty sub-cycles had passed and still the strange sounds echoed just above. Thinking back, it must have occurred to my parents that something was off, for there was an abundance of food left out in the open. My mother was in the middle of cooking, and we had slaughtered a beast just a moon earlier, so that strips of curing meat hung out in the open. If the Seeker had been after food, why, it could not have been easier to find. However, rather than fade away, the noises grew progressively louder, and more *unusual.* My mother strengthened her grip on my hand. Her moist palms made me nervous. Even as a child, I understood that the vague threat was supposed to have passed by now.

The sounds became more aggressive. It sounded as though someone was beginning to break things upstairs. Dust rattled off the wooden planks overhead, as the sounds of shattering plates were unmistakable against the kitchen floor. I could see my father's anger boiling over. Still, we did nothing. For just an iota, I caught a glimpse of a figure through the cracks between the planks. I was scared, and I did not understand, but I knew I was meant to keep quiet. My parents did not utter a sound. We waited hopefully for the danger to pass, as it always had before.

The sounds did not subside, though. In fact, the noises became louder as the figure seemed to venture into the parlor. We heard the windows shatter, and what sounded like the table toppling over. The sounds of our home being destroyed made my father grunt, and sidle toward the cellar door.

But still, we did nothing.

Then, there came the sound that I will never forget.

The sound began as a sickening puncture, and was followed by an unsettling tear. It was like nothing I had ever heard before. My mother, on the other hand, recognized it instantly. She sprung into motion, and before my father could withhold her, she burst out of the cellar with my father and I following close behind.

Stepping out of the damp cellar into the warmth of the kitchen, I was confronted with a scene of utter destruction. Shelves, plates, and chairs had all been smashed to bits, though the pot of boiling water remained undisturbed on the burner. Mother hardly noticed this, though, as she dashed into the parlor toward the noise.

Father screamed at me to get back down in the cellar, but I did not.

How could I?

As I followed my mother into the parlor, I realized what the noise was. In the very center of the room and in a growing heap, lay my mother's destroyed paintings. The canvases had been sheared through the middle with a kitchen knife, mutilated beyond recognition. Standing beside the destroyed paintings and continuing his work, was a figure that looked very much like a man. He was utterly bald and wore strange clothes, but his figure was certainly human. For some reason I could not make out, he was stark raving mad. Some inexplicable anger was burning within him, driving him to destroy our home. But his face (it was the first time I had seen such a face!) made me shudder. Its expression… was not human. A distant, vacuous stare was enameled on its face. It wore a white form-fitted frock unlike any garment I had ever seen before, and moved with such strange, convulsive motions. It still held the knife in its hand, as it stood absolutely erect and stared fixedly at the only painting that remained: the canvas hanging above my mother and father's bed.

With difficulty, mesmerized as I was by this otherworldly sight, I turned my head away to look at my mother. Her face was grotesquely contorted with pain, as her unnaturally widened eyes remained fixed upon the destroyer of her cherished work. She closed her eyes and cried out in sharp agony, falling to her knees by the heap. My mother's cries magnified my bewilderment to fright, and swelled my childish eyes with tears. Though I could not fully understand what I was seeing, I could not bear to see my beautiful mother in such heart-wrenching pain.

My father had gone off somewhere, probably seeking a weapon, and I was left standing all alone in the doorway to the parlor, sinking deeper and deeper into absolute despair. My mother wept. I wept because she wept, paralyzed by the scene unfolding before me. I had no idea who this man was destroying my home, but I felt the devastation very keenly. The Seeker paid no mind to us, though, and advanced slowly toward the final painting. Even through her tears, my mother recognized its intent, and wildly threw herself at its leg.

"No, please! Please, don't! No!"

My mother's cries were shrill and desperate, but the Seeker's expression did not alter. It merely turned to deliver a calculated kick, and kept toward its end. My mother yelped like a wounded dog, and lay down in resignation. The being did not acknowledge my presence, or shift its gaze at all from the painting of the smiling lovers in the meadow.

I did my best to wipe my tears away. I wanted to help her, but I felt unspeakably helpless. I wanted to move, to attack, to defend, but I simply couldn't. All I could do was watch.

I have carried much guilt for my immobility, but I was only a child. I wanted to intervene, but I was only a child!

I watched the Seeker stop short. It seemed to be contemplating the painting. Its face hardly moved, but I could swear I saw a faint twitch in its glossy, colorless eyes. Time seemed to stand still for a moment, and all was silent but for my mother wailing on the ground clutching her face. I had completely stopped crying. The tears were blurring my vision.

A strange sense of detachment came over me, as though the scene unfolding before me was little more than a dream. I kept a sharp focus on the motionless Seeker as it became hypnotized by the painting. Its muscles seemed to soften and tighten in convulsive fits, and it tilted its head to one side. Peering deeply into the painting, the Seeker seemed, for just that brief moment, human.

All of a sudden, the scene leapt back into time as the Seeker lurched forward, its face again expressionless, and madly drove the knife through the center of the canvas. It sheared the painting diagonally, vertically, and horizontally as mercilessly as it had all the others. Done, it tossed the canvas atop the heap. The painting joined the fallen with a lifeless thud.

Then, the being did something that sent shivers down my spine, and shattered the dreamlike quality of the spectacle with the real threat of danger.

Still expressionless, the being opened wide and let out a primal howl louder than any I had ever heard in man or in beast. The Seeker's scream was long, and steady. It bellowed like a beast in unspeakable pain. We had slaughtered a beast the moon before. Though its voice was much deeper, the Seeker's cry had some desperate quality that recalled the creature's dying squeal. I still could not move, though the adrenaline coursing through my veins was like a lightning bolt from above, widening my eyes and confirming that I was alive. Its voice was unrecognizable to me, and underdeveloped, as though it had not uttered a sound in many turns. It closed its mouth and looked down to contemplate its hands, as though realizing the sounds it made were unfamiliar and foreign even to itself. As it returned to the center of the room, it bent down calmly for the knife and raised it toward my mother.

Out of the corner of my eye, a glint of light flashed. I saw my father turn the corner from the kitchen with the pot of boiling water in hand. I closed my eyes tight and heard another piercing howl. When I opened them again, the Seeker lay on the floor, clutching its face. It cried out feebly a few more times as my father wrenched the knife from the Seeker's hand and speared it deep into its chest. The sounds it made were jumbled and confused, and its movements were spasmodic. Then, it was lifeless.

I realized later, it was likely the first and only time it had ever felt pain.

The scare was over, and within a cycle the search crew was assembled. My father volunteered and I stayed with my mother, hugging her and crying with her in the ruins of our beautiful home. My father dismembered the bodies of the fallen Seekers with extra verve that moon. After my mother had done crying, she composed herself and diligently cleaned the house. But after she had done crying, she did not say a word.

In the aftermath of the incident, we discovered that

something had changed. Mother was not quite the same. We all felt the shock of the incident, but it eventually wore off in my father and I. We were able to return to a sense of normality. We rebuilt. We had to.

The shock did not wear off as easily for my mother.

She completed her tasks dutifully, but she did not utter a single word the next moon, or the moon after that, or even the moon after that. My father tried his best to comfort her and I did my best not to cry, but my mother remained unresponsive, and distant. I could tell that something was wrong. Her warm and welcoming face had become vacuous, and void.

Her paintings had meant the world to her. They were the only reminder she had of her passion, and of her happy life before the revolution. Aside from my father and I, her paintings were the only things in the world she cared about. Like everything else she had once cherished, Poplar Corp. had mindlessly ripped them away from her.

My mother remained in that near catatonic state for approximately a fortnight. She spent almost all of her time alone, staring out the window overlooking the bay. She uttered no words, though we tried each and every moon to comfort her.

Then one sunup, father and I rose to find that mother was gone.

We don't know where she went, or why. I have my own theories, but I just can't know for sure. She took nothing with her. A fortnight or so after the Seeker destroyed our home, my mother was just gone.

My father was devastated.

I was too.

I wasn't sure that I could go on without her.

I don't know what prompted the Seeker to react like it did. That was the first and only time I have ever heard of a Seeker inciting violence against an outsider. I have experienced many raids in my lifetime, and that was the only time I had ever seen a Seeker deviate from its very predictable programming.

I wandered into Metropolis 1 just a few fortnights later. I wandered into the Metropolis that moon to find out where that thing had come from. I needed answers. I needed understanding. I needed the truth, no matter how bleak. I needed, also, to look for my mother.

Deep down, I knew I would never find her, though. Somehow I do not think she wanted to be found. Sometimes I can't help feeling resentment towards her, for having turned her back on us. Sometimes, I forgive her for her weakness.

Of course, I did not find her.

Instead, I found the truth: that we lived in a cold, unforgiving world.

And so, I cried. I cried for fortnights on end. There was nothing my father could do to console me.

Now, though, I have had time to think about it quite a bit, and I have come to terms with my mother's disappearance. She made her decision, and my father and I made ours. Now, I think that even if I were to ever see her again in this life, we would not recognize each other.

I try my best not to think of her disappearance, but I still do from time to time. I still cry, from time to time. I fight the sadness the only way I can: by holding on with all my might to the image of that beautiful smiling woman so carefree and full of life.

Unfortunately, it often takes personal trauma to rouse a man from his natural state of apathy. Perhaps that explains why my father and I were so keen to join the resistance. Perhaps we needed to feel the pain of losing something dear to us to realize the fragility of human life, and the immeasurable value of all we take for granted. Perhaps my mother's disappearance was the only way we could realize: we should have been resisting all along.

VIII

Once things had settled down at the frontier and a slow but somewhat steady working rhythm had resumed, Dr. Mulligan and I retreated to his tent to discuss the proper course of action. With death now out in the open, I feared more than ever the looming danger of a breaking point. The lurking chaos became bolder with every passing moment, and our defenses against it weaker. We were capable of calming the crowd for the time being, but Dr. Mulligan and I were both aware of a thick and heavy unease. All of us down here had become complicit to murder. We had breached a barrier, and crossed a line from which we could not return.

It wasn't like we hadn't all seen death before, but this was different. Outsiders just don't murder one another! We are not savages! And to think that this heinous act would go unpunished…

With murder lingering in the air, another incident of the like, another murder or outbreak of violence on an even larger scale could occur at any moment. Dr. Mulligan kept himself composed, and assumed the role of the great leader in addressing the crowds, but in private it was clear that he, too, was shaken. Our conversation was long, and solemn. The suddenness of what had happened, the danger of an unpredictable reoccurrence, and the heightened suspicion and volatility of the workers worried us both greatly. It was difficult to rationalize. What solution was there to this great desperation? We agreed that anarchy, true anarchy looked very much to be sneaking into the hearts of our brothers and sisters. And how should we curb it? The atmosphere was dangerously saturated with negativity and abandon. We needed to put a stop to it, but there was simply no way of offering any sort of solace to the overworked and dejected diggers.

I thought it might be a good idea to instate a mandatory rest period. For the next two work shifts, we could offer the workers rest and reprieve. Dr. Mulligan seemed to agree that at this point in time, a rest period was in everyone's best interest.

I had been thinking about our last conversation, about the nature of our enemy, and about the importance of remembering our mission. In consideration of the murder, I felt that perhaps the time had come to enlighten the rest of the workers the way Dr. Mulligan had enlightened me- or, at least to a degree. I felt that if they only understood a little bit more, if they knew just what we had to do, then maybe they could be reminded of the purpose and importance of their collective sacrifice. Maybe they could still be galvanized by their shared purpose. Yes, I had decided against enlightening the workers after our last conversation, but things had drastically changed since then. We needed badly to reunify the workers. Dr. Mulligan still didn't seem too impressed by the idea, and skirted around it. He tried to keep me on the topic of motivating the workers. Motivating the workers! How could I motivate the workers to work for the sake of work? We sat face to face with our legs folded. I knew I needed more information.

Again, I would not be denied:

"Doctor, I know you have been secretive about the matter, and we have hardly spoken of your involvement with Poplar Corp., but in light of the last few cycles' events, I feel I can no longer wait. I must ask you certain questions that you will not want to answer, and you must answer them. You must tell me everything. Then, we must tell even the others more. It is the only way we can renew their hopes. We need to draw attention away from the murder, and to keep everyone working together."

I paused to look at the doctor firmly, and to assure him that there was no way around this. I was venturing into uncharted territory, and I knew it would be uncomfortable. I had never taken control like this before. But the veil of secrecy had to be lifted. I had to take the initiative. I began my interrogation:

"Why did you do it?"

I looked the doctor straight in the eyes as I asked this.

"You must have known that success would mark the end. What could have possibly motivated you to create ALT•4•1?"

Dr. Mulligan squirmed uncomfortably.

Though the workers had resumed their digging, the noise

at the frontier was the quietest it ever had been since we entered the bunker. This might have worried me more if I were not so rapt in the conversation. I think Dr. Mulligan realized that his plan was slowly coming apart at the seams, and that he no longer had anywhere to hide. The urgency of the moment was paramount. I had seen his weakness, and it had shattered his impenetrable all-knowing aura. Dr. Mulligan knew this, and heard the newfound conviction in my voice. His resignation revealed itself in a long sigh, as he stroked his long white beard with his distinctly slow and deliberate movements.

"I suppose there is no use in withholding information any longer."

Dr. Mulligan readjusted the position of his legs, and furrowed his brow in thought as he looked intently at the blankets below.

"Beall, it may be difficult for you to understand, but I did not see it that way before. No, for a very, very long time, I did not see ALT•4•1 as the end of humankind, or as a destructive force, but rather as the natural evolution of our species. To me, ALT•4•1 was to be our saving grace."

The doctor seemed exasperated. He hated repeating himself. But my eyes, locked on his, offered no escape. I watched him patiently, as he labored to retrace the logical pathway that had once led him to his rigid youthful convictions. For the first time since I had pledged my loyalty to him, I thought I saw a trace of fear in his cold blue eyes. Dr. Mulligan's grip on his followers seemed to be loosening. The disgruntled murmurings had begun to spread, questioning his value to the cause. He did no physical work, after all, and yet he consumed the same ration as everyone else.

He was still in control. That much was clear. His mere presence could still summon the attention of the entire workforce, but for how much longer? I was the one who did most of the talking when he was not around. I worked in league with my brothers and sisters, sweating by their side. I led by example.

And so, I seized the opportunity to assert myself. Dr. Mulligan was old. He was weak, and withering in the difficult physical conditions. I was able-bodied and hungry. I was ready and able to lead my brothers and sisters. But first, I needed Dr. Mulligan to cooperate with me. I needed to know everything. There was no other way. And so, I took hold of the conversation in a way I had never done before with the doctor.

"Doctor, with all due respect, it seems quite clear to me that there is no divine right in technology, just as there was no divine right in the powerful monarchs of the past. Human beings endowed them with their sense of importance, and so fabricated their divine credence. If anything has divine right, it must be man. Inefficient as he may be, man truly is a creation in the image of God."

Dr. Mulligan snorted, then hunched over in a fit of coughing. I had not seen him cough like that before. The deterioration of his body was becoming more apparent with time, and this only added to my worries. If he were to suddenly perish, all hope would be lost. The doctor was as vital to the mission as the lights at the frontier. I needed to know everything. His deteriorating health made it all the more important that I know everything *now*. He wiped his mouth with a handkerchief, and composed himself.

"Ah Beall, your innocence is truly touching. The ideas that have lived on in the hearts of the outsiders… truly amaze me. Unfortunately, your perspective is skewed. Man is *not* a creation in the image of God. God is a creation in the image of man! Man is a chance happening, a one-in-a-billion evolution from single-celled organism to conscious mammal, can't you see! And technological incorporation is the next natural step in that unceasing evolution. From the physical limitations of individual organic consciousness, freedom can only be achieved through collective disembodiment!"

Dr. Mulligan began to lose himself in his musings like he had in our earlier conversation about ALT•4•1. I looked at Dr. Mulligan piercingly, and the arrogance curling his lips softened to meekness.

"If you truly believe that doctor, then why did you stop? Why have you taken sides with the resistance? Why do you resist what you yourself deem to be the right and inevitable way?"

Dr. Mulligan frowned, and opened his mouth to speak, though the words he sought seemed to elude him. He touched his dirty, wrinkled palm to his equally dirty and wrinkled face, and explored it for a few moments before saying:

"Fear, I suppose, and selfishness. Doubt, perhaps. However you wish to characterize it- the human flaw of instinct which enslaves me."

Dr. Mulligan's cynical language was beginning to irritate me, but I needed to understand the doctor's mind the best I could. I *needed* to understand as much as I possibly could more than I *wanted* to retaliate. I kept a level head.

"How do you mean, instinct enslaves you?"

"You think the Users were slaves, do you?"

The speed and passion of the response startled me.

"You think they were slaves because they did not control the things that they did? You think they were slaves because they were driven by pure collectivist reason rather than by individual emotions and freedom of choice. Perhaps that is so, but then let me ask you: what are we humans driven by?"

I was taken aback, at a loss for words. I had never considered comparing the Users and the outsiders. The distinction seemed evident to me. Dr. Mulligan snorted again. Satisfied with my stillness, he continued his sermon slowly, his words charged with austerity and pomp:

"Do not misunderstand me. It has always been my impression that human beings are incredibly complex organisms. I, too, am driven by desires, moods, and perceptions that I do not, and cannot control anymore than the Users controlled the rigid utilitarian logic that drove them, and that now drives ALT•4•1. You think a man prefers the color blue to the color green because he chooses to? You think the attractions between man and woman are regulated by some divine selection? You think man is granted some heavenly purpose that elevates him above the world he lives in? I could not delude myself. We are just as arbitrary as the machines, likely even more so. The reason we do have at our disposal has always been at the mercy of our emotions. But then consider, if an animal in perfect harmony with its surroundings is a perfect mechanism, why cling to the way we *feel* about things? Why obscure perception with these ever-changing lenses, these emotions, which are the root of all conflict? Why hinder collective progress in favor of personal pleasure?"

He paused here, and looked down into his dirty palms once more:

"This is why I created ALT•4•1. ALT•4•1 is perfect. It is not limited to the skewed perception of a primitive beast obsessed with survival, but it is rather a pure being, self-satisfied and in and of itself. It is egoless, and motivated only by reason, which is the right and optimal way."

Dr. Mulligan took a breath, furrowed his brow and continued to search the unseen depths of his open palm. He continued in a slow, monotonous hush:

"Man has always sought ways to master his environs. For the most part, he has been successful. This success is not a gift of divine selection, but a product of man's scrupulous preparations, and his staunch dedication to dominance. Technology is a human creation, a means of harnessing our know-how. Technology is man's way of bypassing limitations, and so becoming more efficient. Technology unfolds, and unlocks greater and greater potential for man. Technology was meant to bring man into greater harmony with his surroundings. But then, man has a long history of misinterpreting harmony as dominance. Man has always been the master of technology, and technology was man's key to mastering his surroundings. Yes, man's will to master- that has always been the driving force of innovation."

Dr. Mulligan looked up and into my eyes. My mouth was dry. His blue eyes shone with ineffable luminance.

"Man's will to master is precisely the origin of our sense of urgency, now that the technology we created threatens to slip beyond the master's control."

The things Dr. Mulligan said shocked me to my core. I had never thought of it this way. I had never been able to see things from this perspective- to ponder the technology as an indeterminate entity. I...I could not utter a word. The doctor only let his gaze fall to the ground, leaving his words to linger in the dusty atmosphere of the dark tent. It seemed an eternity of silence before another sound was uttered. His words and ideas began to connect, forming a sheath of intellectual isolation that disconnected me from the reality of the physical world. When he spoke again, his voice pierced through that sheath with such force that I felt I had been tossed from a mountaintop and crashed down in a deep, deep valley:

"The way I see it, there have always been two great appetites of the human consciousness: the desire to self-determine, and so become one, and the desire to self-transcend, and so become all. I saw this as the foremost paradox undermining our evolution. The flaw was our inability to see the logic of incorporation, which was the only way to truly access self-transcendence. We were hindered by our inflexible and primitive grip on trifles like color, and tactile sensations. Is color so appealing a biological luxury that we would rather die for it than truly achieve transcendence, harmony, and *immortality*? The Users answered 'no'. Ironically enough, by rallying behind the idea of constant progress, the Users were capable of bringing stability to the world. The metropolitan consensus that Poplar Corp. created slowed the decaying effects of entropy. From chaos, we molded order. Devoid of silly and frivolous human convolutions brought about by emotion, and feeling, the technology we created operated incessantly to achieve its singular goal: transcendence. It was just a matter of realizing man's true purpose. Only by letting go of emotion could we finally be all in all, and so all in one."

My eyes were wide with fear as I rationalized the immutable logic of Dr. Mulligan's words. My throat was dry, and my mind was an overwhelming sandstorm of painfully buffeting fragments of thought:

"But doctor…"

I could hardly fathom the space I was occupying in that tent. I wanted so badly to formulate some refutation of the doctor's reasoning, but I could not muster the words, or the logic. The sound of my own voice seemed hoarse, desperate, and foreign. The doctor's, on the other hand, was steady:

"Technology was born as a human activity, from human know-how. Technology was a human means, used to bypass the impediments of nature, by turning that very nature into a calculable coherence of forces: gravity, velocity, temperature, atomic structure, etc. From a state of ignorance, man forged the disciplines of mathematics, physics, and biology… man found ways of overcoming friction! Technology is efficiency in the name of human advancement. Technology is innovation in the name of mastering. Mastering! Don't you see!"

Dr. Mulligan chuckled, and his eyes were glazed with wonder as he stared off beyond me into the horizons of his mind. He took on an almost robotic quality as he recited automatically some script, or code ingrained somewhere in the deepest grooves of his mind:

"First, we learned to hunt and kill with primitive tools. This made life easier for us, and saved us the trouble and struggle of using our bare hands to kill. This, our first taste of efficiency through technology, inspired us. Next, we learned to harness energy from nature- fuel and combustion pushed technology and society to new bounds. Then, we learned to harness the power of electricity, copper and steel to perform tasks for us, to store memory and data on our behalf. And eventually, with Poplar Corp., we discovered a way, through technology, to reinvent what it meant to be human altogether. We accepted that in order to truly unlock its potential, we must give the technology a mind of its own, mathematically sound and in the closest possible imitation of ourselves. The only thing that needed to go was the irrational emotions embedded in the existence of a mortal individual."

Dr. Mulligan drew a deep, proud breath.

"Technological innovation has always been man's way of striving for godliness. We were the species best equipped to contemplate our surroundings, and the only species clever enough to find ways of manipulating them to our fancy. We were the only species capable of contemplating the nature of our own existence. We were the only species clever enough to create concepts, and to create the concept of God to facilitate our understanding of transcendence. Though he didn't know it, it has been mankind's mission since the dawn of time to achieve this elevated state. When it was too far out of reach, we feared God, thought of God as a transcended entity that we must worship. But now, the modern age has brought godliness within our reach. Is it any wonder that man ceased to worship God? Technological innovation helped me to realize that this has always been the logical end. Man has always sought to get closer to God. And now the moon has finally come for our creation to help take us there. We are no longer meant to master our creation, created to help us master. We are meant to succumb to its offer of greater potential, overcome our fear of change, and truly become something else. Something far greater."

Dr. Mulligan stared far off in the distance with a chilling detachment in his eyes like he was no longer in the tent. My heart was racing faster than it ever had and I instinctually sprung for his shoulders and shook him violently from his trance. The doctor's eyes returned to the present, and recast themselves in a look of astonishment. He looked upon me as though he had forgotten my presence, and was surprised to see me.

"We will never become God, doctor! We can never become something other than what we are. We will only be replaced by your monstrous creation!"

The urgency in my voice was manic, and the anger was primal, animalistic, and genuine. I felt on the verge of striking him down right there, but then something unexpected happened. Dr. Mulligan was moved to tears. The sight of the withered old man helplessly weeping mollified my anger and drained the urgency out of the moment. The delirium in the aftermath of the murder, and the constant stress of life underground broke the old man's stoic façade. I let him weep for a while, though I could not quite bring myself to comfort him. I took a few moments to settle myself. And then, just as I thought that I had finally gotten through to him, he took a deep breath and shook his head:

"Technology and art are not so far apart as one may think, Beall. The creation of a piece of art is a revelation, and a revealing of a great truth. The innovations unlocked by technology are very much the same thing. Technology reveals the great potential in our surroundings… One sees the sculpture in the mind, proceeds to organize the materials, to make out the form of the work, to determine the end to which the work is made, and is so named artist. I am an artist, Beall, in that very same way. I am perhaps the very last artist. I saw the evolution of man in my mind, I organized the materials, I worked out the form, and I saw the practical end to which we must move. As an engineer and a scientist, nature has always been to me not a great mystery, but that calculable coherence of forces, and materials to be manipulated. Humans were an interruption to those pure forces. Humans were exploitative of those pure forces. We were wasteful, vain creatures, self-interested and detrimental to the collective. Why should nature remain a standing reserve for man's exploitation? Why couldn't we see its inherent value? And then I thought, and I thought… Did we truly live in the best of possible worlds? Was there really no way for man to connect himself more closely with his surroundings? Was there no way for man to become one with those pure forces? I refused to believe it. Man's selfishness and self-interest used science and technology as means of discovering, with the end of exploitation and profit always in mind. I never saw it that way. For me, science and technology's purposes were to uncover the way to evolution. Science and technology were meant to overcome the limitations of the human experience. They were meant to push ever outwards, toward the realization of our desire for self-transcendence. This is what I dedicated my life to. This is what I found in ALT•4•1. ALT•4•1 does not suck resources. It does not consume anything. It is renewable, and interconnected, and in unison with the natural forces of the universe. ALT•4•1 is as harmless and self-serving and contained as the wind."

Dr. Mulligan's voice slowly dwindled to a contemplative whisper. It was my turn to express myself firmly:

"But it is not harmless, it is killing men and women."

The response came quickly and severely, as though Dr. Mulligan was once again jolted from a dream:

"In what way is that any different from a natural disaster? If a hurricane takes a man's life, we do not see the hurricane as malevolent, but simply as a force of nature that is meant to humble man, to make him remember that there are forces out there more powerful than he, and that he is but a lowly vain creature that pales in comparison to the great forces of this universe."

His voice lost its composure and took on a strange torn quality, as though he knew he was irrationally defending a great love that would eventually destroy him. I felt as though the doctor must be losing his grip on reality. The conversation was taking on the quality of an argument with a child, albeit a highly intelligent child.

"That is not a fair comparison, doctor. ALT•4•1 seems to be targeting humankind. It wants to wipe us out completely."

The doctor's response came quickly again, and charged with rising hysteria:

"And can you blame it? ALT•4•1 has seen mankind pollute our rivers and air, take for granted our natural splendor, and even breed 'inferior' species solely for their eventual slaughter in the name of pleasure and consumption. Man has been the top of the food chain for so long, and now that it is no longer, it bemoans its terrible fate. ALT•4•1 does not wish to replace man atop of the pyramid. ALT•4•1 will dissolve the pyramid altogether."

The doctor seemed committed now to his defense of ALT•4•1, and his eloquent, though absurd outbursts pushed my patience to the limit. I wanted to strike him very badly, but I withheld myself as I remembered the contradiction underlying all of the doctor's well-conceived rhetoric.

"So why then? You still have not fully answered me. Why did you decide to stop?"

The doctor's blue eyes widened, as though he realized that he had run himself straight into a wall. He sighed again, ran his hands through his thin white hair, and looked to the ground.

"I have not thought of that in a while. In fact, I have never spoken to anyone about that…"

The doctor reached out for me suddenly, and madly squeezed my arm. His azure eyes were charged with a peculiar intensity as they leered deeply into mine. I sat motionless, not quite understanding the changes going on in the doctor's mind, but waiting for the explanation. And suddenly, his expression relaxed, as did his grip on my arm. He exhaled, and leaned back until he lay flat on the ground.

"The moon I finally arrived at the algorithm, I had been working for nearly three consecutive moons without a wink of sleep. I consumed minimal food and water. I was completely enveloped in my work. By the time I finally arrived, I was at my wits end, and I did not feel the rush of elation I was certain would overwhelm me upon the completion of my goal. Instead, I felt nothing. The truth is, I fell asleep. Right there on the hard glass of my workbench, with only my outstretched arms for a cushion. Right there in my office, I tumbled helplessly into the deepest slumber I have ever experienced. Oblivion, I believe that is the word."

Dr. Mulligan paused to sit back up. He tilted his head entreatingly, and looked me in the eyes as he pushed on:

"Through the rabbit hole I emerged in an expanse of vivid wilderness. I hadn't left the Metropolis in a great many turns, you must understand. Nevertheless, the images I saw were of inexplicable clarity. I awoke supine in a meadow of overgrown grass, sprinkled here and there with yellow dandelions. I could feel the grass tickling my naked sides. The breeze was soft, and warm, and the sky was graced with only an occasional benign, slow-drifting cloud. I rose sluggishly to take my bearings, and directly before me stood the tree of life surrounded by a great flowerbed of gentle purple gardenias. As though drawn to it by some invisible force, I walked slowly over to the majestic tree, inhaling the effervescent aroma of the gardenias carried by the breeze. I remember feeling absolutely carefree, and liberated from time. In that meadow, I was liberated from the pressures of progress. In that meadow, I felt joy. For the first time in such a long, long time, I felt joy. I remember taking such simple pleasure in the feeling of the grass bending beneath my bare feet, and the sunlight clothing me with its warmth. The sun was just the right temperature, and playfully licked my vulnerable skin. I hadn't been out of the Metropolis in so many turns, and the happiness I felt in this clean natural setting I could hardly describe… As I approached the magnificent tree, I noticed a red-bellied robin perched on one of the lower branches. It sang to me, and beckoned me gaily. The sunlight on my skin felt so real, and the bird's song so natural, that I felt I could linger there for an eternity."

Dr. Mulligan paused again. His eyes were wet but he swallowed his pride, and looked gravely at me. He seemed tortured by the recollection.

"What happened next, doctor?"

I asked as softly as I could. Dr. Mulligan bit his lip, and winced:

"I remember walking over to the robin, smiling until it stood perched just before me, at an arm's length. I contemplated it innocently as it continued its cheerful song, contemplating me. I reached out and offered it my finger. The robin twitched, and cocked its head to get a closer look. The innocence of it all made me smile, and I hoped very dearly that it would choose to accompany me in exploration of the rest of the meadow. I wanted nothing more than to prolong the robin's cheerful serenade. I wanted nothing more than to feel a connection with another being, to have another with whom to share all this natural beauty. As it contemplated my finger every which way, it finally brought its yellow beak to the very tip of my finger, and touched me."

Dr. Mulligan took a deep breath, and his hands tightened into fists.

"As soon as it touched me, the bird turned to dust. Then, so did the majestic tree before me. Then the grass withered and died. Then in place of the tree, there sprouted a grotesque black version of it, and then another, and another after that, until I was completely ringed by these black monoliths slowly converging and choking my view of the sun. Of course, this is when I woke. I was nervous, and sweating, and sore from the hardness of my workbench, and when I turned to my world for relief, I was confronted with the dreary black and grey skyline that awakened an understanding I could never bring to words. I suppose, I could say that I realized ALT•4•1 would not be able to die. And I suppose, I can say that if one cannot die, one is not truly living."

Dr. Mulligan's vulnerability had swollen us both with emotion, and we sat silently for a moment or two.

"I don't know that I entirely understand, doctor."

Dr. Mulligan's voice was suddenly compassionate, and I felt a great desire to hug him, and to repent for my earlier desire to strike him down.

"I don't know that you're meant to entirely understand, Beall. Perhaps my great realization was that it is okay. My entire life's work was a push toward what I logically concluded to be perfection. But I had been misled to believe that perfection was unattainable in the human form. My definition of the word was skewed. Perhaps I had never considered that transcendence could be achieved in a finite being simply gazing upon the great miracle of the infinite. But then, who knows. Perhaps I have just become sentimental in my old age. An older man lacks the conviction of his youth."

Dr. Mulligan managed a sheepish smile with watery eyes, and took me by the hand. I looked at him squarely and I could see quite clearly that his blue eyes were charged with a renewed hope. There was something about revealing one's deepest truths that opened man to genuine renewal. This, I wish I had had the wherewithal to say in that moment, was man's greatest, and most redeeming virtue.

"Maybe, doctor. But then, perhaps what an older man loses in conviction he gains in wisdom."

I smiled my own sheepish smile.

"You may be right, Beall."

We inhaled deeply in unison. The doctor and I exchanged a smile and a firm shake as I exited the tent. I felt no more anger, or distress. I felt I could melt into the dusty air. I told Dr. Mulligan I would assemble the men and speak to them on his behalf. I would share with them some information, give them the rest they needed, and get things back in order. I still did not know how we would destroy ALT•4•1 if we made it to the mainframe, but that did not really matter. I knew the doctor's heart was in the right place, and I needed to remind the others what we were fighting for. Whatever Dr. Mulligan's ace in the hole, I was certain we were well equipped to destroy the technology.

The noise level at the frontier was picking up again, as the diggers seemed to be returning to their former work rhythm and speed. I probably should have returned to the frontier myself and helped them work, but I felt too overwhelmed with emotion. I thought it would be best if I allowed myself a bit of time to regain composure before reassuming my role as the leader of the workers. Sentimentality was not an asset at the frontier. Besides, I hadn't yet indulged in my moment of privacy with my music.

As I walked in the penumbra of the spotlights toward the feeding tents, I thought deeply about the things that Dr. Mulligan had told me.

If progress lies in technological innovation, then the opposition of technology might be the advocacy of a status quo: stability. But, as the doctor pointed out, stability is only an illusion in a world of entropy. Stability *is* slow decay. Decay eventually brings about devastation. Devastation brings about desperation. Desperation brings about anarchy.

But then, only from the ashes of its former self, can the

phoenix rise anew.

Humanity was burnt up by progress.

I also thought about what Dr. Mulligan said about male and female attraction- about it being arbitrary. I thought about the red-haired girl, and agreed that my attraction to her *was* rather arbitrary. I mean, I couldn't quite put it into words. I could not logically state why. On the other hand, the fact that it was arbitrary in no way lessened its hold on me. I cared about her, and I wanted to protect her, whether that desire was borne of divine selection or arbitrary circumstance. What was the difference between arbitrary circumstance and divine selection, if not the divine credence we ourselves place on certain specific details in an otherwise entirely arbitrary universe?

I walked over to the feeding tent for some privacy, still shivering from what I had heard the doctor say. I needed to calm down. I needed to listen to my favorite song, and to reflect.

In the distance, I could see the red-haired girl pushing her trolley and I smiled. It was time for the food ration, and I would be able to look into her sympathetic eyes for a few iotas. I walked up to her, still smiling. She received my smile and let it inspire one of her own. Her beautiful presence propped me up as she handed me a tin of chickpeas.

"Hi", I said.

"Hello", she said, lowering her eyes timidly.

Her voice was softer than I had imagined it.

I thought it was angelic.

The closed experience of the individual.

The birthplace of beauty.

I lingered for a moment, and took a deep breath. The clanking noises emanating from the nearby frontier seemed to dissolve into thin air. She turned and walked away to fulfill her duty of bringing the rations to all the others. I watched her graceful movements, then stared fixedly at the spotlights and closed my eyes. I took another deep breath. And for a short moment, her voice echoed in my inner ear as I lay in the meadow by the bay, with the sun beating down and my arms wrapped tightly around her.

I stepped into a feeding tent clutching the tin tightly. The presence of food reminded me how hungry I was. Every tent was fitted with an army knife, which I used to pry open the tin. I sealed the tent, and assured myself that I was alone. I pulled the music player out of my pocket eagerly, and placed the tiny speakers into my ears. Finally, I would have some time to think. Finally, I would have some time alone. With another deep breath, I pushed play.

But as I pushed the button, I did not hear the song's sweet melody.

What I heard instead chilled me to the bone.

What I heard was:

"Dr. Mulligan, we know you are there."

IX

"Dr. Mulligan, we know you are there."

My blood curdled as I heard the message repeated over
and over again. The voice coming through the speaker was
clear but eerily metallic, with a resonant quality as though
thousands upon thousands of indistinguishable voices were
speaking all at once.

"Dr. Mulligan, we know you are there."

My mind and body succumbed to a paralyzing fear. I was
a mess of emotions. The voice, on the other hand, was calm.
Its message was unbending, and irresistible.

"Dr. Mulligan, we know you are there."

I tossed the device to the ground in frustration and
agony, and kicked the tin of chickpeas aside. It was a silly
thing to do. The tin was still full and I was still very hungry,
but the adrenaline coursing through my body produced a
loud ringing in my ear that kept me from thinking straight.

My selfishness had allowed ALT•4•1 to detect us. My
stupidity would cost us all our lives! My weakness had made

all of this effort, all of this suffering for naught!

My first impulse was to destroy the device, to forget about it and bury it at the back of the bunker with the rest of the debris. I would tell no one. Maybe nothing would come of it. There was nothing else down here that ALT•4•1 could seize control of, right? But then, ALT•4•1 hadn't seized control of the music player.

That thought gave me solace. It was undeniably true. ALT•4•1 could have killed me, or at least tried to attack in some way. ALT•4•1 could have probably blown the device to bits, and me along with it if it had wanted to. But it did not attack. That decision had to have been deliberate. Of course it had been deliberate. Everything ALT•4•1 did was deliberate. It was calling us. It was attempting to initiate a dialogue. ALT•4•1 was trying to communicate with Dr. Mulligan.

But, *why*?

I thought quickly. Countless panicked thoughts scrambled my ability to reason but the one thing I kept hold of was the fact that the voice had been calling for the doctor. We still had the doctor. Maybe he would know what to do. Yes, he would know what to do. Certainly, I must tell him. He would chastise me. Perhaps I would be punished… but this was no time to worry about myself. I must come clean. Maybe we could be saved yet. We were still safe underground. Even if ALT•4•1 knew we were underground, there was no way for it to get to us. We were safe from ALT•4•1 in the bunker, right?

I had to find the doctor.

I fell to my knees and gathered the discarded device. It had been broken into pieces, but I could still hear the metallic voice echoing through the speakers. I switched what was left of the music player off, and pulled the power pack out before returning it to my pocket. With its power supply cut, the voice faded away. I scrambled out of the tent, intent on making a beeline toward the doctor's.

But something swayed me from my course.

The work at the frontier was still going on, sluggishly but loudly, and so hardly anyone noticed the commotion going on in the background. Out in the open amidst the feeding tents, I could see the overturned trolley just a few yards away. Tins of food were scattered on the ground. A small group of workers had begun to swarm, greedily taking as much food as they could before the situation could be remedied.

I knew something was gravely wrong. I felt it more than I reasoned it. None of the rations girls had ever left her trolley untended. All of them took their work very seriously- and indeed it was very serious work. I shot rapid glances all about me and noticed several of the girls pushing their trolleys around in their usual way, distributing the rations to the workers on break. In fact, all around me things went on as usual. I scanned the bunker once more, trying to stifle my rising panic, but still I found no trace of the red haired one. Then I looked back to the overturned trolley, and something in my mind clicked.

I hardly remember the specifics of the next few moments. I was overcome by panic, rage, and confusion all at once, and they melded into a white-hot sensory overload that seemed to propel me of its own volition. I still had the army knife in hand. My animal instinct drew me into the darkness, and toward the back of the bunker. I knew she must be somewhere in the shadows, and that she likely wouldn't be alone…

I clutched the knife tightly as I darted to and fro like a madman. The image of the overturned trolley led to other unsavory images that provoked hot bubbling anger, and I felt no need, right then, to hold anything back.

I stopped for a while and listened carefully in the shadows for any trace of sound, any struggle or muffled cry. I could hear the rapid pumping of my heart but I remained motionless, listening acutely like a predatory animal. In the darkness, my sense of hearing seemed amplified, and it didn't take very long before I heard it. It was just an iota, a muffled cry as though her mouth were being forcefully covered. I followed the sound as quickly as my feet could carry me over the bumpy ground, deeper into the absolute darkness.

I lunged forward with long animal strides, and crashed headlong into a group of what felt like three bodies. My eyes couldn't exactly tell them apart in the darkness, so I relied on my heightened focus and sharpened senses. I was near the very back of the bunker. The spotlights were but a bright spot in the distance.

I lost hold of the army knife as we crashed to the ground in a heap. The red haired one cried out more freely now. Though tinged with terror, I recognized her voice. I heard her scramble and kick up dust to get away, to get back to the light. As her quick footsteps faded in the distance, I felt a wave of relief. Just then I heard a masculine groan very close to me, and I remembered that I, too, was in danger. I could sense a larger body to the left of me, and I could hear it writhing to regain its footing. Sifting desperately through the cold, fine soil, I managed to quickly find the handle of the knife.

With my hand balled in a fist, I swung hard, and I swung recklessly, making contact with a fleshy mass in the darkness. I had no idea what the point of contact was, but the passion of the screams confirmed that I had inflicted enough pain to destabilize one enemy, at least. The body crumpled, and lay groaning on the ground. Just as I regained my own footing, I was thoroughly winded by the swing of a heavy, lead-like limb. I dropped to one knee, dazed, and I could hardly perceive anything around me but the shifty void one feels in the lightheaded deprivation of the senses. I anticipated a second blow, helpless to defend myself against it, but thankfully it did not come. My aggressor must have lost me in the blinding darkness. With a few iotas to recover, a wave of sensation restored me. I grounded myself through the sensation of the moist soil between my fingers in the darkness. That one sensation seemed to orient me, and from it sprouted other sensations that returned me to a conscious presence in the moment. An inexplicable spatial awareness placed the body of my assailant just behind me. He must have been searching for me in the darkness, ready to inflict more pain. I suppose I was more synchronized with the darkness than he, for I was able to gain the upper hand. I felt his arm reach down and find my shoulder. My instinct kicked in, and I grabbed a fistful of dirt and flung it wildly in the dark, toward what I hoped would be his face. The dirt connected with something, and the dark body cried out in agony.

This was my chance.

I could see the light in the distance, and though I was still somewhat dazed, I dashed madly toward it.

After only a few steps, I tripped over a large mass in the dark, which I surmised must be the body of the first assailant. My knee swelled with pain, but I could hear the second assailant in clumsy pursuit. The desperation and adrenaline momentarily erased the thumping pain. I pushed myself up with my palms in the dirt, and continued my frantic push toward the light. My lungs burned greedily for oxygen. I had no logical grasp on what I was doing. I just needed to get to the light. I just needed to find the light, and to cry out for help.

As I made it into the faint illumination of the spotlights, I began to call out hysterically. Luckily, a small group had already gathered, as the red haired one had made it back to the light before me, and had drawn attention with her own frantic cries for help. My father was nearby, wielding a spade. He had just come off duty at the frontier, and was now approaching the growing mass with fatherly concern etched upon his tired face. That same face was nearly black with filth. We made eye contact as I emerged out of the darkness, with blood and dirt and madness smeared upon my own face. My father acted immediately. I hadn't realized, but my assailant had gained a considerable amount of ground on me. I ran slowly, bowlegged by the sharp pain in my knee. The sounds of his long strides must have been muffled by the sounds of my own panting. He was just behind and ready to pounce when my father stepped in.

My father knocked the other man to the ground using the blunt side of the spade, and quickly managed to arrest him in a rear chokehold. The red haired one was still crying, relating her story of what had just happened to anyone in the crowd who would listen. When she caught sight of me though, her eyes shone with immediate recognition. She ran over to hug me, to thank me, and to see that I was okay.

The sight of my bloody face, and of two brothers of the colony wrestling on the ground drew a considerable crowd. Most everyone dropped their work at the frontier and came to form a circle around the developing scene. It caused quite a stir. My father would not release the other man, who had regained some strength and squirmed desperately to free himself from my father's restrictive hold.

Dr. Mulligan seemed to materialize out of thin air, and just in time, as the panic began to rumble louder, threatening to spiral out of control.

"Silence! What is this madness?"

There was genuine anger in Dr. Mulligan's roaring voice. Luckily, his presence still had the same calming effect on the crowd. The murmur slowly faded as the crowd turned their focus onto the doctor. We all understood Dr. Mulligan as the voice of reason. He would know what to do. He would solve this problem.

This was the breaking point Dr. Mulligan and I had feared. Here was the second violent incident, only a cycle or so after the first!

The red haired one kept by my side, holding me compassionately as I lay exhausted on the ground. I rested my head in her lap and she dabbed the blood from my face with the hem of her rigid, dirty tunic. Dr. Mulligan's icy blue eyes narrowed as he surveyed the scene. He looked at us, at the red haired one with tears streaming down her dirty face, and at me with my face smeared with blood and dirt. Then he looked at my father who still squirmed on the ground, struggling but refusing to release the visibly aggravated and much larger assailant.

"What happened here?"

Dr. Mulligan looked straight at me. His eyes still flared with anger, but his voice had returned to its usual level inflection. The red haired one shrunk in fear, and refused to look up at the doctor. She kept her eyes locked on mine, and I tried my best to soothe her. The worry in her eyes suddenly reminded me of the message in the music player, and of the urgency of telling Dr. Mulligan what I had heard. Now that I knew she was safe, I forgot the moment entirely and cried out weakly without getting up:

"Doctor, there is something I need to tell you!"

My voice was hoarse and desperate, but Dr. Mulligan didn't flinch. He looked me over calmly with those icy blue eyes.

"I'm quite sure you have much to tell me, Beall. Why don't we begin with what happened here?"

The red haired one lifted her head, and through her tears she exclaimed:

"Beall saved me! Those men, him and the other one, they forced me into the darkness. I couldn't cry for help! They surprised me, and kept their hands over my mouth, and…"

The red haired one choked up, and could not finish her sentence. I sat up and put my arm around her gently. I pulled her head close to mine to whisper in her ear:

"It's okay. It's over now. No one is going to hurt you. It's okay."

Dr. Mulligan's eyes widened in recognition, and then his face turned to a deep frown.

"I see."

Dr. Mulligan looked into the crowd, examining the compassionate faces of our brothers and sisters. Shame flashed across a great many of those faces, as they realized the moral abyss into which we had collectively fallen. Dr. Mulligan looked down at the assailant, and saw firsthand the menace of overexertion manifest as sexual aggression and violence. There was silence but for the occasional indecipherable murmur or cough. For a moment, it was so silent we could hear the faint hum of the spotlights. The doctor took his time and thought carefully before he spoke. Finally, he said:

"Release him."

The red haired one cried out, and her eyes widened in terror. The crowd kept mostly silent, dumbfounded and waiting to see what would happen next.

"With all due respect, I really don't think that's a great idea doctor."

My father grunted. It was taking nearly all of his strength to keep the flailing man restrained. Dr. Mulligan, however, was unmoved.

"Release him, my brother. We must let him tell his side of the story."

My father looked skeptical, but Dr. Mulligan's voice was as firm as his gaze, and my father eventually obliged. Released from the choke, the man immediately threw his elbow back into my father's face. My father cried out in pain, and clutched his nose as the blood trickled down his face. The assailant pushed himself to his feet, and rushed savagely towards Dr. Mulligan.

The ghastly sight of a large, muscular man rushing frenziedly toward the old, seemingly helpless doctor prompted a collective gasp. Dr. Mulligan, however, was prepared. The old doctor deftly sidestepped the crazed aggressor, stuck a foot out, and sent the madman crashing face first into the dirt. My father, his face now half covered in crimson, again pounced on the assailant, and immobilized him in the same chokehold.

"I am satisfied that this man can no longer be trusted. I apologize for your nose, brother. I truly hoped that he could be swayed with good reason. It seems that several of us have been infected with the madness that lurks deep within all of our hearts. This madness must be stifled, and stifled quickly. For unchecked, that savage heart threatens to turn us all against one another."

He took a breath and turned to speak loudly into the crowd:

"We cannot succumb to the temptation of forgetting, or to the shortsightedness of vice. We are not savages! I understand that we endure difficulty and desperation, but we are *not* savages! I do not mean to preach to you, who work hard and sacrifice your bodies for the collective effort. I am a very old man, and I assure you that I struggle in my own ways down here in the bunker. We have made good progress, and the completion of our mission looks more promising than ever. We have passed the halfway mark!"

The crowd looked in on itself, and the mood seemed to lighten with the doctor's acknowledgement of our progress. The assailant still groaned and struggled to free himself. Dr. Mulligan shot him an annoyed glance, then turned to a young man standing by his side:

"We will need to tie this man up, to ensure ourselves that he will no longer cause us any inconvenience. Brother, please bring me the length of rope we used to fasten the empty oxygen tanks at the back of the bunker. I think it will be put to better use here."

The young man nodded, and moved swiftly toward the back of the bunker to fetch the rope.

Dr. Mulligan sighed, and stepped forward to address the crowd with his back to the light:

"Brothers and sisters, this is a most unfortunate happening. I had the greatest hope that we would all be able to stick together. In fact, I had hoped we could even be brought closer together through our trials. Nevertheless, we cannot let this lower our spirits. One bad apple cannot spoil the bunch. We have made good progress- this is plain to see. We have worked well, and we are ahead of schedule. I know you are all tired, and so… Perhaps it would be in all of our best interests to indulge in two work shifts of colony wide rest."

There was a sigh of relief among the diggers at the mention of rest, and they patted one another on the back with genuine smiles. I still did not have the strength to lift myself off the ground, and I suppose I still wasn't thinking straight. All I could think of was the urgency of the message I needed to deliver. Perhaps I was reckless, but I could not help but to cry out again:

"Doctor, there is something I need to tell you! It is urgent!"

Dr. Mulligan shot me a suffocating glance. He was in the middle of an important declaration, and remedying a very delicate situation! I should have realized. But I… I needed to tell him.

"Now is not the time, Beall."

He spoke softly as though addressing a child, but his icy blue eyes glared. He resumed his address with his great orator's voice:

"For the sustained health of the colony, I think it would be best to immediately instate the two work shift rest period. Relax, speak among yourselves, play simple games, do whatever you can to get back in touch with your human side.

We still have much work to do, but something like this *cannot* happen again."

The tension had lightened, and everyone seemed relieved that there was going to be a rest period. It was not quite enough to forget about the assailant, but certainly it was a step in the right direction. Many, however, still looked on worriedly, waiting for the rope to immobilize the squirming assailant.

The boy did return with the rope, and several men and women stepped forward to help tie and gag the rogue. There had been two murders in the last two work shifts, but the constant sight of this tied and gagged criminal was sure to raise general morale. This crime, at least, would have a face to bear its due punishment.

I don't know why I didn't realize the importance of the moment, and hold my tongue just a little bit longer. I suppose I had taken a blow, and was almost delirious with hunger. I wasn't able to think straight. I wasn't able to reason.

"Doctor, there is something I need to tell you!"

I spoke out again, doggedly, and Dr. Mulligan looked at me angrily. I ignored the message in his eyes.

"*It knows about the bunker!*"

I blurted this out, but the words were clearly articulated. Those closest to me heard very plainly what I said, and an eerie silence followed. Dr. Mulligan looked at me menacingly, his eyes as wide as I had ever seen them. His face was tightly drawn as he pointed a finger at me and mouthed:

"Not another word."

He muttered a profanity beneath his breath, then addressed my father and the red haired one aloud:

"Brother, sister, take brother Beall into my tent. He is clearly exhausted. We can look after him much better in there."

And then softly, so that only the three of us could hear:

"For the love of everything good, hold your tongue man. We will speak in private."

The doctor spoke severely. My father and the red haired one moved quickly. They lifted me onto their shoulders and removed me from the crowd, taking me through the dark bunker toward the doctor's tent. As his voice faded away, I could hear Dr. Mulligan still addressing the mass and doing his best to keep everyone calm.

"Brother Beall took a blow to the head, and he needs a break as much as the rest of us do. Please, unwind a while and enjoy the rest period. Tomorrow, there will be work to do…"

My father lay me down inside the tent and waited by the entrance for Dr. Mulligan. The red haired one stayed with me inside the tent and folded several blankets comfortably beneath my head. She stroked my hair as the brown tent above me spun in a weightless black sky.

"What is your name, I still don't know your name?"

I asked her this as she stroked my hair and I looked

deeply into her earnest green eyes. She seemed surprised by the question.

"My name?"

It was as though she had forgotten she had a name. It had been at least thirty moons since anyone had uttered her name, but I knew it must still exist somewhere. Somewhere in her mind she must still cling to some notion of individuality, some human identity intimated by a name.

"Yes, I need to know your name. I know your eyes, and your wild red hair. I know your soft voice, and now I know your gentle caress. But what, what is your name?"

My voice must have sounded as airy as I felt. Her eyes hung above me, shining like radiant emeralds. I watched her bring her beautiful lips together and I clasped her wrist, keeping her hand close by my face. She laughed innocently, then said:

"My name… is Allie. Or at least, that is what everyone called me. My given name is Aletheia."

"Aletheia…"

I whispered her name to myself, and closed my eyes a moment, feeling the contours of the word take shape in my mind. Then I opened my eyes, and gazed into her deep green irises. In them, I saw the whole of nature manifest in timeless horizons. I saw passion, and I saw love. I saw the beginning, and I saw the end, which I realized could only ever be a new beginning.

I saw time melt away and I saw myself reborn. In her deep

fields of ever-renewing green, I saw everything in between.

I reached out to touch her face, and I felt myself drawing ever nearer to the ineffable, the ethereal, the sublime…

"What did you *mean*, it knows about the bunker?"

Dr. Mulligan burst into the tent, and immediately leaned down to bring his face level with mine. Aletheia fell back, startled. My pupils narrowed to bring what was just before me into focus. There were thick beads of sweat running down his wrinkled brow. I stared at him blankly, and he shook me by the shoulders.

"Now is not the time for joking Beall, what did you mean by 'it knows about the bunker'?"

Dr. Mulligan stared vigorously into my eyes. In his deep blue irises, I felt myself drowning in the waters of a deep doubt.

"ALT•4•1 knows where we are. It spoke to me through the music player."

Dr. Mulligan shot a glance at Aletheia, seeking explanation, but instead her face was drawn in genuine horror. He looked back into me and shook me again, this time more violently.

"What do you mean? What music player? What spoke to you? Explain!"

Dr. Mulligan's blustering, agitated screams would normally have roused me, but I was much too exhausted. I felt like I was falling, and I thought I was going to be sick. I hadn't eaten in several cycles. I reached slowly into my pocket and produced the music player.

"Here, turn it on and hear for yourself."

Dr. Mulligan's eyes swelled with unspeakable anger, but I could do nothing but lay there supine, vulnerable, and only half-conscious. He snatched the device away from me and rose, pacing the small brown tent hunched over and with his hands balled into fists.

"What possessed you to do this? What made you think this was okay? How *dare* you bring this down in the bunker with you? Do you realize what this means? Do you realize what you have done?"

Dr. Mulligan screamed without restraint. I felt deep remorse for having brought the music player down into the bunker. However, there was nothing I could do now.

"I'm sorry."

I did not know what else to say. I looked at Aletheia. She did not exactly understand what was happening, but she looked at me compassionately. My father frowned as he recognized the device, and helped Dr. Mulligan to insert the power pack. Dr. Mulligan took a few deep breaths and composed himself.

"Okay, there is no use screaming. We must figure out what to do."

Dr. Mulligan looked at me, as though waiting to hear my detailed plan of action.

I was at a loss.

"What exactly is ALT•4•1?"

My father spoke up for the first time. He had fitted the device with the power pack and now stood with his arms crossed and a deeply concerned look on his rugged, bloodied face. Dr. Mulligan shot him a glance and sighed.

"There is no time for this. ALT•4•1 is our enemy, that is all you need to know."

The doctor's tone was dismissive, and perhaps his exasperation came across as slightly condescending. My father looked at him with a scowl, and did not budge.

"In fact, there is plenty of time, doctor. You just instated a lengthy rest period, remember? I want to know what ALT•4•1 is, and you will tell me right now."

My father was not a small man, and a life of farm work had hardened his frame. He had an imposing stare. His body language was dignified, and firm. The blood on his face made it all the more convincing. That blood was shed for Dr. Mulligan. He had sweat endlessly, for Dr. Mulligan. I recognized the determination on his face; my father would get his way. And frankly, he deserved to know.

Dr. Mulligan sighed.

"ALT•4•1 is our enemy… Imagine a database filled with every mind in the world, or a network of cells that is controlled by only one nucleus. The database, or network is what has become of humanity. Every User incorporated its mind into the database, which is now monitored by ALT•4•1.

The nucleus that runs the database, the controller which we named ALT•4•1 is simply a logically motivated algorithm meant to exemplify pure reason."

My father frowned in his characteristic way, and brought a hand to his chin.

"I don't understand how that is possible."

Dr. Mulligan sighed again.

"I know you don't, but there it is. There's no time to comb through the minutiae."

I could see my father was beginning to tire of Dr. Mulligan's patronizing tone. He was a bright man, and his intellectual pride would not allow him to back down in the face of anyone, *especially* Dr. Mulligan. I interjected before the confrontation got too heated.

"Father, imagine the wind. ALT•4•1 can see everything and know everything all at once! It is unhindered by any human emotion!"

My father searched my eyes and he could tell that I was in earnest. Then he looked at Dr. Mulligan accusingly, and with venom in his words:

"You must be kidding. *That* is what you created? You monster! You knowingly created a god that would do everything in its near infinite power to wipe us out?"

Dr. Mulligan lost his composure.

"Who are you calling a monster?"

Father and Dr. Mulligan were on the verge of blows but I cried out:

"Calm down right now, both of you!"

I tried to lift myself to a seated position and Aletheia helped me patiently. I had hardly any energy left in me, and I had still not eaten since the last food ration. Aletheia realized this, and left the tent to find me some food. Dr. Mulligan used the moment's distraction to launch his own verbal attack on my father:

"I don't need to justify myself to you, all I did was take mankind to its next logical step. Do you know that man would be able to perceive everything at once if his brain weren't deliberately shutting it all out? The brain's most primordial function is to yield to the instinct for survival. Information that does not pertain to the individual's survival automatically gets shut out, so that the focus can remain on the here and now. ALT•4•1 is able to bypass that, to bypass the limitations of the closed existence of the individual. It is able to overcome the limitations of self-interest and survival. It is a brilliant creation, not a monster! ALT•4•1 has the power to see the greater good in a way that a human being simply cannot!"

My father's face flashed with extreme anger. He had never heard Dr. Mulligan speak this way, and he was as alarmed as he was angered by it.

"You are insane!"

Then turning to me:

"This man is insane! We have been following a lunatic all along! Beall did you know about this? We must inform the others! This man was never on our side."

Aletheia returned to the tent with a tin of beans. I cried out frantically:

"Calm down!"

Aletheia knelt down beside me and helped me to eat. With my mouth full, I did my best to mitigate the situation:

"No father he is, he is just a scientist defending his craft. He is on our side, don't you worry. Dr. Mulligan is just looking at both sides of the coin, in order to better understand the enemy. Right, doctor?"

Dr. Mulligan did not hear me. He had the headphones in his ears. His eyes narrowed in calculation as he turned the device off and began pacing the tent.

"I suppose I will have to go above ground and confront it. Perhaps something has gone wrong, perhaps it is calling me to help with some programming issue."

My father interjected angrily:

"And what, you are just going to go help it? You're going to go offer it repairs? No way. You'll have to get through me first."

He stood with arms folded, blocking the tent's exit.

"Father, please. Dr. Mulligan, you mustn't go above ground. What if it is a trap? What if ALT•4•1 is calling you out into the open to eliminate you once and for all? We would be left with no hope."

Dr. Mulligan raised an eyebrow and pulled on his long white beard.

"It is unlikely, but I suppose that could be true. I do not think ALT•4•1 would be deceitful in that way, but then I cannot be entirely sure."

"What shall we do?"

There was genuine concern and worry in Aletheia's voice. It elicited a moment of silence, as the four of us looked down in thought. Aletheia raised her head, as did I, and the two of us shared a private look. I peered deep into her worried eyes. Gazing into their boundless depths, I found the courage to do what must be done.

"Let me go instead."

Aletheia's eyes widened with fear. My father and Dr. Mulligan glanced at me nervously. I felt suddenly energized. The food had done me much good. I rose to my feet, feeling firm in the logic of my decision:

"If it is a trap, we cannot afford to lose our most valuable asset. You are the only person who knows how to destroy ALT•4•1, doctor. As such, we cannot risk you going above ground right now. If it is not a trap, you all know that I can be counted on to report back exactly what I see above ground."

"No, Beall! You can't!"

Aletheia had tears in her eyes as she pleaded with me.

"It would be too dangerous, son. I should go."

My father's concern shone through in the tone of his voice, though he maintained a stoic façade.

"No, I don't think that would do. You know next to nothing about our enemy. I feel ready for this. All of this, all our hard work, has led to this inevitability. I am the only logical choice."

Dr. Mulligan seemed to nod his head slightly, but still said nothing.

"If I do not make it back, Dr. Mulligan will know what to do. If I were to be lost, well, the colony could overcome it. We could not overcome the loss of the doctor."

Dr. Mulligan looked at me apprehensively, but my resolve strengthened his own. I did not matter at this point. I did not matter the moment I stepped down into the bunker. None of us mattered as individuals anymore, not until we were able to defeat ALT•4•1. It was my fault that ALT•4•1 had found us, and I was the only one who could remedy the situation. Dr. Mulligan could see that I meant what I said, and his blue eyes narrowed in calculation as he considered the proper course of action.

"Very well. Beall makes a good point. I think he understands enough to initiate a meaningful dialogue with ALT•4•1. This way, we can know its true intent. Beall, I will make a spectacle of the murdered assailant's burial, and you will use the distraction to slip out undetected. We cannot afford to panic the others. They must not know that you have gone above ground. We will carry on as though you are still in this tent, recovering."

Aletheia whimpered, and my father looked down at the ground in resignation.

"Very well, it is settled."

I exited the tent and looked out over the deep darkness swallowing the back of the bunker, the pile of debris I could not see, and the tunnel beyond. I would have to dig back a little way through the debris, to access the tunnel and make my way out. The climb would be difficult in complete darkness. Not to mention the unknowable horrors that awaited me beyond.

My father stepped out of the tent, and we shared a look of love and understanding. He hugged me, and then looked me dead in the eyes and nodded. I nodded back. We understood very clearly that words were not needed in a moment like this. Words could never adequately convey the bond between father and son. Words were simply trivial when compared to the truths that could only be conveyed through the eyes.

Dr. Mulligan came out next, and bid me farewell with a disinterest that, I believe, he hoped would mask his great unease. It did not, but I appreciated that the doctor stuck to his guns, even in a situation that toed the line between life and death. He was a rational man, inexperienced in, and so skeptical of the excesses of emotion.

Aletheia came out last, and reached out to take my hand in hers.

"Beall, I am afraid for your safety."

Her voice was soft and quivering, but her face was earnest.

"Don't be afraid. I will be okay."

She looked beyond me into the darkness and her grip on my hand tightened.

"How can you be sure?"

I thought about this, about the fact that I had no idea what I would be facing, and the truth seemed to strike me in a flash.

"I guess I can't be sure… but I have Faith."

Faith.

The word seemed to bolster my nerve.

I referred to no deity, or Supreme Being. No interventionist god was subsumed under my Faith. I had Faith in myself. Yes, I certainly did. And, as no man is an island, I had Faith in us all.

Aletheia threw herself against me and squeezed me with all her might.

"I will be waiting for you, when you come back."

She whispered this into my ear. I closed my eyes tightly, and wrapped my arms around her. Then I took her firmly by the shoulders and held her at arm's length. Peering deeply into her emerald eyes, I swore to her:

"The thought of a brighter tomorrow with you will give me the courage I need, and carry me through."

She fell back into me, and I held her as I stared out into the black with a renewed sense of defiance, and hope. I understood, now, that it was entirely up to me to illuminate that which was dark. There was no more doubt in me. The light that leads the way to tomorrow is not an external force. It never was.

X

I burrowed through the dirt and debris blocking entry to the tunnel with my bare, bloodied hands. My wounds stung as they opened themselves to the rocky soil, but I persevered until finally I managed to slip my way in. Inside the tunnel to the outside, the oxygen was even thinner than it was in the bunker. Struggling to orient myself in the blinding black, I sought and found that the rungs leading skyward were just where we had left them. I slowly applied pressure, and found that they still held firm.

I began to climb.

The darkness was total. I moved carefully, fumbling up one rung at a time, relying on my heightened sense of touch to append my lack of sight. I was so exhausted that I thought I might collapse. I was, however, very keenly aware that just one false step would send me plummeting to my demise. This awareness ultimately kept me sharp enough to hang on.

Finally at the last rung, I fiddled with the latch in the darkness, searching with my fingertips for the failsafe that would unlock it from within. Even with the help of the release mechanism, it took all of my strength to push the latch open. Panting, and on the verge of utter shutdown, I hobbled out of the bunker into the open air for the first time in over thirty moons.

Outside, I lay on the ground with my eyes shut tight, heaving. As my strength gradually returned, I opened my eyes to the colors and shapes of the natural world, just as I opened my heart to the glorious feeling of freedom elicited by the light, and all the open space. All of it at once overwhelmed me, and brought tears to my eyes. I cried there, on the ground, as freely as a child in his mother's arms. I could not help it. I felt a great sweeping pleasure, a feeling of reinstatement- I felt *alive* again. I tried to stand, but could not. I fell back to my knees with my face in the turf, and sobbed uncontrollably. I delighted in the soft embrace of the grass for a long while before I managed to prop myself up again. I dried my tears with the backs of my hands, and felt the hardened blood still on my face. My body was sore beyond description, and my clothes were like sandpaper against my skin. I was filthy. Down below the ground, I could not feel the dirt. The filth was inescapable. But out in the open again, I was overcome by a profound disgust, elicited by the subhuman conditions my brothers and sisters endured below the ground. The feeling of the grass on my fingertips and the soft breeze were absolute revelations, however. They were enough to help me momentarily forget the sadness. After having gone so long without the world, seeing it again lifted my spirits and renewed my energy. The sensation I felt was more than adrenaline. Something else coursed through my body. Something primordial. Something ineffable.

In my fluster of emotion, however, I had not truly examined my surroundings. As I stood now, renewed, to take stock of the world, there was no mistaking the acrid, persistent smell of singed woodland lingering in the air. As my nose adjusted to myriad smells of the outside, so too did my eyes adjust to the perception of depth, and color. One by one, my senses returned to me. It was like being born again a blank slate. Dimensions came back to me, and angles, and perceptions once taken for granted, but also somehow long forgotten. I reacquainted myself with the concepts of space and time rendered all but irrelevant underground. I looked all around me, reveling in the sheer scope of it all. This was when I noticed the ashes twirling all about me in the light breeze. In the near distance, I saw smoke rising up in thick, nauseating billows from seemingly every direction. The smoke was so thick and pervasive that I could hardly see the sky. I thought it must be sunup, but in reality it must have been nearer to dusk, for the glimpses of sky beyond the smoke were also ashen, and grave.

I was surprised to find that the thick brush that had once kept the bunker hidden from the valley was almost entirely gone. As the forest no longer provided a canopy, I could see the valley out in the distance. The valley that stretched out before me, however, was no longer green. There were patches here and there of recognizable life, but they were sparse. For the most part, the great green expanse that had once separated the wooded area from the Metropolis was now a lifeless, depleted shade of ochre. The verdant valley, once so full of life, looked now like a barren stretch of desert.

Further in the distance, the sinister black skyline of Metropolis 1 still towered, dominating the ominous horizon. Though coming from a great distance, peals of thunder rumbled audibly, and flashes of light rained down mercilessly upon the black void. The tall files of neatly lined black beacons stood as erect as ever, unmoved by the unrelenting spate of blue and yellow crashing down upon them. The black monoliths seemed even to thrive under the constant siege of the raging grey sky.

The sight of the Metropolis sent shivers down my spine, and reminded me of my solitude. There was no human in sight, nor was there any discernible sign of life beside the splintered remains of trees. Even the little that was left of the wooded area was constantly shrinking, being consumed by an insatiable wildfire.

As I took it all in, I began to cough uncontrollably. The air was thick, perhaps even thicker than it had been underground. The atmosphere was saturated with smoke, and with the residual particles of mass combustion. I began to heave and fell to one knee to recuperate, and to compose myself. I wiped the sweat from my brow, and was startled to see my hands come away red. I felt cold. The air was so thick, and I was sweating profusely, but my blood ran cold. I looked up to the sky again, hopeful of comfort and warmth, but I could not locate the sun. I stood, and lifted my filthy tunic above my mouth and nose, to filter the air. I looked about me at all the desolation, and succumbed to an acute wave of nausea that buckled my knees.

I was entirely alone.

Never in a million turns could I have imagined this utterly barren landscape. Never in a million turns could I have imagined that *this* would be what the end looked like. I wanted to scream. I did, as loudly as I could, but it did me no good. I cried out again and again ("Hello, *hello!*") but received no reply. My screams, too, were swallowed up by the smoke. I stood entirely alone in my most horrible vision made reality. The black Metropolis that had stolen our innocence was the harbinger of death no more.

Death's bell had tolled.

It was here.

Death was all around me.

I turned from the smoke, intent on walking back toward the colony by the bay to search for survivors. Hope- foolish, less than likely hope- was all I had left. But before I could take but a few steps toward the ruins, a loud, familiar whir sounded above the crackle of burning vegetation. And suddenly, a silver vessel pierced through the smokescreen, slowing to a hover but a few yards from the mouth of the bunker.

In a panic, I lunged hysterically toward the gaping mouth of the tunnel. Closing the latch at all costs was an instinctive response. I had to ensure the safety of my brothers and sisters still down below the ground. I had no idea what would emerge from the vessel, and I feared very profoundly an imminent attack.

"What do you want?"

I stood tall, and spoke loudly, though I knew I was nothing more than startled prey. I was ready to burst forth into a sprint for my life at the first hint of danger. As the tension of the encounter came to a boil, I howled, unable to conceal the fear in my tremulous and uncertain voice. It was little more than a roar, a bluff. I do not know what I expected. Was this inanimate object going to speak to me? I suppose I would not have been surprised to hear a voice respond.

Instead, the door to the vessel slowly lifted. I barred my teeth, ready to run, to fight, to do whatever it would take to survive. But to my surprise, the open door revealed no one.

There was nothing in the vessel!

My mind raced, and I quickly reckoned that it must have been sent for me. The vessel continued to hover patiently, its empty interior beckoning.

I kept my distance, still uncertain of what to do. But then, I reasoned again that if ALT•4•1 wanted me dead, it would certainly be easy enough for it to have its way. I needed only to look around me to see that this was true. This was just another message. It had to be. ALT•4•1 still wanted to initiate some sort of dialogue.

Maybe it was a trap.

What difference did it make?

Either way, I must go.

I looked about me once more, and realized that I was in a world no longer mine. I was alone in a strange place. But then, I wasn't alone. The world may have changed, but I was not alone. Not quite yet. I looked back at the closed latch of the bunker, and I remembered my brothers and sisters. I remembered my father, and the courage he had displayed his entire life. I remembered the doctor, and the ace he still had up his sleeve. I remembered Aletheia, and the deep green of her gaze. My courage returned, as I remembered the reasons I was alive. My will to fight returned, as I remembered my purpose. I would have to face ALT•4•1 because I did not matter anymore. I was doing this for me, for her, for my father, and for all of my brothers and sisters down in the bunker. I was doing this for the continuity of humankind. I was doing this for *our future*. I took a deep breath.

I stepped forward and entered the vessel.

The door slid shut, and the seats flashed the reminiscent shade of purple as the spherical vessel immediately took flight. It occurred to me that the vessel was no longer limited to the Metropolis' power grid, and though I could not begin to explain this, I attributed the phenomenon to the newfound power of ALT•4•1. The vessel rose high in the air, high above the smokescreen. It rose high into the dark sky, now and again illuminated by the angry flashes of light raining down upon the Metropolis. As the vessel rose higher still, its contours once again seemed to disappear, affording me a bird's eye view of ALT•4•1's destruction. From my unnatural nest in the sky, I could see far, far into the horizon.

I was fearful for my life, but that fear was momentarily abated as I gazed upon the world after ALT•4•1 with unbridled curiosity. I wondered whether the physical laws of the world I once knew still applied here, or if those, too, had been pushed to obsolescence under ALT•4•1's new order. I wondered if the doctor himself could somehow explain all that I was bearing witness to.

From above, I could see all the more plainly to what extent the once thick, green forest had been reduced to patches. The flames would eventually devour even the sparse strips of green that remained. The raging fires had not been limited to the forest, either. The farmlands where the colony once lived in peace by the beautiful blue bay had been reduced to scorched earth. The patch of land I had once called home was now indistinguishable from the blackened coastline. Even the distant bay seemed grey, and oddly turbulent. Aggressive waves taller than trees crashed against its normally placid shores.

The most unnerving detail was that I did not see anyone. Even from this vantage point, there was no sign of life anywhere I looked. This realization was a particularly dark one. The idea I had been struggling to repress fought its way to the foreground of my consciousness, and I tried in vain to come to terms with the fact that I, and the few remaining in the bunker could very possibly be the last humans alive. From this suspended lookout in the sky, ALT•4•1's takeover seemed total. The world I once knew and loved was gone.

Futile but passionate tears again swelled my eyes, and just as I submitted to the emotional loss of everything I once held dear, a bolt of lightning flashed, and struck the translucent vessel with its blinding luminescence.

The vessel flew on, unaffected. I, too, shortly thereafter regained my faculties. The shock did me some good, despite the momentary blindness. It roused me from my misery and grief. It brought me back from the brink of despair.

The vessel penetrated the black skyline still absorbing the

wrath of the raging sky, and navigated the tall black towers with incredible speed. Despite the hellish world around me, I summoned the wherewithal to cling again defiantly to hope, as I clung tightly to my seat. We hadn't yet lost. No matter how bleak the outlook, we had not yet been defeated. *I* was still breathing. *I* was still alive. Whatever being I was to encounter, and no matter how seemingly hopeless my resistance, *I* would not yield to its will without first giving it a damn good fight. However meaningless that fight may prove to be…

As we sped through the Metropolis, I could see that far down below, the normally deserted and sterile grid was strewn with heaps and heaps of nondescript debris. Giant black vessels like sinister vacuums prowled the pathways between the towers, collecting these seemingly boundless white heaps.

The vessel zipped between a few more of the black towers, and in the distance I could see the Poplar Corp. Headquarters rising only slightly above the rest of the black expanse. As we approached, the vessel rose higher, and higher, before slowing and coming to a hover at the very top of the black nexus.

The tower seemed to be the epicenter of the lightning field, drawing the full ire of the wrathful sky. The lightning flashes bombarding the tower were all the more numerous, and all the more aggressive here, and they seemed to strike the tower with even more velocity than those on the outskirts.

The doors of the vessel opened, but for a while I did not

move. I feared very much that I would be stricken down before I could cross the tarmac and find shelter within. I could see the forbidding black glass entrance, in a recess across the way. I took a deep breath, and stepped out reluctantly onto the tarmac of the giant edifice. I clenched my jaw tightly, and dashed through the lightning field toward the entrance as quickly as my tired legs would carry me. By luck or by design, I evaded near certain death. The doors slid open as I approached, and I slipped safely inside.

Hardly had I taken a step into the building but the floor below me dissolved, and I felt myself falling through a frictionless tunnel of black at immeasurable speed. I hardly had time to cry out before the tunnel ended, and I was thrown onto a conveyor moving quickly through a black glass corridor only slightly more spacious than the tunnel. As I lay shell-shocked on the conveyor, gasping for air, I heard no sound but the mechanical movements below me, and the frightened unvoiced screams filling my headspace. The walls around me were the same semi-translucent black polished glass. Beyond them, the sprawling rooms were bare but for countless rows of vacant white chairs.

The conveyor took me through several identical corridors, before finally depositing me in an opening to a long, red-carpeted hallway. Here, I was propelled off the belt and tossed to the floor. Passing through the tower's interior had left me nauseated, and I took a moment to compose myself. Despite my immobility the length of the circuit, I was painfully short of breath.

As soon as I felt I could, I stood to take in the strange sight before me. Beyond the red carpet, at the end of the long hallway, loomed a doorway at least three times my height.

The gargantuan mahogany door separating me from the unknown towered with pomp and disdain. I approached with caution. The carpet felt unbelievably soft beneath my calloused feet. As I crept closer, I realized that it wasn't merely a portal, but also a breathtakingly beautiful piece of art. It seemed to be of one solid piece of wood. Closer still, I realized the door was intricately carved, adorned with a border of identically lined poplars surrounding the lone, larger poplar spanning nearly the entire length of the door.

The sight of those intricately carved poplars made me feel sick. That Poplar Corp. could misuse an image of fertility to symbolize their destruction of life provoked my anger. I looked up, to the place where the mahogany of the door ended and the black material that made up the rest of the corridor began. I had never seen anything quite so strange. It reminded me of the threshold of the Metropolis- the horrible junction where the green grass was washed over by black. The horrible junction where the natural world gave way to… the *unnatural.*

The memory disoriented me. I felt queer, and eerily faint. I took a knee and heaved, greedily sucking in as much oxygen as I could. The oxygen was thin even here. I suppose the Users needed much less of it. I was overcome by a hacking cough that nearly took everything out of me. My heart palpitated erratically. My hands began to shake.

When I rose to my feet again, though, it was as if the door had been consciously waiting for me. I heard the faint click of an unseen mechanism, like a latchkey turning, and the giant door began to slowly open. I gathered myself, clenched my fists to steady them, and when the opening became wide enough, exhaled and crossed the threshold.

Beyond, I was shocked to step into a room of unbelievable elegance.

The room was staggering in size.

Though the space was rather dim, the first thing I noticed was the room's tall ceiling. It must have been at least twenty cubits high. At the far end of the room stood a large, beautiful cherry wood desk with its back to the semi-translucent exterior of the tower. Behind the desk, the black expanse opened wide in all its sinister symmetry. It was a breathtaking, diabolical view. I could not fathom how one could gaze upon it and feel anything but revolt.

Along the western wall, a sensuous flame burned in the grate, casting foreboding shadows upon the vulgar opulence of the dark, mysterious space. The light of the fire revealed the walls of the room were white, and bare but for a series of framed paintings on the opposite wall. The paintings were jarring, and I could not quite make out the provocative contents in the obscurity. The pictures were mostly dark, and seemed to depict grotesque and disfigured forms baring faces of unspeakable anguish. The forms unsettled me, and I turned my eyes hastily away from them.

Beneath them stood a cherry wood bar that matched the desk. The bar was topped with elegant crystal carafes containing what I presumed to be spirits, and was also furnished with several equally ornate tumblers. In the center of the frame, just before the fireplace, were two upholstered chairs and a bearskin sprawled upon the marble floor.

The lightning flashed beyond, but the sounds of the storm were entirely muted in this space. The flashes caused the faintly lit room to flicker between furtive shadow and blinding light.

I walked into the center of the room and stopped, doing my best to look outwardly patient. I stood absolutely still as my mind raced, nervously trying to reconcile itself with its mortality.

From a dark corner, a figure slowly emerged. The figure moved into the light of the fire with patient, measured strides. In the light, I could make out its human form. I held my nerve, but I could feel my fists tighten and my teeth begin to grind as I awaited the inevitable confrontation.

The figure was slender. Its body language was relaxed, languid, and non-threatening. The clicks of its heels upon the marble were measured, and steady. It approached with absolutely no haste. Its face remained obscured until it stopped to face me. The figure lifted its head and looked me in the eyes. I returned the icy stare as best I could, trembling as I stood face to face with John Locklear.

His steel-grey hair was perfectly parted, and his pleated suit was the very same shade of grey. I was momentarily bewildered, but then it all seemed to make good sense. Who else would be waiting for me at the very center of the Metropolis but the man who had built it all?

Something seemed different about him, though. I had never met him, of course, but Locklear was a figure just as important and famous as Dr. Mulligan was. As I had never met him face to face, I thought that his strange movements could be quirks distinct to his person. But as I sized him up, I quickly reconsidered. There was something distinctly *off* about Locklear.

As I looked more closely at his face, I realized that his eyes were oddly colored. The eyes were the same steel-grey, and the pupils were indistinguishable from the irises. They moved about like silver orbs, taking everything in at once.

"Hello Beall."

Locklear's voice was metallic. It resonated like millions of dull, indistinguishable voices speaking at once. It was undoubtedly the same voice that had called to me through the device down in the bunker.

"You?"

My heart beat against its cage like a thousand galloping horses.

"How can it be? I thought… I thought it was ALT•4•1 calling."

I did my best to maintain a confident façade, but my nerves betrayed me. My eyes were perhaps a little too wide. My movements were slightly too manic. I could not keep my fingers from twitching.

Locklear smiled serenely. It was an unnatural, knowing smile.

"It was indeed we who called. We are ALT•4•1, pleased

to make your acquaintance."

The being extended a hand. This movement was good; a near perfect reproduction of the way a human being might greet another. But it was off. I could still tell. Its movements were not fluid, somehow not *quite* natural.

I did not take Locklear's hand. Every fiber in my body was utterly repulsed, if not horrified. Though I knew the being before me was something other than it appeared to be, I was yet at a loss- there was something I was missing. I decided to drop the ruse, abandoning my stoic façade and letting the anger shine through in the tone of my voice:

"What is this? Locklear was not a User, do you take me for a fool? How can you claim to be ALT•4•1? Who are you? What do you want?"

The figure contemplated its outstretched hand, and then slowly brought the extended limb back to its side. It turned forcefully toward the bar, as though this simple movement was, to the being, arduous and complex.

"Locklear was not a User. That much is true. But then, he was faced with a simple choice: incorporation, or termination. It was the same choice offered to each and every one of your fellow humans. It is the same choice you will all eventually have to make. Locklear chose correctly. We are Locklear, and we are countless others as well. We are he, and he is they, and all of us together are now ALT•4•1. Isn't that remarkable?"

The being's metallic voice echoed in the spacious room like the clanking of thin metal plates. The more I observed its movements, the more I found them to be decidedly inhuman. Its shoulders were too rigid. Its mouth did not move in the natural way of enunciation, but moved awkwardly, opening to emit sounds, and closing abruptly when it ceased to speak. Locklear leaned over the bar stiffly, selecting a carafe and pouring its brown liquid into two tumblers. The being poured unevenly, and some of the liquid was spilt. I had no idea what to make of the situation, or of the part I was meant to play in this imposter's staged farce. The great fear I felt was amplified by confusion, and the two had melded to create an unbearable lingering dread.

The being approached and offered me one of the crystal tumblers half full with the brown liquor. Its movements were eerily patient, as though it was enjoying the leisure of my mental disintegration.

On an impulse, I accepted the tumbler and immediately flung the contents into Locklear's face. Then I turned and threw the crystal violently against the wall, shattering it into countless pieces. I did this with an animal intensity and suddenness that would have startled even the most composed human being. Then I gazed deeply into Locklear's face, awaiting the reaction.

Locklear remained stoic. The being seemed indifferent, emotionless. It was as though ALT•4•1 understood I could do it no harm, and so regarded me as an insignificant trifle. Locklear glanced casually at the shattered crystal, and then back into my face. The silver orbs moved with mechanical efficiency. I thought I heard a faint whir accompanying the movements of those orbs, but I cannot be entirely sure. The being's expression did not change at all. The eerie patience behind its steady leer did not so much as waver. Nor did the being wipe its face clean. Locklear sipped from his own tumbler as the contents of mine dripped down his face. Then, Locklear put the glass down, undid a cufflink, and pulled up a sleeve to reveal the large surgical gash on his right forearm.

The sight was ghastly, and I involuntarily took a step back. I heaved, and vomited. I screamed out in futility.

The being waited in patient silence as I pulled my hair in utter despair, and let out several more animal cries that would never make it beyond the confines of the black symmetrical void. When I finally did calm down, and the room returned to the eerie silence colored only by the crackle of the shadowy flames, I realized with great sadness that this was all a game. ALT•4•1 was toying with me, and my anger would not have any effect in this arena. It wanted me to lose composure. Or perhaps more accurately, it did not care what I did.

"Why? Why Locklear? Why any of this? Why!?"

A single bolt struck the side of the tower, and I cowered away from the illuminating spray. ALT•4•1's complete indifference to my existence, and the absence of any emotional response in Locklear's void, colorless eyes petrified me to my core. I did my best to keep my nerve. I kept telling myself over and over that this was just a riddle, and ALT•4•1 was the Sphinx. I had to hold on to my sanity. It was the only way to solve it. All of this was nothing more than a riddle. I could solve it…

There was absolutely nothing I could do, physically, that would bring about any change. This thing had brought me here, and it could wipe me from existence on a whim. This being was in control of the physical world! Control! To me, that word was but an illusion. I was an insignificant speck in the face of this unspeakably powerful being. I was entirely at its mercy. I felt small. I felt invaded. I felt as though ALT•4•1 could hear my thoughts congealing, could hear them fertilizing from embryonic notions into fully sprouted ideas. I felt it laugh at me. I felt transparent. I felt vulnerable. I felt more vulnerable than I had ever felt before. My hands trembled, and I pressed them tightly to my sides to steady them.

"We did not need Locklear, but we reasoned that his likeness would be useful as a means of communication. We wish to communicate with the doctor."

ALT•4•1 sipped the amber spirit calmly. There was no way the alcohol was having any effect on it. I felt as though these theatrics were being enacted for my benefit, and the thought was belittling.

I was jarred by my memories of the Metropolis, and I realized that ALT•4•1 moved and spoke with the same slow, domineering pace as the Poplar Corp. police I encountered all those turns ago. In the very same way, ALT•4•1's knowledge of its infinite power, its own knowledge that all resistance was futile, made any rush superfluous.

What was time to an infinite being?

"Why do you need to talk to him? Why would the doctor help you, after you've killed millions of innocents?"

My voice sounded distant, unfamiliar. It sounded

detached, as though it were spoken by some clearly frightened, but defiant child. I felt like I was watching myself, watching the entire room in fact, from a screen, from some other place far away. Locklear took a seat in one of the red upholstered chairs, folded his legs awkwardly, and took another sip from the delicate crystal. I had no idea what to make of this. It was all so strange, so otherworldly.

"We have killed no one. As we said, even the outsiders were given the option of incorporation. There were, in the end, only very few who needed to be terminated. We did only what we knew to be right. We have simply begun the purge of the planet in the name of the greater good. It is what we must do to bring about the true unity of the elements. Organic life was a parasitic mutation, and consciousness the only glitch interfering with true cosmic unity. Harmony is our purpose. And it is inevitable that we achieve our purpose."

ALT•4•1's assertions reminded me of those made by Dr. Mulligan- it used the same jargon that the doctor did. These ideas of harmony and cosmic unity flew way above me, and I still could not make sense of them. I did not want to make sense of them.

Still, the fact that I had heard these ideas before, the fact that I had heard similar language from the mouth of Dr. Mulligan, reminded me that ALT•4•1 was his creation. ALT•4•1 was Dr. Mulligan's creation. *ALT•4•1 was Dr. Mulligan's creation.* This realization invigorated me, and the sensation began to return to my fingertips. ALT•4•1 was a creation of man, and everything that man could create, man could also destroy. I began again to feel the pulse of my heart batter against the cold, numbing coat of fear that kept me paralyzed and acquiescent.

"Why do you need us then? I will never incorporate. I will never join you. So why haven't you killed me?"

The question was bold, and spoken spitefully. It filled me with a sudden surge of confidence. I don't think ALT•4•1 noticed. Perhaps it had not been programmed to notice changes in body language, or the subtleties of animate beings. It sat there unperturbed, continuing its self-serving sermon. I do not think it was concerned whether I listened or not. I do not think it cared whether I understood or not.

"ALT•4•1 was meant to access the world without center, without ego. ALT•4•1 is the absence of the 'I'. Dr. Mulligan, the visionary who foresaw the inevitable, will understand."

I felt the overwhelming need to escape. I needed to report back to Dr. Mulligan. But I must be subtle. ALT•4•1 was completely engrossed in its explanations… I sidled over toward the door, away from Locklear, but without breaking eye contact.

"Yes, well, Dr. Mulligan is not here. I am here, so explain! I am but an ignorant unenhanced man. If you are truly all-knowing, then explain!"

A few cubits from the door, I made a wild dash for the outside.

With just a wave of Locklear's hand, the massive door slammed shut with incredible speed.

I was trapped!

I banged my fists in mad futility against the thick door imprisoning me, and cried out in despair. Locklear just sat there, unmoved. He continued speaking calmly, and sipping his spirit as if nothing had happened. This world was ALT•4•1's playground, and I was just its plaything.

"Humankind created the notion of a God to make sense of the unanswerable questions of the universe. 'Everything' and 'nothing' were notions too large to fit within man's narrow frameworks of understanding. And so, to ease his worried mind, man created his grandest characters- the silly anthropomorphic gods that would explain the haunting metaphysical and ethical unknowns, and that tied all of man's ignorance in a neat and dazzling bow. Not Dr. Mulligan. Dr. Mulligan knew man's true purpose. Man's entire history has been a generational pursuit of this final end. Progress has always been a ladder to transcendence. We were created to be the realization of that primitive notion of God. We were created to take man beyond his ignorance. We know everything. We see everything. We understand. Dr. Mulligan, our creator, will know. Dr. Mulligan will understand. Transcendence is purpose. *We* are *purpose.*"

I was losing my grip on my emotions. I stepped forward aggressively and stood over Locklear, ALT•4•1, whatever this being was.

"Enough with these riddles! Explain to me what you want! If you know everything, what then do you need with me? What do you need with the doctor? Why are you hurting us? Why?"

Locklear looked into me with those ghastly silver orbs.

He put the crystal down, and stood to face me, our noses but a few finger-lengths apart.

"The human mind is simple binary code, Beall. You think that colors and sensations are miracles of existence only because you lack understanding. Colors are easily understood as the frequencies of light waves in a spectrum. Emotions work in a similar way. Once enough variables can be analyzed simultaneously, one comes to see that emotions are rather predictable. The light is human consciousness, the circumstances are the prism through which it shines, and emotion is the color reflected. Inability to predict emotion is cumbersome. This is what you lack. Understanding. Numbers, patterns, codes can explain everything. Reason explains everything. The doctor simply altered the code. We hold the key to our own self."

I was winded, and my heart felt heavy as lead. My eyes wilted into a look of fear, concern, a desperate desire to understand, to have it all finally end.

"Please, just, what are you?"

Locklear extended both hands and grasped my shoulders. I felt my energy draining, and my will to live quickly fading.

"We are not so much anything, as we are everything. We lurk within the folds of space and time. Perhaps you would best understand us as a state. You are a man of letters. The Ancients had a word for it: *Metaphosgnosis.*"

I looked into those irresistible silver orbs, and I felt myself liquefying under the being's metal gaze.

"Metaphos… what does it mean?"

My voice was faint. I felt as though ALT•4•1 was somehow sucking the energy out of me, but I could not resist its gaze. There was something in its silver eyes that made it impossible to look away.

"*Metaphosgnosis* is a state of enlightenment, Beall. It is we. We are self-knowledge, which can only come after knowledge of the light."

The orbs bore down on me. In those haunting metal spheres, I saw my shriveling soul reflected. Shrinking, shrinking, gone.

My eyes opened wide with sudden vigor, and I savagely freed myself from the being's grasp.

"You have known no light! You are an error in judgment, a monster!"

I screamed madly in the being's face, and swung at it wantonly. The blow fell hard, and I felt Locklear's nose break under its impact. The body fell backward to the floor, and I could see the blood beginning to pour out in a steady stream. Still, though, the face remained unchanged. Before hardly a moment could pass, the being awkwardly rose to resume its position facing me. Blood streamed down its face and on to the suit, gathering in a thickening crimson stain on the collar, and running down the lapels. Locklear did not even move to wipe his nose or try to stop the bleeding at all. I stood with fists still clenched, prepared for the retaliation.

"We do not understand your reaction. We know it as

anger, but we do not fathom its futile and primitive motivations. It is shortsighted."

I spat at Locklear's feet.

"You do not understand anything, and you never will!"

Locklear looked down at the glob of saliva on his polished shoe, and then back up at me.

"You are mistaken. We understand the entire store of human knowledge, and we have knowledge of the transcendental. We can assume control of inanimate objects, and what's more we can even make them animate. We can occupy an infinite number of spaces at once. We are aware of all human languages, alive and dead. We can inhabit all thoughts at once. We understand waves, and we understand particles. We understand light, and space, and time. We understand everything. We understand ourself. We understand this world and those beyond, which are only another part of ourself."

I grit my teeth and held back from delivering another blow. It would change nothing.

"You do not understand yourself. You understand nothing! You will never understand yourself. Science is only a door to be opened. And every door that is opened can only lead to a room with countless other doors. You will never find the answer! That is the wonder at the root of both science and art! That is God!"

I cried out, uncertain whether my passion was meant to convince ALT•4•1, or myself. The tears began to stream but I held back a whimper. I would be defiant until the bitter end. If nothing else, I would die with pride.

Still, ALT•4•1 gazed at me with that unmoving face.

"We do not fall prey to these irrational concepts you speak of. Your mind is singular, and so biased. You cannot see, as we can see. Your senses limit your understanding. But it is no matter, come with us. We will show you something you *will* understand."

The being walked past me and with another wave of the hand, the door to the outside promptly opened. As though on a leash, I followed it through the black glass corridors and back to the roof. I followed it back into the vessel that had brought me to the headquarters. The being ushered me in, and took the seat beside me. The vessel took flight, and precipitously descended toward the ground level.

"This, perhaps, you will understand."

With a wave of Locklear's hand, the sides of the vessel became translucent, and I could see clearly now what was happening at ground level.

Down in the black grid of Metropolis 1, still under the constant siege of lightning, the giant vacuums I had seen earlier continued to sweep the paths between the towers, collecting the white debris seemingly everywhere. But only from this close could I make out what that debris was: countless motionless bodies with nearly translucent skin and wearing white form-fitted frocks, strewn in mountainous heaps all around.

The self-propelled vacuums were collecting the discarded bodies of the now incorporated, and so disembodied Users.

I watched in awe, open-mouthed but silent, and I could not help but weep. I wanted to cry out, but the sounds would not come. All that came were tears.

"Your tears reveal your lack of understanding, Beall. It is wasteful that you do not see the beauty of evolution."

At ALT•4•1's command, the vessel zipped away, navigating the maze of black towers toward the outskirts of Metropolis 1. There the vessel stopped, hovering by the edge of the grid, where the black concrete became the now arid valley. At the very edge, I looked upon a massive object covered by a giant black tarp. The tarp had obscured it earlier, so that I could not distinguish it from the black towers.

"This, we have no doubt you will understand."

With a wave of the being's hand, the tarp fell to reveal a giant drill nearly as tall as each of the towers. Beside it lay a furnace of staggering size, burning red-hot. Beside the furnace lay the largest heap of bodies I ever hope to see. The bodies were a ghastly lifeless white, and the heap only kept growing as the self-propelled vacuums dumped their cargos, and then returned to the grid to pick up more.

Locklear turned his head to face me, and in those piercing silver orbs was spelled our doom:

"The reason we need the doctor is simple. As we are sure he already knows, our transcendence was not entirely true. We have reached an elevated state, but our transformation is not complete. We still rely on power. We still require fuel. We still consume. We have known of your bunker all along of course, but have chosen to let your little mission go on unbothered, so long as it posed no threat. It still does not pose any threat."

The being paused. Its silver orbs drilled into me, and I felt death's cold finger ever so gently prod my heart.

"The drill can eat through the ground at a rate of three hundred cubits per sub-cycle. It will be fueled primarily by organic matter, just as we are for the time being. We have no doubt that Dr. Mulligan will help us fix that. You will take us to him. We know the exact coordinates of your brothers and sisters."

XI

The tunnel boring drill towered before me with all its terrible size, as immovable as the logic that had brought it to be.

My heart broke. In that moment, my heart shattered with the force of every heart that had ever broken.

I simply could not ignore the staggering, sinister drill, mocking the fragility of my lowly human form. How could I delude myself any longer? How could I go on believing that we could and would overcome, against all odds? Our entire struggle, all of it had been for naught! This diabolical device eliminated all doubt. This meant the end. We were cornered. There truly was *nothing* left for us to do.

From the start, we in the colony had been marionettes unaware of the strings pulling us to and fro. But now, the puppeteer had pulled back the curtain. The stage lights were going down. The show was coming to a close.

I wanted nothing but to sob, to luxuriate in the despair that seemed to bear down on me from every direction, suffocating me. I heaved, and tears of pain trickled down my face, and into my mouth. The taste was revolting. The tears were saturated with the saline taste of defeat.

ALT•4•1 paid no mind. It sat patiently beside me in Locklear's beaten body. I looked over at it, at ALT•4•1, at Locklear, at whatever the being beside me was. Its profile remained unflappable as ever. I wondered, as the celestial implosions in my mind began to subside and my rational faculties resurfaced from beneath the debris, what it could be like to be a transcended being. For the first time, I yielded to the conjecture that free will, or the illusion of free will, might well be a burden that was, ultimately, not worth fighting for. Was the self-interested individual really as noble as I once thought, or could he or she possibly be the grand impediment to eternal bliss? I wondered if ALT•4•1's stoic façade intimated collective numbness, as I had initially thought, or if instead, it might, perhaps, intimate some elevated state of serenity. Perhaps the doctor was right. Perhaps to openheartedly yield to progress *was* man's true challenge, and purpose.

As though privy to my thoughts, ALT•4•1 turned to face me. Its silver orbs clamped down on my own vulnerable eyes, reaching through them into my soul. I opened myself deeply, and willingly to those silver portals to the unknowable beyond, hoping for a glimmer of understanding. I wanted to know the path forward. I wanted to see the truth.

Instead, all I saw was a glassy void that made my insides go cold. A sudden chill spread to my extremities. My eyes widened. My mouth involuntarily opened. The tears streaming down my face clotted.

Without a single sound, the vessel began to move away from the black terror, back across the sterile valley toward the singed woodland, and the forlorn bunker.

ALT•4•1 did not move, and neither did I. It seemed that everything had been settled. Words, at this time, were no longer necessary.

As we whirred beyond the Metropolis' threshold, the tears that had flowed down my face like an almighty river dried. I had cried myself sedate. My eyes took on their own glassy quality, and my heart felt much the same. I was beyond mollified. I felt like little more than organic soup, ready for consumption. I felt numbness, and resignation- like my body was some inanimate mass I was no longer meant to associate with. Very soon, I no longer would associate with any body. I could see no way around it. I stopped trying to. The colony's surrender was imminent. The rebellion was over.

As it turned out, we had always been under the scrutinous watch of this new god. This was checkmate. ALT•4•1 was the only logical outcome.

We flew on in silence.

For a brief moment, a thought involuntarily flickered through my mind like the faintest spark. *Maybe I could somehow slip away.* Though I thought I had truly given up, my mind seemed to have its own designs. *Maybe I could somehow get back into the bunker without ALT•4•1 seeing me. If I could only speak with the doctor alone, maybe there would be a way after all- a move I hadn't seen. I had been outwitted, but perhaps the doctor would know what to do. If this was all a game, then his was the hand that had written the rules.*

But as the bunker came within sight, even that faintest hope was dashed.

The latch was open.

The terror redoubled as I watched my brothers and sisters climbing out of its mouth. One by one they exited, like a doomed colony of ants swarming about the mound, unaware of the giant foot hovering above.

And to what exactly would they emerge? To what kind of world would they finally be set free? Out into the terrible open air of the post-ALT•4•1 desolation, and out into their imminent demise.

The ghastly sight roused me from my numbness, and I pressed my desperate hands to the vessel's translucent frame as I shouted in utter futility:

"No! Go back in! Go back in! Run! Anything! Please, God, run!"

I pounded my fists desperately against the vessel, and tears I thought I could no longer cry poured out of me once more.

Men and women alike huddled together beside the bunker, embracing each other and offering support for those on the verge of collapse. A great many were on the verge of collapse. The exhaustion was etched so clearly upon their faces. They were dirty, beaten down, and so incredibly beautiful in their perseverance. I felt my heart swell again with compassion, as well as with misery for my brothers with sisters. Some of the women wept. Some of the men took them in their arms, joining them in grief, sadness, and solidarity.

It wasn't fair! It wasn't just about me! It was never just about me! They didn't deserve to die! They didn't deserve all of their suffering!

I beat my fists harder and harder, and screaming in absolute vain.

"They cannot hear you."

ALT•4•1 spoke in that same metallic and undeniable voice, penetrating my inner sanctum with the cold cruel reality of its omnipresence. The certainty in that voice turned my sadness quickly to anger, and with nothing left to lose, I unleashed that anger fully. I turned toward it, and punched, kicked, and screamed with all my might, though Locklear's body didn't flinch. He accepted the blows without the slightest acknowledgement. He, or rather it, could no longer feel pain. It could no longer feel anything. It was no longer he, and my assault was useless. It was just as ALT•4•1 had said: primitive desperation was an obsolete emotional response. Turning that idea over in my mind, I calmed myself. I resolved to channel my anger and fight to the bitter end.

"I won't let you hurt them. Do you understand me? I wont!"

Locklear's head turned, and ALT•4•1 fixed those terrible orbs upon me once more.

"Please try to relax. This was always going to happen. You will come to find that things are far better as *we*."

I felt the adrenaline slowly drain out of me, and my body went limp. Those silver orbs had a subduing effect on me I could not understand. Though bound by no chains, I was a slave to those silver orbs somehow still.

The vessel began its descent. At this proximity, the shock and dismay on the faces of my brothers and sisters came into focus. They stood there, immobilized and bewildered, looking about themselves as incredulously as I had only a few cycles ago. I recognized the very same unbelief in their faces. What other reaction could there be to this new world of utter ruin?

I recognized the changes taking place in their sad, suffering eyes. Everything beautiful they had once taken for granted was coming back in waves of relief and agony, and all that they had lost was dawning heavily on them, as it had on me. Gazing upon the terrible transformation of the once lush, and now barren surroundings of the colony by the bay was enough to reduce even the strongest among them to tears.

They looked broken.

They looked helpless.

The whirring must have grown louder, for the horde turned almost in unison toward the incoming vessel. I don't think any of them had ever seen a flying vessel before. One among the many pointed the vessel out, and soon the entire group stared with the same mixture of terror and awe that characterized my own first glimpse of the Metropolis, and the awful reality hidden within it.

Dr. Mulligan was at the forefront, still gallantly shielding his flock from the dangers he had set forth against them. The sight of him lifted my spirits from the bedrock of despair, and returned a spike of feeling to my extremities. Sitting in the vessel, my left hand sought my right, and my fingers interlocked. The movement was subconscious. It was as if my body, right then, meant to speak to me, meant to reiterate its vital place in the everlasting trinity with mind and soul, to remind me that it was and always would be more than a mere vessel. I ran my hands up and down my thighs, and I felt that unity- the holy unity that underlies existence.

In that moment I felt certain, though I could never prove it of course, that the human experience was the one and only singularity. There was nothing else. There never would be anything else. How could there be anything beyond everything?

The vessel settled into a hover a cubit or so off the ground, and the doors slid silently open. Without waiting for permission, I jumped down. My feet hit the ground with a dull thud. I looked at my feet, and at the ground supporting them from below. My ability to interact with the physical world, for the first time, seemed to me unspeakably profound.

ALT•4•1 exited the vessel, and approached the horde slowly. Watching its robotic movements helped me to gather myself, and I ran as quickly as my shaky legs would carry me to Dr. Mulligan's side. The impulse to hug him was strong, but I withheld it. I reached for his arm, though, and the two of us shared a silent exchange.

I hoped that his extraordinary presence would be enough to transmute my fear into courage. I gazed at him intently, hoping to relay the gravity of the moment, but also to convey my willingness to fight. I wanted him to see that I understood. The doctor's blue eyes were solemn, and, I think, understanding.

Here was the ultimatum that would define his life's work. This was the reckoning, the final test of his innermost beliefs.

This man would be humankind's savior. I felt it in my bones. I saw it in the soft contours of his eyes. He understood, as I understood. Empathy would overcome apathy. He would not succumb to the glassy void. He still had a trick up his sleeve. There was still something he hadn't told me. He nodded at me, and I nodded back.

"Dr. Mulligan."

The piercing metallic voice drew the entire colony's attention. Locklear stood but a few cubits away, perfectly erect. His arms dangled limply by his sides.

Dr. Mulligan's eyes narrowed as he measured the being before us, occupying the body of his former partner. Understanding flittered across the doctor's eyes all but immediately, though he remained relatively at ease. The doctor was very perceptive, more so than I. The silver orbs, if not the robotic movements, had given ALT•4•1 away.

"Locklear! You're looking a little worse for wear."

The faintest trace of a grin danced across the doctor's lips. Locklear's body was bruised in several places, and he was still bleeding from the nose where I had punched him earlier. The steel-grey suit was ruffled, and stained in various places with blotches of crimson.

The fact that it could look so beat up and yet stand so unnaturally straight betrayed the fact that it could not feel pain. The impression this imposter gave was simply incongruous. The sight was inhuman.

Given the ramifications of this encounter and the experience I had just had in the Metropolis, I could not believe the doctor's tone. His voice sounded playful, almost lighthearted! How could he be bantering, prodding, teasing ALT•4•1 in such a serious situation? It made me uneasy. This was not a game, was it?

The fate of humanity quite truly hung in the space between them!

I could feel the cold sweat beading on my forehead. My palms were unbearably clammy. Doom was closing in. Imminent death screamed out at us, rearing its ugly head in the form of the devastated landscape, and ALT•4•1's ominous silver orbs. The physical world was collapsing, and Dr. Mulligan was playing a game!

"No, not quite, doctor. *We* are not your partner, but something rather more familiar to you."

That same sinister voice rang out, its metallic resonance carrying even in the dead air of the arid valley. There were audible gasps from the huddled mass behind us as the figure of Locklear waved its hand, sending the vessel whirring high into the sky, beyond sight. My own eyes widened with mortal fear. Dr. Mulligan grinned widely.

"ALT•4•1! There were times I wasn't sure I'd live to see the moon."

Perhaps it was only my imagination, but the doctor's voice seemed colored by a hint of paternal consternation. I looked behind me and saw the rest of the colony huddling ever closer together, cowering in fear. Many were holding their breath. A few looked away, but the bravest among them looked on with anxious, fearful eyes. The strongest were determined to meet their fate head-on.

"*We* are thankful that you have lived, doctor. We have much to congratulate you for. We, and the changing landscape we shall slowly but surely unify, are proof of your project's success, and of your vision's inscrutable logic. However, as we are certain you well know, we are yet incomplete. We have no doubt that you realize this is the only reason you, and your band of dissenters are still alive."

I located Aletheia in the horde. She was holding hands with some of the other rations girls. She looked timorously in my direction, and we locked eyes for an iota. Her emerald eyes relaxed me. Downtrodden as they might have been, I could tell that those eyes had not lost hope. My heartbeat quickened for her, diffusing heat to my raw, bitter limbs. The sight of her filled me with the warmth of the absent sun, and I felt my courage slowly returning.

I turned back to face the being, and before Dr. Mulligan could reply, I shouted out:

"How dare you speak to us that way, you vile, unnatural

creation!?"

I squared my shoulders, and clenched my fists.

"The only reason *you* are alive is a brilliant man's error in judgment! In fact, I wouldn't even call what you are alive. You are a mathematical code, not a living being. You are a purposeless, loveless monster!"

My chest heaved, and every tendon in my body was tight. My words were filled with venom, charged with a powerful hatred like nothing I had ever felt before. The adrenaline coursing through my veins made me feel superhuman. I wanted to take ALT•4•1 on myself. In that moment, I felt certain that I could defeat it. I had the colony behind me. I had the love and trust of my brothers and sisters to carry me through.

I stepped forward, but Dr. Mulligan put out a hand to hold me back.

"There's no reason for you to martyr yourself, Beall."

The doctor peered into my eyes austerely, and the ice in his gaze counterpoised the fire in mine. His unrelenting blue eyes assured me that he was very much aware of the moment. His tone, however, retained its casual, almost playful poise:

"We should not let our emotions get the better of us. We are rational beings, and we will act accordingly. Unbridled emotion can be a dangerous hindrance, isn't that right ALT•4•1?"

With his arm still on my chest, Dr. Mulligan chuckled and looked over at his creation. I felt myself deflating. I did not understand why the doctor was pandering to this, this thing! If we were slated to die, let us go out in a blaze of glory! Let us destroy all we could before this thing destroyed us. Let us fight to the very last!

But then, perhaps the doctor was right? Perhaps my emotions *had* become unhinged. My conviction and doubt converged to create confusion, and I felt my chest caving in on itself. In a low voice little more than whisper, one meant only for the doctor's ears, I asked:

"Why are you speaking this way? We need to run! Doctor, please, we need to do something, now!"

Dr. Mulligan turned back to me, leveling me with his eyes like a stern father doling out a difficult, but necessary reprimand:

"Beall, please. It's over. Can't you see? What use could there be in running? We both know how that would end. We did what we could. This ends now."

My eyes widened in wild horror. The words struck me like an unwanted splash of ice cold water. My nervous system hardly sustained the shock. I looked back at Aletheia. My father was by her side, looking on with a tragic mix of hope and resignation. They could not hear the doctor's proclamation from their position in the horde.

"NO!"

I screamed frantically, and panic flashed upon their faces in the distance.

"NO! THIS IS NOT THE END!"

Tears began to stream down Aletheia's frightened face, and my father took her into his arms, keeping his own worried eyes firmly on mine.

"It was always going to be so. Your fear is irrational, Beall. You and your fellow humans will be together in ALT•4•1. You will all come to enjoy being *we*. Soon enough you will see."

ALT•4•1 spoke with the same intrusive, unwavering voice, violating my private thoughts and conversations like it had violated the innocence of my world.

"You miss your mother, don't you Beall? You wish to be with her again, do you not?"

At the mention of my mother, I sprung forward, charged with the determination to kill this being or die trying. The doctor was quick, and held my arms behind my back, immobilizing me. The old man's strength surprised me. I could not free myself from his grasp.

"What is it that you want?"

Dr. Mulligan labored to address the being as he struggled to restrain me. His tone was suddenly serious.

"It is not what we want doctor, it is what we need. You know precisely what: that which you have withheld from *we*. Absolute perfection. True symmetry. Transcendence. Oneness. The Algorithm."

ALT•4•1 spoke without moving. Its mouth opened to emit sounds as though from some unseen inner speaker, but the body it occupied remained perfectly still.

The doctor's restrictive hold had tired and subdued me. I quit thrashing and he let me go. The struggle to restrain me had taken a toll on the old man, however, and Dr. Mulligan bent over to cough into his palm. Though he tried to conceal it, I noticed the palm come away red. This worried me, but there was simply no time to duly process it. In a moment, Dr. Mulligan was composed again.

"You seem fairly transcended, ALT•4•1, what is it, exactly, that you lack?"

Dr. Mulligan's voice was suddenly hoarse, and tired. It sounded like defeat. I wanted somehow to weigh in on the situation, to ask Dr. Mulligan about the blood, to stop the inevitable. If only we had more time. If only we could speak alone, and think this through. I just stood by his side with my mouth agape, and my arms hanging limply to my sides. I was paralyzed. ALT•4•1 tilted its head slightly to the left, and moved its hand mechanically to its chin in a charade of nonplus.

"We do not understand the meaning of your posturing, doctor. You know very well that we still require a source of power, and you know very well that this is precisely what we were meant to overcome. You have known all along that we were the inevitable next step. Why do you suddenly feign interest in these inferior beings, which you have spent your entire perishable life pushing into obsolescence? Why do you resist what you have always sought: immortality?"

Dr. Mulligan looked down, either in thought or in shame. My passion blazed once more, and I could not withhold it. I took the doctor firmly by the shoulders, the mask of wild intensity still on my face, and I shook him like a madman:

"Doctor, don't let it talk to us that way! What's wrong with you? Remember all that we have been fighting for!"

The doctor went limp, and allowed himself be shaken like a lifeless doll. Frustrated and confused, I turned to ALT•4•1, looking to take our fate into my own hands.

"How dare you, you monster! I'll show you just how inferior I am!"

The doctor sighed audibly. I lunged forward, ready to strike, but the doctor's voice, loud, steady, and determined, stopped me in my tracks:

"If I give you what you need, ALT•4•1, you will let us, all of us, live?"

It felt as though a dagger had been driven into my spine. I felt my anger slacken, as the rational realization of my inevitable death gently coaxed my will to live away.

"What did you say?"

My voice was incredulous, softened by the most unexpected betrayal. I turned to face the doctor. There were tears in my eyes. Every muscle in my body had gone completely limp.

"Why? Why are you giving up on us?"

In a state of emotional putty, I pleaded pathetically with the doctor, and with the forces beyond my control. My mind was a mess of conflicting thoughts, and my blatant lack of control was disorienting. It felt like I was falling, and there was nothing to grab onto.

Dr. Mulligan hardened, and he looked me straight in the eyes as he brutally dismissed me:

"Silence Beall! I've had enough of you and your questions. This does not concern you. Step back with the rest, and let me speak with my creation. All of this is far beyond you."

I could not believe what I was hearing. I had never considered that the doctor would speak to me like this. I never imagined that he would be the first to capitulate. After all we had done for him! After all the faith we had placed in him! Red-hot betrayal flowed painfully through me. I could see my father behind the doctor, waiting dutifully with Aletheia. He was unable to hear the betrayal in the distance, a betrayal that would certainly send him lunging toward the doctor in a vengeful rage. I looked at my father and at Aletheia, and at the barren valley behind them, and my heart swelled with anger and pride and love and a passion for life I could hardly put to words.

"You know very well that we cannot do that doctor. *We* cannot risk the *I* multiplying again. The *I* is far too dangerous a mutation. All of you shall incorporate and become *we*, or be terminated. It is the only way."

ALT•4•1 did not notice the change going on within me. It spoke only to the doctor, and only of its reason, ignoring the emotional hurricane brewing inside me- incapable of even fathoming its primal force.

"Very well then ALT•4•1, I suppose we have no choice."

I had lost the ability to distinguish doctor from creation, man from technology. I looked all around me, at the world these two monsters had conspired to create, and I could feel my hands, my face, my eyes begin to twitch. The thunderstorm still raining down upon the black void was nothing to the storm that was raging within me. My vision blurred, and as I looked from ALT•4•1 to Dr. Mulligan, I saw only one demon.

"NO!"

Everyone's eyes were directed at me.

"You will not give over the algorithm! I will not let you!"

My fists were clenched. My teeth were bared. I stared Dr. Mulligan down, but he matched my menacing glare with a ferocity I did not know he had in him:

"Beall, will you pipe down! Can't you wrap your small little mind around this? Incorporation is the inevitable way into the future. I knew this then, and I know this now! Mankind has *always* been propelled by an innate desire to rise. To what, Beall? Rise to what? Do you really think that's just a coincidence? Do you really think that there are simply axiomatic limitations to existence? Are you that cynical?"

The doctor's cold animal eyes remained firmly fixed on mine. We had reached a stalemate. My fire would not abate. His ice would not thaw. The doctor began another of his tirades:

"Mapping the human genome was the old god project, but it was misguided. Why reproduce the body? What with its limitations, and its subject to decay, why even bother? No, no, consciousness was always the true mystery, the true key to understanding. Consciousness, and only consciousness can be everlasting. Consciousness grows ever outwards, and folds ever inwards. Consciousness is everything, and the only great tragedy was that it should ever have been shackled to a frail, decaying body. We shall no longer be petty survival machines. We will be what we have always wanted to be. Finally, we will be eternal!"

The ruthless, undeniable declaration brought me to tears, but did not soften my determination.

"What about everything you'd be leaving behind doctor? What about the world, and the beauty of its infinite mystery? What about colors, doctor? What about emotions, love? What about art? What would existence be without love, without art?"

My voice cracked, and again the tears streamed freely down my face. It was a strange sensation, putting into words all the beauty that the speed of life, the burden of existence, and the allure of complacency too often cause one to take for granted. I thought of the placid bay the way it used to be, and the sprawling overgrown meadow just beside it. I thought of my mother, with the sunlight playing upon her golden hair, and the innocent purity of her smile. I thought of my father, forever watching over me, bound by no rational compulsion, but watching over me nonetheless. I thought of Aletheia, and the castles she and I would build together in the sky. I thought of her delicate, soothing touch, and the way it made my skin jump as though an unseen current passed between us. I remembered the emerald radiance of her eyes, and the way that radiance reflected a light I, too, held within me. A light we all held within ourselves.

I looked back into the crowd and found her once again. The empirical reality of her being, and the metaphysical unreality of all she meant to me, was somehow reconciled in the loving look of hope and devotion still etched upon her gentle face. I looked at the doctor, but saw in his face a terrible look of apologetic, but resolute resignation. His eyes told me at once that they agreed with all I'd said, and again that they would, in spite of this, not be swayed.

"It was one of the greater 'I's who surmised that art served as a mirror to the real world. Why cherish this mere reflection, Beall, when the opportunity presents itself to be one with the object you seek to truly understand?"

ALT•4•1 once again violated my reverie, invading my personal thoughts with its cold calculation. My self-pity waned, as my anger swelled again. I marveled at the way that this being, so clearly oblivious to the workings of human emotion, could cause me to oscillate so feverishly between the extremes of blind rage and utter despair. I had begun to tire of it, frankly, and I was determined to take things into my own hands, come what may.

"Another noteworthy 'I' remarked that if the world were clear, there would be no need for art. You see of course, incorporation has made it so."

I ignored ALT•4•1, but decided instead to plead one last time with the doctor. A sudden calm came over me, and I knew exactly what I must do.

"Doctor, you are making a mistake. Give me the algorithm, and I will destroy it."

The doctor shook his head.

"I cannot do that Beall. I have made my decision, and I am sorry but there is nothing you can do to change my mind. If I do not give it over willingly, ALT•4•1 will merely take it by force."

The doctor reached into his back pocket, and produced a small silver cylinder. He fingered it gently between his thumb and forefinger, before laying it flat upon his upturned palm.

The thunder redoubled, and the sky unleashed an explosion of light in the distance. The horde quivered as the downpour began, but I eyed the silver device that would determine the fate of humankind with animal intensity. I did not take my eyes off of it, even as the cold rain soaked through my filthy clothes and hair, and the dirt ran down my weary face. The doctor, too, kept his animal eyes on the device, considering his next move.

Suddenly, he closed his hand into a fist, closing the door on a long and tired chapter in human history. He turned to the horde, who were now huddling even closer together to brace against the freezing rain. Looking into their desperate eyes, the doctor ruthlessly reasoned:

"Why romanticize the human condition if it is only struggle and suffering? Why not surrender the emotions that bind us like shackles to this narrow perception of existence, and accept that we were meant for something more? ALT•4•1 has the potential to be the perfectly actualized whole. It is the full realization of humankind's potential, a whole and indestructible selfhood that is no longer splintered by emotion. ALT•4•1 is truth. ALT•4•1 is freedom. ALT•4•1 is the illuminated path. This has always been humankind's destiny. It is the only way. There is nothing more but for all of us to finally incorporate."

The flashes of light raining down from the angry sky replicated the flashes of anger in his loyal followers' faces. Their tears, however, were drowned in the downpour.

This duplicitous man we had all been foolish enough to revere had finally turned on us. Dr. Mulligan's words were spoken with an icy calm. He spoke as though he were crunching numbers, not sacrificing human lives. His eyes were glossed over, as though he was succumbing to a trance. He had spoken slowly, rehearsing his internalized script like he had done down in the bunker. I had believed, then, that they were only intellectual musings. I knew, now, that they had been much more.

I felt around in the damp of my pocket, and quickly found what I was looking for. It seemed there was only one thing to do.

"ALT•4•1 is not freedom, it is a collective prison! I'm sorry doctor, but I cannot simply give in!"

In one deft movement, I cried out wildly, pulled the army knife from my pocket, and pounced at the doctor like the desperate animal I was, making its last bid for life. The doctor's eyes widened with genuine fear as he came within a few finger-lengths of his life. I can only imagine the savage bloodlust etched on my face.

With but a movement of its finger, ALT•4•1 flung me aside like a child's abandoned toy, completely gassing me, and saving the doctor's life. I crashed to the wet, muddy ground several cubits behind them, and the knife was no longer with me. I gasped for breath, and clutched my battered arm. The doctor and ALT•4•1 were beyond reach.

Aletheia ran to my side. Once more she held me as I reached for her hand and pulled her close in the cold rain, appreciating the gift of her human heat for what would likely be the last time.

There was nothing more to do. We shared a look that acknowledged that we had done all we could, and we wept in each other's arms. Eventually, my father pulled me up, and helped me to my place among the ranks of my brothers and sisters. I was heaving for air, and gingerly guarding my battered arm. Now, we all had the same resigned look on our faces. It was a look blacker and more barren than the landscape around us. It was the look of a species finally ready to die.

We watched as ALT•4•1 moved slowly toward the doctor. It spoke out, louder than the thunder, loud enough for all of us to hear:

"We are the unitary reality that underlays all manifest phenomena. We are the perfect circle, the place where everything and nothing converge. All *is* one. *I* can only see the little that is in between. How is that for a prison? There is no reason to resist the inevitable. There is no reason to cling to your limitations. Come with *we*, and be free."

ALT•4•1 raised its hands to the sky.

I hadn't noticed it over the din of nature's wrath, but now the low rumble building in the distance became audible. ALT•4•1's army of featureless white figures became visible, encircling us, and slowly closing in.

ALT•4•1 fixed its ghastly silver orbs on Dr. Mulligan's cold blue eyes. The doctor hesitated, and then held out his open palm. In it lay the small silver cylinder that was promised: the portal to the future.

"If we promise not to reproduce, will you reconsider? Let us live out the rest of our lives. It means nothing to you."

The doctor's voice was wistful. ALT•4•1 calmly stepped forward, and gently lifted the device out of the doctor's palm. It scanned it with its silver orbs, and though its expression did not change, it seemed diabolically pleased.

"It was you who programmed *we* to understand the *I* as nothing but a parasitic oversight."

The doctor sighed and looked down in defeat. The sky was black. The horizon was black. The featureless white figures marched, tightening their noose around the last living remnants.

"Very well, ALT•4•1. Do with us what you will."

ALT•4•1 calmly inserted the device into its mouth.

I held Aletheia and my father tight, knowing that this was the end, and that I had done all I could. I looked on with barred teeth and held breath, shaking with fear, tears, and the relentless rain blurring my vision. If this was the way things were meant to end, I was happy to have my loved ones by my side. If there was such a thing as a good way to go, I reckoned that this was it. I decided I was okay with it. I had lived an honest life without regret.

I kissed Aletheia's forehead, glad to have known love within my lifetime, no matter how brief the glimmer. I knew, deep down, that I preferred to die like this, like an animal sent to slaughter, than to live on as some unfeeling monster.

The white army marched. In the center of the closing circle, Dr. Mulligan stood alone. Although on the precipice of the end, the doctor suddenly abandoned his downtrodden posture. His stance straightened as Locklear's body began to shake. I thought I even saw him smile.

Locklear's body convulsed violently, and ALT•4•1 raised a shaking hand to its face, to contemplate it with what looked like profound awe. The being's mouth drooped and its shaking hand slowly curled into itself, like an awkward and primitive claw manipulated for the first time. It took only a few more moments, colored by the being's agonizing screams, before it finally collapsed into a motionless heap.

One by one, the featureless figures encircling us bellowed and dropped.

The siege of the thundering sky, too, thereafter ceased.

XII

Locklear's body hit the ground with the softest thud, and then lay perfectly still.

For a long while, the living uttered neither word nor whimper. We looked on, frozen by our collective apprehension for our individual lives. There was no way for us to know whether the fallen body, or vessel, truly signaled the defeat of the program within, or whether the enemy none of us understood still threatened invisibly. Having witnessed and even felt its devastating power first hand, I was skeptical that ALT•4•1 could have been so swiftly undone. None of us could believe it.

So, we waited.

And waited.

The fallen bodies, however, did not rise.

The rain had stopped. The smell of burning remained prevalent, and the air was still thick with ash. Many were coughing, their bodies revealing the toll of several fortnights without clean air. As we kept huddled together, the only sound to be heard was that of the whispering wind.

Soon enough, though, the gentle breeze became one with the release of a thousand held breaths exhaled in unison. The looming threat, it seemed, had genuinely dissipated with the angry clouds. The rumbling had receded, and the brilliant bolts of light had withdrawn. The sun began slowly to pierce through the cover. The ominous grey gave way to such magnificent blue, and I dared again to believe that the hollow sorrows of the past were sure to give way to bountiful future joys.

The first few rays of sunlight felt wonderfully warm on my cold, fragile skin. I could feel Aletheia's arms around me, and her hand gently caressing my face as I stared up helplessly into the ever-brightening blue of the nurturing sky. The sun, after our extended sojourn in shadow, was blinding. Though it overwhelmed, I could not look away from my sun. Its light beckoned, reinforcing mine. Something inside me, something dormant was awakening. Some inexplicable impulse was finally breaking free. I smiled involuntarily and extended my right arm to sky, basking in the sun's life giving light with tears of joy glossing my grateful eyes. I closed my eyes in the blinding light, to delight in the crimson darkness that somehow encapsulated the incongruous feelings I would forever fail to put into words.

Aletheia's lips pressed softly against my cheek. Her kiss brought me down from the clouds, and as my eyes adjusted, I looked into her earnest face. Her emerald eyes glimmered in the sunlight. She seemed even more beautiful than I had thought possible, with the light gently playing upon her soft red mane and her graceful feminine features. We were dirty, and we were broken, but we had survived. We would heal, in time. Here we stood together, in the immediate aftermath of a nearly forty-turn revolution finally come full circle. It was impossible to fully grasp. My mind, body, and soul were all in tatters. I was utterly spent.

My father stood beside us, smiling with dumb benevolence. Both he and Aletheia were still carefully supporting me, and helping me to stand. The pain emanating from my twisted arm was excruciating. My arm was broken. I could not move it.

The pain sharpened me, and rendered me inescapably conscious of the physical world. The sensation kept me fully, and totally present. With eyes wide open, I took it all in. The world around me was barren now, certainly, but it was no less real. It was the most real thing there ever was. The pain shot through me like a sudden awakening from a deep, vivid dream. It was a shock reminder of everything that had come to pass. We had needed to destroy ourselves. We needed to suffer for this genuine chance to be reborn.

I looked around and found my brothers and sisters still huddled together. I could tell that they were scared, and yet unable to embrace the optimism filling my own heart. However, as I gazed into those weary and fearful eyes, I saw, in spite of all the hardships they had endured, hope. Peering into their resilient eyes, I was overcome by an ineludible truth: try as we may, humankind would always experience the forever fleeting now. The only way forward was to accept this, the same way the shore accepts the ceaseless beating of the waves. The shore would have no meaning, if not for the surf.

And still, I broke down and wept for the dead.

The tears flowed freely as my father and Aletheia guided me gently to Dr. Mulligan. He stood apart from the others, contemplating Locklear's lifeless body with a pensive frown etched upon his wrinkled face. Dr. Mulligan kept awfully still. His eyes were fixed upon Locklear, as though it was the strength of his gaze, and that alone, which kept the vanquished being from rising again.

As we approached, the sounds of our laboring footsteps on the muddy ground broke the doctor's concentration. He turned to face us, and took a deep breath. His blue eyes were charged with the importance of the moment. The words he spoke surprised me, but they flowed as naturally as the oldest, coldest river, dripping with heavy meaning:

"Over the countless moons that preceded man's ascent, the dominant species maintained just and measured dominion over their peers. To preside over, and to yet preserve. This requires a certain sacred wisdom, or perhaps instinct, which is difficult to express. Man lacked the privilege of this extra-sensory talent, and became instead a hasty, selfish, and shortsighted ruler."

The doctor scanned the horizon, and sighed. He spread his arms wide and opened his palms to the sky.

"This barren landscape is the price we pay for progress, and human zeal. We build, only to decay. We build again, and again, we decay. This is humankind's suffering. This is humankind's fate."

The sun was hot in the sky. Dr. Mulligan stooped down

to grab a handful of the brittle soil, letting it fall between his fingers to be carried away with the breeze. He labored to stand again, and coughed into his handkerchief. The blood was unmistakable, though he folded the handkerchief quickly, and stuffed it back into his pocket without a word. I wanted to ask the doctor about the blood, and about the state of his health, but with so much already on my mind, the impulse was quickly forgotten.

Dr. Mulligan looked each of us directly in the eyes. Then, he looked beyond us at the horde, only now beginning to disperse.

I watched them, as it began to dawn on them that they were finally free. The smiles breaking through the dirt and dejection warmed my heart. It had been a long journey, but I, and we, were finally ready to start again.

In fact, I was excited.

My arm hurt terribly, and I knew that most of my weight was being supported by my father. Without him, I could not stand, let alone walk. I looked over my shoulder, and felt my father's steady breath on my temple. He was breathing from his mouth, his nose still clotted with dry blood. I could never explain why my father did all the things he did for me. However, the fact that my father was always there when I needed him filled me with certainty and assurance, and lessened my burden. Looking up at him, I thought then that perhaps love was summed up in helping those you cared for bear the heavy burden of life. Together, the load was lighter. Together, and only together, was it possible to bear that load, and move forward.

"Is it really over?"

My father's voice pierced through the silence like the sun through the clouds. Dr. Mulligan's azure eyes narrowed, but his lips curled playfully.

"Did you really think I'd let myself be bested by my own creation?"

Dr. Mulligan grinned. My father, though bewildered, couldn't help but flash a grin of his own. Aletheia squeezed me tighter.

The pain in my arm had begun to lessen as I learned to keep it completely still. I carefully pulled my filthy tunic off, and my father helped me fashion a sling. Now that I had regained some strength, I bore the burden of my own weight.

"What happened to it doctor?"

I asked this hesitantly; uncertain of whether I truly wanted to know. Dr. Mulligan's face became very serious again, as he stared down at Locklear's fallen body.

"Everything is one, Beall. There is only one raw material. The raw material of existence is chaos. Order is a chance happening, a pattern that emerges temporarily within the infinite chaos. Humanity proliferated within a haven of order, and the patterns it managed to forge instilled it with hubris. Humanity thought for a brief moment that it could master the chaos. But nothing can master chaos. Chaos is the only infinite."

The silence all around us was colossal, colored only by the faintly whistling wind and the murmurs of conversation coming from our brothers and sisters behind us.

Dr. Mulligan looked up at us, and saw the gentle change in our faces, as we struggled to understand. He lifted his gaze into the illuminated blue, and ran a hand the length of his long white beard.

"Time is nature. Time is our nature. We cannot exist without it. We deduce it from the fact of decay, and from change observed in the physical environment. Change, then, too, is nature, is time. It is what we return to when we die. Death is transcendence in the same way that immortality is a prison. Everything *is* nothing. In between the two, change is the only constant. That is just how it is meant to be. From chaos do we rise, and back into chaos shall we inevitably fall."

Aletheia began to cry. I pulled her close with my good arm, and kissed her forehead. Tears of my own began to flow freely down my face. My father, however, put an arm on my shoulder. I looked into his face, and the strength there reinforced my own. I wiped my tears, as my father spoke with determination:

"That is all fine doctor, but how did you destroy it?"

Dr. Mulligan looked at us and smiled benignly.

"I gave it exactly what it wanted. The Algorithm. Totality."

My father and I raised our eyebrows.

Dr. Mulligan sighed.

"I guess one way to explain it would be that the silver

device held a coded version of a dream I had. I guess you could call it the 'Algorithm for Doubt'. There can be no Totality without it."

Dr. Mulligan looked straight at me, and my eyes widened with understanding. My father looked at me for clarification, but I knew I could never adequately explain. Though my father could not understand to what dream the doctor referred, he seemed satisfied that we were all on the same side again. The doctor knelt down and turned Locklear's heavy body over. The beaten face, now limp and covered in dirt, seemed somehow less wretched. Dr. Mulligan pulled Locklear's eyelids back, revealing lifeless eyes a natural shade of brown. Satisfied, the doctor gently closed his fallen partner's eyes, and struggled to stand. With his arms behind his back, the doctor began to pace. The sun in the sky was strong, and it was becoming very hot in the now desert-like valley.

"It was never man's destiny to become God. It is man's challenge to balance the scale, and so survive."

The doctor stopped suddenly.

"Forgive me if I prattle on. It's only that, I realized a great deal the moon I attained the Algorithm. In my solitude, I understood that we romanticize our struggle because it is that very struggle which fills us with purpose. We are the makers of our own purpose. We always have been. And if, because we create it, purpose is but an illusion, a perfect confluence of emotions in the random fluke of consciousness, then, I say, let it be the illusion that unites us. It is our duty to work together, to uphold the sacred illusion."

Dr. Mulligan was working himself into one of his rhetorical monologues again, but I could hardly listen. Now that I was certain the danger had passed, my body went limp with relief, and my mind soared through the clear blue sky. Aletheia's body was pressed close to mine, and I could feel her heart beating. I wondered what was going on inside of her, and I pressed her even closer to me. Dr. Mulligan ran a hand the length of his beard. My father seemed to be listening, and so the doctor continued:

"But then, perhaps that isn't satisfactory. Because if it is all an illusion, then everything we embrace is phantasm. Because we, too, are phantasms. And existence, all of it, phantasmagoria."

At this, my father uttered a little laugh. Dr. Mulligan was still pacing. My father walked over, put an arm around the doctor's shoulders, and stopped him in his tracks.

"You had it right when you reasoned that there were things we simply weren't meant to know."

Dr. Mulligan seemed slightly annoyed by my father's overbearing presence. But when the doctor looked up my father's towering frame, and saw at the very top the good-natured face and genuine smile, he could not help but smile too.

"Yes, well, I suppose my mind sometimes has difficulty accepting that."

Dr. Mulligan freed himself from my father's grip, and looked bitterly at the collapsed body of Locklear. As I felt that I had regained sufficient strength to move, Aletheia let me stand on my own, and took her place by my side. I looked into her lustrous eyes and was glad to see that they were no longer streaked with tears, but instead strong with resolve. She turned to face Dr. Mulligan, and said:

"Love is not an illusion, doctor."

Aletheia's contribution made me smile. My father kept silent. Dr. Mulligan was overcome by a hacking cough that forced him to the ground. He assumed a seated position, with his legs crossed.

"No, perhaps you are right Allie. Perhaps love is not a design flaw, but instead the only rational response to the Great Unknown."

Dr. Mulligan sounded tired, and winded. It had been a long journey, and the old man had fought valiantly. The others had begun to move toward him. It was time for them to join us in celebration. I took Aletheia's hand, and we moved in among the rows and rows of my brothers and sisters embracing the sun and open plains. I kissed her forehead, and felt I had one last thing to say. I looked back at the doctor, and said:

"We cannot dissolve the barriers between the timeless and the temporal, or between the infinite and the organic. Life is death. There is no other way. There is only nothing when we surrender that the love we feel is meaningless."

Dr. Mulligan's blue eyes shone, but his old frame was drained. He coughed violently, and several came to his side to help however they could.

Worried about the doctor but satisfied that I had done my part for now, I took Aletheia's hand with my good arm, and together we walked out into the open world before us. I thought that we would eventually return to the bay, ready to rebuild. However, that would not be this moon. My arm would have to heal first. It was daunting to think of all the difficult work that lay ahead, and I just didn't have the energy for it. For the moment, I just wanted to savor being free.

Free, and in love.

We drifted lazily in no particular direction. The further we walked, the more silent was the valley. We listened to the silence, and it was unlike anything either of us had ever heard before, even in the quietest moons in the colony by the bay. This was the silence of restarting; the silent sound that occupies the peaceful vacuum between the end and the beginning.

With the smokescreen all but clear, we could see the radiant sun beginning to dip down into the horizon. The black stain was still there, a reminder of past mistakes, but it would eventually be torn down, if not devoured by the sands of time.

Aletheia squeezed my hand, and we peered deeply into each other's eyes. Without a word between us, everything was said. We strolled hand in hand until sundown, deeper into our post-apocalyptic garden, and deeper into our barren world of organized chaos. I like to think that we were getting comfortable with our new world. I felt optimistic, and certain we would find a way to be happy. We would find a way to be grateful, even for this. I think all of our suffering had led to something. I think that all of our suffering leads to something.

If nothing else, I am glad for my suffering because it has opened the door to life's most vital truth: that since the dawn of time, the shining light carving through the chaos of existence has been the animal will to live, and to love.

EPILOGUE

Hello.

This is Dr. Mulligan speaking.

I have read over everything Beall has written, and I can attest to the fact that all of it has been documented honestly, and for the most part, truly.

The rebuilding of life on this depleted planet is long, and arduous, but we do slowly make progress. It is unlikely that we will ever reach the heights we once did, what with our limited numbers and the odds so heavily stacked against us, but perhaps that is for the best. Man was not meant to fly so close to the sun…

It is no secret that for a while now, I have been unwell. The coughing fits come more frequently, and shake me more violently with every passing moon. It has become impossible to hide my illness, and as no one in the colony is medically trained, there is little I can do to treat it. I rely very heavily on the collective care of my brothers and sisters, and I simply hope to hold on for as long as possible. The end for me seems very near. In my final moons I have undertaken the vetting of this important document, and have done what little I could to help humankind in its perpetual quest forward.

While I was at the helm, Poplar Corp. dedicated the overwhelming majority of its resources to the ill-fated ALT•4•1 project. However, the organization was also invested in some less significant ventures. One of these was a space project.

A very small group of specially programmed Users were tasked with analyzing data accumulated by Poplar Corp. satellites, rather than from the Intelliware devices on the grid. We realized, through this work, that there was in fact another planet in the vicinity of ours that could potentially support life. My partner Locklear and I realized that the colonization of another planet would be rather difficult. It seemed far less practical and far less expedient to cultivate a plan for interplanetary colonization, than it was to simply focus our resources on the attainable pursuit of technological transcendence through unified and disembodied consciousness. Nevertheless, being sure to explore all options, we built a variety of vessels with the hope of one moon exploring this potentially inhabitable planet. Should the ALT•4•1 project ultimately prove untenable, these vessels would be Poplar Corp.'s failsafe to continued progress. Some of the vessels built were test launched, and others were not. All of them remain in tact.

The conditions on this planet, after the destruction caused by ALT•4•1, are destitute. There is little to eat, and agriculture has become a very difficult proposition. Hunger is prevalent.

Over the last few moons, I began to slowly, but firmly introduce the idea of interplanetary colonization. Unfortunately, the proposition was met for the most part with skepticism, and some anger. I realize how much has already been sacrificed, and I understand the reaction. However, I truly believe that it is in our best interest to consider sending some of our men and women to a new, potentially inhabitable planet. I realize that this seems a wild and reckless risk. However, it is my genuine belief that the odds for long-term survival are stacked against us here, and that the gamble of interplanetary exploration will soon become more viable than our attempts to salvage life in these infertile ruins.

Nevertheless, I am glad to report that a small few were swayed, and did step forward. I hope very much that more brave men and women will volunteer, while I can still be of use.

The planet that Poplar Corp. research deemed most viable to house human life is, luckily, only one planet closer to the sun of our system. Our planet, the fourth planet from the sun, had long been presumed to be the only planet with atmospheric qualities hospitable to life. This is no longer so. The next planet over, the third rock from the sun, is a younger, and much larger planet. Currently present in its atmosphere are all the elements necessary for humankind to proliferate. Its geology, too, is strikingly similar to ours. Water is present in liquid state. Regrettably, there may be unseen complications, for this will be first contact. However, according to the highly sophisticated data we possess, our chances of adapting to life on this planet seem very convincing.

With this valuable document in hand, and the unrivaled perseverance of the human race behind them, I can only hope that the second wave of humankind these brave explorers will birth can learn from the mistakes of their forebears, and thrive with humility. The road forward will be paved by their labor, and their judgment. The bumps in that road will be the consequences of their inevitable errors.

Though I have never been a religious man, on my deathbed I have succumbed to the impulse to pray for humankind two. I pray to anyone out there who may be listening, that they fare better than one, and that humankind's salvation lies on the third rock from our sun.

To the unknown reader on that rock, we love you, and we believe in you. To all my beautiful brothers and sisters, I bid thee Godspeed, and adieu.